"What do you want from me? Absolution?" I felt panicky all of a sudden.

"You know what I want from you, Nicki."

"I already told you back in Savannah that I wasn't going to recruit any souls for your army. I don't need that on my conscience."

"At least you have one," Sammy said. "What does it feel like?"

I was hardly qualified to answer that question. "Just leave me alone."

He shook his head, not taking his eyes from me. "I can't do that. When I'm in the flesh, I'm 'in the flesh.' "

My throat went dry.

"Your flesh calls to mine, and when that happens, I'm powerless against it."

The Devil had the hots for me.

By Terri Garey

YOU'RE THE ONE THAT I HAUNT
A MATCH MADE IN HELL
DEAD GIRLS ARE EASY

TERRI GAREY

YOU'RE THE ONE THAT I HAUNT

AVON

An Imprint of HarperCollins*Publishers*

AVON BOOKS
An Imprint of HarperCollins*Publishers*
10 East 53rd Street
New York, New York 10022-5299

Copyright © 2009 by Terri Garey
ISBN 978-0-06-158203-5
www.avonromance.com

First Avon Books paperback printing: March 2009

Avon Trademark Reg. U.S. Pat. Off. and in Other Countries, Marca Registrada, Hecho en U.S.A.
HarperCollins® is a registered trademark of HarperCollins Publishers.

Printed in the U.S.A.

10 9 8 7 6 5 4 3 2 1

YOU'RE
THE ONE
THAT I
HAUNT

Life's a bitch, and then you die.

Usually.

My name is Nicki Styx, and a few months ago, I found out the hard way that even though death may come for us all, not all of us are willing to go quietly. Some of us even get kicked out of the afterlife with words like, "It isn't your time", and "Go back and do unto others as you would have them do unto you." Heart failure in my twenties had come as quite a shock, but being sent back to do good in the world was the real kicker. I mean, life's hard enough, but does death have to be that way, too?

Back in my goth days (not so long ago, if truth be told), I always figured that the "good die young" because being good all the time left them no reason to live. Now everything's changed, and this former bad girl has to be a "do-gooder" or pay the ultimate price. Unfortunately, the people I have to "do good" to are people who are already dead—the ones who refuse to go quietly.

Never let anyone tell you the universe doesn't have a sense of humor.

CHAPTER 1

"Always remember that you're unique . . . just like everyone else."

The TV behind the counter was blaring when I walked in the door of Handbags and Gladrags. My partner, Evan, was glued to the set, watching his favorite midmorning talk show.

"Self-hypnosis can provide important past-life information that can help you understand your present life and transform yourself into the *you* that you were meant to be."

"Oh, please." I slid the box of vintage jeans I was carrying onto the counter, glad to be rid of its weight. "You're not buying into this crap, are you?"

"Shh." Evan waved me impatiently away, not even bothering with our usual "good morning" hugs and air kisses. "She's just getting to the good part."

"My new book, *Reincarnate Your Way to a New You*, is available now from Atlantis Books, and can be yours for the low, low price of nineteen ninety-five."

"Nineteen ninety-five for a book on reincarnation? Not in this lifetime." I giggled to myself at the unintended pun.

Evan's sense of humor seemed to be missing this morning, though his sense of fashion was, as usual, in perfect place. He was wearing gray pin-striped pants with a silky black button-down shirt, patterned with green Chinese dragons. "Shh," he said again, "I wanna hear this."

I shrugged and went into the back room to lock up my purse and pour myself a cup of coffee. The TV was too loud to block out, and I couldn't help but be glad the store was currently empty of customers. Business would pick up after lunch.

"*Reincarnate Your Way to a New You* will give you the tools you need to tap into the three major dimensions of your psyche: your past lives, your preexistence, and the lives you've lived between lifetimes. Visualization is the key."

"It sounds like English, but I can't understand a word she's saying," I called out, unwilling to pass up an opportunity to tease my best bud. "What do you think will happen if I visualize her with duct tape over her mouth?"

The TV went dead, leaving blessed silence in its wake.

"It worked," I shouted triumphantly. "Visualization IS the key!"

"Ha, ha," said Evan from the doorway. "You're awfully close-minded for somebody who sees dead people."

"Any connection between that woman's reality and mine is purely coincidental. You know perfectly well I'd prefer *not* to see dead people, thank you very much, and I don't scam poor suckers out of their hard-earned money." The coffeemaker was empty, pot missing. "Unless they want quality vintage, which they will have to pay for. Now where's the coffeepot?"

"In the trash, where it belongs." Evan leaned against the door jamb, crossing one sandaled Prada casually over the other. "*Somebody* forgot to turn off the burner yesterday."

Ugh. I got a quick mental flash of the muddy black mess we'd found at closing time yesterday—that "somebody" would be me.

"How about a couple of large Mocha Lattes

from Moonbeans?" I gave Evan a hopeful smile. "You fly, I'll buy."

"Oh sure"—Evan sniffed—"ask the fairy to fly. How very politically incorrect of you."

"Somebody has their panties in a twist this morning." I grinned, taking the sting from my words. "Anything wrong?"

Evan sighed, giving me a mournful look. "I think Butch is losing interest."

"Impossible. The guy's nuts about you!"

"He's been spending a lot of time on the computer late at night, and this morning I found out he'd changed his e-mail password."

I lifted an eyebrow at him. "You've been reading your boyfriend's e-mails?"

Evan shrugged. "Of course. Doesn't everybody?"

Remembering how I'd sneaked a peek at *my* boyfriend Joe's computer recently, I had no room to talk. But that didn't stop me. "No. You must learn to respect your partner's privacy."

Evan looked at me, and I looked at him, then we both burst out laughing.

"Okay. Okay. But just because Butch changed his e-mail password doesn't mean he's losing interest. You're overreacting."

"Imagine that," Evan murmured sarcastically.

"And you think reincarnating yourself into a new you is the way to get his attention?"

Evan sighed again. "I don't know. Butch is interested in all this 'New Age' stuff. Maybe if I knew something about it, we'd have more in common."

I rolled my eyes. "Tell you what, pretty boy. You park yourself in the catbird seat and keep an eye on the store while I go get us those Mocha Lattes. You can tell me all your troubles when I get back."

Evan didn't argue, which told me more than words could've. He didn't even fuss at me when I stopped to adjust the ruffles on Grace Kelly's ivory chiffon cocktail dress, a sure sign he was deep into depression. All of the mannequins in Handbags and Gladrags were made to look like film stars, and Grace was one of Evan's particular favorites.

I left him flipping listlessly through a muscle magazine while I went out the front door and into the rarefied air of Little Five Points, Georgia.

If Butch was into New Age stuff, he needed to hang out in *this* neighborhood more often. Wind chimes in front of Crystal Blue Persuasion tinkled in the morning breeze, the perfect counterpoint to the weird electronic music they piped into the street every day to attract shoppers. The rich smell of coffee from Moonbeans vied with the odor of sandalwood incense, and if you breathed deep enough, you could smell the fresh fruits and vegetables stacked in bins outside the organic market, Garden of Eatin'.

I dodged a dreadlocked kid on a skateboard, and smiled at an elderly black man who shuffled by, nodding pleasantly, folded newspaper under one arm. The familiar sweet/sour scent of stale beer rose from the alley as I passed the Vortex, skirting the dirty garbage bins ready for pickup.

God, I love this place.

"Two large Mocha Lattes, Amy," I told the girl behind the counter. "Is that a new nose ring?"

Amy, a chubby girl of about twenty who had more tats and metal on her body than most bikers, grinned happily at me as she filled the order. "Yeah. Thanks for noticing. Blue Screwed Tattoos got some new rings and studs in last week. Cute, isn't it?"

I suppose—if you don't mind standing in line at metal detectors.

"I prefer my studs about six-foot-two and built, but yours is supercute," I answered cheerfully. *To each his own.*

"Love the hair," Amy eyed my pink-streaked head as she filled my order. "More pink than usual . . . new highlights?"

"Flamingo Pink glam strips," I said. "Temporary clip-ons. You should try the Midnight Blue—they'd go great with the silver in your studs."

"Cool. Thanks."

I paid and turned away, glancing around for one of the regular neighborhood winos to give my change to.

"Nicki!"

Speaking of studs.

Joe's shout caught me by surprise, very pleasantly so. We'd talked on the phone last night, but I hadn't been expecting to see him until the weekend. He was smiling as he sprinted toward me on the sidewalk, narrowly evading a collision with a fat tourist couple in matching socks and sandals. Dark hair brushed his collar—he needed a haircut, but he looked so sexy. His surgical scrubs were wrinkled . . . he either needed a nap or had just woken from one.

"Hey, baby." I couldn't hug him properly holding two cups of coffee, but I stood on my tiptoes for a quick kiss. "What are you doing here?"

"I missed you," he said simply, and my heart did that little flippy thing it does. The sensation used to scare me, but now it feels like an old friend.

After all, if I didn't have a wonky heart valve, I would never have met Joe.

I kissed him again, a quick smack, which he enthusiastically returned. He smelled like antibacterial soap and male sweat. Running an emergency room was a tough job, one I could never do in a million years. Yet his green eyes were smiling, and his mood was upbeat. He looked terribly happy to see me.

"You look good enough to eat." Joe held me at the waist, checking out the black camisole, the hot pink tee. The jeans were my new favorites—indigo denim flares worn with a pair of thick-soled Louis Vuitton boots, circa 1980.

I gave him a naughty grin, glad he was still hungry. "Later, baby, we'll eat later." I wasn't talking about food, and the gleam in Joe's eye showed he wasn't either.

We'd been dating almost six months now—definitely a record for me. A failed engagement in my late teens had left me a "commitment phobe" for the last decade, until Joe.

"How about a Mocha Latte for now?" I handed one over without a qualm; I'd get Evan another one.

Joe lifted the lid on the coffee cup and inhaled blissfully before taking a sip. "Ah. Just what the doctor ordered." He tilted his head toward an empty sidewalk table. "Come sit with me."

I glanced involuntarily toward Handbags and Gladrags, knowing Evan was waiting to tell me his boyfriend troubles. But I couldn't resist the chance to spend a few minutes with my own boyfriend, so I slid into a chair.

As I did, I noticed a girl watching us. Early twenties, blond hair to her shoulders, very thin. Too thin, in fact—her shoulder blades jutted like clothes hangers beneath her T-shirt, low-cut jeans skimming prominent pelvic bones. She was staring right at us, and she looked pissed.

"What a night," Joe said, bringing my attention back to him, where it belonged. "Gang fight over in Riverdale, and we got the overflow. Forget the gunshot wounds—it's unbelievable what knives and baseball bats can do to people."

"Ugh." I wrinkled my nose, not really caring for the visual images that statement conjured up. "How you handle all that blood and pain on a daily basis is beyond me."

Joe cocked his head, smiling as he reached across the table to take my hand. "It's like a battle," he said, "between me and death." It seemed an odd thing to say, yet it made sense. "Sometimes death wins, and sometimes I do." His thumb smoothed over the skin of my knuckles. "And it's all worth it. All I need to do is look at you to remind myself why I do this."

I smiled at him, squeezing his fingers. "I'm glad you were in the E.R. that night. You brought me back to life." I leaned in over the table, letting my voice go all throaty. "In more ways than one."

"How sweet," came a syrupy voice.

I looked over Joe's shoulder to see the blond girl, now standing right behind him. A nasty sneer curled one corner of her lip, a bony elbow jutted sharply from a hip.

"Excuse me?"

"True, I do know how to make you tingle," Joe said. "Electric shocks, kissing the back of your knees . . ." He gave me an intimate grin, then took another sip of coffee, oblivious.

A chill ran down my spine. I looked at his face, then back at the blonde.

Crap. Not again.

"What's the matter, Nicki?" He lowered his cup. "You look like you've seen a gho . . ." His voice trailed off.

"Isn't he the clever one," the girl said. "Too bad he wasn't that clever last night."

Little Miss Nasty was beginning to tick me off.

"Who are you?" If she wasn't going to bother with the niceties, neither was I. "What do you want?"

Joe swiveled in his chair to see who I was talking to, and of course, saw no one. "Um, Nicki?"

Poor guy. He'd gotten a lot more than he bargained for when he started dating me—a girlfriend who talked to dead people was hardly every guy's dream.

More like a nightmare.

The blonde looked at Joe, her expression getting uglier by the minute. "I'm Crystal," she said. "Ask him if he remembers me."

I didn't take orders well, and I really didn't like her tone. Dead or alive, she was *not* my boss. "Why should I?"

She lifted her eyes from Joe's face. They were filled with hate.

"Because he killed me," she snarled. "And I want him to remember."

CHAPTER 2

I stood up so fast I nearly tipped the table over. Joe made a heroic grab for my cup, and caught it, but spilled lattes were the least of my worries.

"What are you talking about? Joe never hurt anybody in his life!"

"Hey," he said, frowning. "What's going on?"

Crystal flicked him a contemptuous glance, then addressed her remarks to me. "Ask him. Ask him what happened in the E.R. last night."

I glared at her, fully aware that there were people all around, some of them shooting us curious looks. Taking a breath, I slid back into my chair, focusing my attention on Joe.

"Did a girl named Crystal come into the emergency room last night?"

His face went blank with shock. "Don't tell me," he said. "She's here? Now?"

I nodded grimly, ignoring Miss Skinny for the moment. "And she's pissed."

He sat back, frowning. "She blames me?"

Crystal moved around the table so she could look Joe full in the face. She was standing right next to me, hands on bony hips.

"What happened, Joe?" I kept my voice down and avoided looking at the blond bag of bones next to us. Animosity radiated from her like waves of heat.

He sighed, running a hand through his dark hair. "She was sick, Nicki. Very, very sick."

"He's the one who's sick." Crystal reached out, and before I could blink, Joe's coffee splashed all over the front of his scrubs and into his lap. He shot to his feet with a hiss of pain.

I flinched, but it was too late. Crystal moved again, and the second cup hit the wall beside us, splattering, leaving a wet stain on my jeans and a mess on my favorite mural—pink and gray aliens in some sort of bizarre moonscape.

"It wasn't my fault," Joe said tersely, plucking his sopping clothes away from his body. "Tell her it wasn't my fault."

"She can hear you," I whispered, trying my best to keep my cool. I was on my feet, too. People were staring, the couple sitting at the table next to us brushing stray drops of coffee from their table and shooting us dirty looks.

Joe held his wet shirt away from his skin, keeping his voice low. "There was nothing I could do. She was severely bulimic, obviously anorexic. She'd taken an extralarge amount of an over-the-counter emetic, and the resulting electrolyte imbalance stopped her heart. It had been too long, and her body was too weak to respond to defibrillation . . ."

"Joe"—I held up a hand—"speak English. I have no idea what you're talking about."

"Neither does he," Crystal sneered. "Stupid doctors. They all think they know so much." She stuck her face up close to his, though he couldn't see her, and shouted, "Bullshit! It's all bullshit! You don't know *me*!"

The next thing I knew, Joe was stumbling backward. He bumped the table behind us, knocked over an empty chair, and landed flat on his ass on the sidewalk.

"How's that for weak?" Crystal shouted, though no one could hear her but me. She lifted a bony middle finger toward Joe in the universal gesture of contempt.

Joe didn't see the finger—he was still on the sidewalk, shocked and covered with coffee, and couldn't have seen it anyway. The people around us were all staring and making concerned noises to each other, like a flock of disturbed pigeons.

Amy, the girl behind the counter at Moonbeans, craned her neck to check out the commotion. "Nicki? Everything okay out there?"

"Everything's fine, Amy. An accident." I knelt to help Joe to his feet, ignoring Crystal for the moment. "You okay?" I murmured, more freaked by the girl's sudden violence than I'd like to admit. I'd seen spirits manipulate objects before, but this chick was nuts. Dead, but still nuts.

Joe nodded sourly, scanning the empty air for an attacker he couldn't see.

I could see her, though, and she creeped me out. Dirty blond hair to her shoulders, shoved carelessly behind her ears. Her arms and legs were so thin they looked like sticks.

Crystal took a step closer.

"Leave us alone," I hissed, very conscious of the fact that people were watching. As far as they were concerned, I was talking to thin air.

"Make me," Crystal said, and smiled an ugly smile. And I do mean ugly—her teeth were bad. Yellowish brown with stains, bright red gums.

Yuck.

"Anything I can do to help?"

I froze, knowing that smoothly sexy male voice all too well.

"My, my. What a mess you've made, Nicki. Boyfriend trouble, I hope?"

I looked up, heart sinking, to see the sexiest lying bastard I'd ever met. Bright blue eyes, sunstreaked blond hair, killer grin, and cheekbones to die for. Today he wore low-slung jeans with a heavy silver wallet chain, black T-shirt.

Black, to match his shriveled heart.

Joe rose to his feet, me along with him. "Friend of yours, Nicki?"

I clutched Joe's arm for courage. "No. Sammy is no friend of mine."

Joe immediately shifted, putting a shoulder between Sammy and me. Though they'd never met, Joe knew all about the man standing before us—including the fact that Sammy wasn't really a *man.*

He was a demon.

The demon, in fact.

Satan. The Devil. The Evil Big Kahuna.

Sammy, known as Samael to the legions of Hell. He'd shown up not long after my near-death experience, making it clear he wanted me on his side; a lover, a partner, a "soldier for his army."

He wanted me to send the spirits who came to me to the Dark, to keep them away from the Light.

But I couldn't do that.

"My reputation precedes me, it seems." Sammy gave a broad smile. He stuck out his hand, for all the world like one regular guy meeting another. Black and silver gleamed—a ring with a star-shaped pattern on his middle finger. Pentagram, black T-shirt . . . the guy was ingenious. He hid in plain sight. "You must be Joe."

Joe stiffened, ignoring the proffered hand. "Get the hell away from us."

"Hell is so boring this time of year," Sammy said cheerfully. "I like it better here."

Crystal laughed, making me jump. All sharp angles and jutting bones, she reminded me of a scarecrow, right down to the straw-like hair. The planes of her face were so sharp, the muscles so stretched. *Creepy.*

"I see you've met my friend, Crystal," Sammy said, his wicked grin widening to a sneer. "Lovely, isn't she?"

Joe's muscles were tight beneath my palm.

"What do you want, Sammy?" *As if I didn't know.*

Sammy took his time answering, sending me a look that would've scorched paint right off the wall.

Silken sheets and strong thighs . . . heat and desire, hard flesh between my legs and a mouth on my nipples . . .

I knew what the horny bastard was doing—he was putting thoughts in my head. Those wicked blue eyes of his had a way of making me *want* to do things. Bad things. Naughty things.

I squeezed Joe's arm, tight. If I gave in to this particular fatal attraction, I'd be screwed, in more ways than one.

Yet the attraction was there.

Taking the devil by the horns, I switched off the porno movie going on inside my head by asking, "Is Crystal one of your new recruits?"

"I prefer the word 'protégé.'" Sammy shrugged, untroubled by my directness. "My new apprentice, if you will." He raised a pair of cool old RayBan shades and held them to the sun, checking for smudges. "No need to be jealous, Nicki . . . unless you're having second thoughts about turning down the job."

He gave me a wicked smile. Evil personified, yet I couldn't help but be drawn to him. Answered to no one, feared no one, did as he pleased. Flawed, yet glorying in his imperfections—his raw sexuality was a huge temptation, and he knew it, dammit.

"Nicki doesn't want anything to do with you," Joe said, his tone harsh. "Leave her alone."

His protectiveness was comforting, but scared me, too. Joe might not be afraid to go head to head with a demon from Hell, but what could he do against a creature like Sammy? Didn't he know how vulnerable he made himself?

Sammy looked at Joe coolly, then gave him the ultimate insult by dismissing him entirely.

"Patience is a virtue, Nicki," Sammy said to me, as though Joe were invisible. "One of the few I seem to have in my possession." Then he laughed softly, shaking his head. "Possession. Oh, I do love that word."

Joe slipped his arm around my waist, jaw set. "Let's go, Nicki." He had three days' worth of stubble on his chin, and he smelled like coffee and sweat, anger barely held in check. His self-control was obviously at its limit.

"Everything okay out here?" It was Amy, studs glinting, eyes gleaming, having left her post behind the register to come out on the sidewalk. Her tone was far too cheerful, and when I saw the smiling looks she was shooting Sammy, I understood why.

She was *so* checking him out. I knew Amy hadn't had a boyfriend in a while, and I also knew she wasn't shy about meeting new guys. Sammy probably looked like fresh meat to a starving lioness.

"Omigod—you're soaking wet." Amy grabbed a couple of napkins from a nearby table and thrust them at Joe, making a total production out of everything. "Are you okay?"

Joe ignored the napkins, never taking his eyes from Sammy. "Fine."

"He's fine," I echoed.

"Um . . ." Amy gave me an eye roll in Sammy's direction, the girly equivalent of a request for an introduction. She seemed oblivious to the tension in the air.

Trapped between Sammy, Joe, and a bony, hostile ghost, I had a sudden, insane urge to giggle. *Amy, this is Satan . . . Satan, this is Amy.*

Joe saved me from making a fool of myself by taking my elbow. "C'mon, Nicki."

"Oh, no, you don't." Once again, though I'd almost forgotten her, Crystal Meth stepped in front of us, grinning that ugly grin.

Shit.

Joe urged me forward, but I tugged my elbow free, giving him a desperate look.

I couldn't just walk through her. That would be gross in ways I couldn't even contemplate.

Crystal stared at me defiantly, daring me with her eyes.

She knew I didn't want to touch her.

She even had the nerve to get cocky, crossing sticklike arms over her concave middle.

Skinny bitch.

"You look familiar." Amy wasn't giving up the chance to talk to a hottie like Sammy, and went for the direct approach. "I think I've seen you here a few times." She was smiling at him, unaware that standing right next to her dream lover was an angry, emaciated ghost.

"What a fat pig," Crystal said, shooting Amy a venomous glance. No one could hear her but me. "Friend of yours, Chubby Cheeks?"

Chubby Cheeks? Me?

Distracted, I opened my mouth to warn Amy away, but Sammy spoke first.

"I'm Sammy Divine, the new owner of Divinyls."

Amy's face lit up. "Oh, you're the guy opening the indie music store across the street!" She was practically drooling.

In a way, I couldn't blame her, because Sammy was *hot.*

As in *hot.*

"Cool." Amy quirked a heavily studded eyebrow,

tucking her hands into her back pockets in the quintessential "boob display" of the red-blooded American female. "Exactly what we needed in Little Five—there aren't enough good music stores around here. You should get with Moonbeans and do some cross-promoting or something."

I'd known this was coming, but I'd tried to forget about Divinyls . . . like if I ignored it, it would go away. The store across the street had been vacant for months. I'd tried to forget that Sammy was determined to insinuate his way into my life. Into my neighborhood. Into my head.

I took comfort in the fact that my sister, Kelly, was safe in Savannah, learning from our grandmother how to resist him.

Grandmother . . . grandfather . . . whatever. In a family like mine, a seventy-year-old transvestite psychic grandparent was practically tame.

"Nicki, let's go," Joe murmured.

"I can't," I whispered. "Crystal's still here. She's blocking me."

Sammy and Amy were chatting it up like old pals. "Divinyls was voted best alternative music store in Savannah five years running, vinyls and CDs," he said. "But it was time to expand, explore new horizons." He gave Amy a devastating smile, a tilt of his streaked blond head. He was wearing it longer these days. "And you are?"

Amy was putty in his hands. Pierced, studded, and tattooed putty.

"Amy." Melted putty. "My name is Amy."

"Well, Amy"—Sammy smiled at her like she was the prettiest girl he'd ever seen—"that's a beautiful rose tattoo on your neck. Very sensual."

She blushed, her tattoo turning a bluish purple.

"I'm filming a commercial for my new shop, and I'd love to use some of the locals. Would you like to be in it?"

"A commercial? On TV? Cool."

Oh, he was good. I had to give him that.

"Just some advertising for the new store— thought I'd shoot it right here on the sidewalk. Little Five Points is such a"—Sammy glanced around, taking in the murals, the shops, the tourists, the freaks, the stoners, the punks and the pin-striped—"such a unique neighborhood. Great setting for a commercial."

And just like that, a guy with a video camera on his shoulder stepped up from somewhere behind Sammy. I honestly didn't know whether he'd been there all the time or just magically appeared. Either way, his camera was rolling, and he was taking footage of the storefronts along Moreland, scanning the sidewalk with his lens.

Another guy appeared, holding a long black stick with a microphone on the end.

Sammy turned his bright blue gaze to Crystal, the Invisible Walking Stick. He smiled at her, intimately, as though they were old friends. "Do you remember our agreement?"

Anyone who heard him would assume he was talking to me.

Crystal's bony edges seemed to soften. Her form wavered once, like a mirage. "I do, Master."

"Then let it begin." Sammy looked me directly in the eye, ignoring Joe, Amy and the anonymous coffee drinkers who watched us curiously over their overpriced cappuccinos and flavored lattes.

"Showtime," he said.

And just like that, the guy holding the camera swung it in my direction. The guy with the microphone came in closer, standing right next to Crystal, though he couldn't see her. Crystal ignored him, smiling her ugly smile and waiting for me to get the gist of what was about to happen.

Enlightenment dawned, but it was too late. Her image wavered again, coalescing into a strip of fog, writhing and coiling, as thin as Crystal herself. Quick as a snake, the fog shot straight toward me.

I would've fallen, would've shouted, would've screamed—but terror rendered me frozen, and a sudden, shocking awareness of my own body rendered me dumb.

Because I could feel her there.

She was *inside* me, all bones and sharp edges, stealing my breath and poking her way into every nook and cranny, every joint, every blood vessel, spreading like a cancer.

"Nicki?" Joe's concerned face swam before my eyes, but I couldn't answer.

You feel me, don't you, Chubby Cheeks? Crystal's voice whispered inside my head. *The Master has given me power.*

To my horror, I heard myself chuckle, as though my body was in on the joke.

Power over you.

I swayed, and felt Joe's arms come around me. Instead of giving me comfort, his touch made me claustrophobic.

"Let go of me," I snapped. The hurt look on his face tore my heart, but I couldn't stop myself. "You murdering bastard."

No one was more shocked to hear those words come out of my mouth than I was.

The camera rolled, Amy gaped, Sammy smiled, and Joe stood like a statue. There was a rush of wind in my head, a blast of ice and fury.

"You killed her," I said. "Crystal Cowart had her whole life ahead of her, and you killed her." My throat was tight, neck stiff, as I struggled to keep the words from spewing forth. But they just kept coming. "You told me so yourself, not two minutes ago. You didn't do anything to save her. You should be arrested for murder."

I managed to take a breath, gasping for air and fighting for control over my body.

You can't win, Chubby Cheeks. Crystal's voice whispered in my ear. *The Master is on my side.*

Another blast of cold rage overwhelmed my brain. "Dr. Joe Bascombe, attending physician at Columbia Memorial Hospital." My arm shot out, stiffly, finger pointing at Joe. "You killed Crystal Cowart."

"Nicki, you're not yourself." Joe's jaw was set, face somber. "Let me take you home."

"Hold on." Sammy stepped forward. "My lady friend here just accused you of murder. I don't think she should be going anywhere with you."

His lady friend? I wanted to laugh, but my body wasn't my own anymore.

Joe's temper flared. "Leave us alone!" He rounded on Sammy, glaring at the cameraman and the guy holding the microphone, too. "And get that camera out of my face."

"Hold on there, buddy," said Sammy, raising his hands. "No need to get violent."

This was a nightmare—Crystal seethed within me, her anger leaving me rigid. I fought her as hard as I could, biting my lip and *willing* her to leave my body.

"I'm fat," I heard myself say. "I'm a fat pig with chubby cheeks. My name is Nicki Styx, and I'm a fatty, fat, fat, fat."

Amy—who I'd forgotten about—choked back a laugh, covering her mouth with both hands. Beside her, Sammy barely hid a grin, and their amusement infuriated me.

It was my body, dammit. Not hers. And there wasn't a damn thing wrong with it.

I was not fat.

"I pretend like I'm so cool and hip and gothic," I went on, like a ventriloquist dummy at the State Fair, "but I'm really just a pathetic loser. Oh, and dead people talk to me." My cheek muscles lifted in a grotesque semblance of a smile. "Come visit me down in Little Five Points, and I'll help you speak with your lost loved ones. I'm channeling right now, in fact. Crystal Cowart has more to say, and I am merely her vessel."

Okay, that's it.

No hateful little bag of bones with an imaginary axe to grind against my boyfriend was going to make me play the fool.

Grimly, in my mind and in my heart, I fought Crystal's possession. She poked and jabbed at the edges of my psyche, at my very soul, but I closed my eyes, concentrating. There came a sudden rush of sound in my ears, like wind and rain through an open window, and in that instant, I knew I'd won. Sensation flooded me, all of it my own. Unprepared for the suddenness of Crystal's exit, my knees buckled.

Joe caught me before I hit the ground, and this time, I didn't push him away. I clung to him like a drowning man clings to a life preserver.

"I'm sorry, baby," I gasped, "that wasn't me. I would never have said those things. It was Crystal." I was completely drained. My head felt too heavy for my neck, so I let it fall against him.

Joe's jaw clenched, and he didn't answer, but his hands were gentle. His arm was warm and strong against my back as he drew me closer.

"Let's just go," he murmured, and before I could blink, he slipped his other arm beneath my knees and swung me high against his chest.

Dr. Bascombe was in the house, and I was more than happy to let him take charge.

"Well, there you have it, folks." Sammy gestured at the cameraman to turn the camera in his direction. "Another one of the eclectic characters in this wonderful little Atlanta neighborhood called Little Five Points."

He didn't pay any attention as Joe swept me off

down the sidewalk, training all his bright blue charm on the camera.

"That was Nicki Styx, owner and manager of Handbags and Gladrags, a cool little vintage store right here in Little Five."

The bastard.

"Guess Nicki's reading tarot cards in the back room these days, hm?" Sammy winked at the camera as though it were an old friend, making a joke at my expense.

"Hey," I made a weak-sounding protest over Joe's shoulder, but we were already too far away to do any good. Besides, people were looking at us strangely enough without my getting into a shouting match with a guy who was filming a commercial.

Exhausted and embarrassed, I tucked my head under Joe's neck and let him carry me back to my store.

The rest of the day was sure to be a complete loss. Joe insisted on driving me home, and I didn't argue. A worried Evan promised to bring my car home and check on me later. I laid my head back in the seat, drained and stunned, as Joe drove.

"Punk." His anger was icy, contained, and thankfully, didn't seem to be directed at me. "You'd think a guy who claims to be the Devil could fight his own battles instead of getting a girl to do it for him."

I didn't answer, knowing he had good cause to be angry.

"Every day in the E.R., I see things most people would never believe—shootings, stabbings, battered wives and girlfriends, children who've been abused or neglected. I see his hand in all of it."

I risked a glance at his face. His jaw was set in a hard line.

"If he thinks I'm going to turn tail and run because he showed up in the flesh, he's sadly mistaken," Joe said grimly. "I've beaten him before, on the operating table, and I'll do it again, in the real world." He shook his dark head, gaze turned inward despite his attention to the road. "I'm just sorry the bastard is using me to get to you."

He reached over and took my hand, and I never wanted to let it go. "You know that's what he's doing, right?"

I hadn't thought that deep yet, but I knew Joe was right. Sammy was letting me know just how vulnerable I, and those I loved, were.

I wondered sickly about the many different ways there were to torment a person.

"Don't let him rattle you, Nicki. I'm a big boy. I can take care of myself. You just concentrate on staying strong."

Considering how, at the moment, I bore more resemblance to a limp noodle than I cared to admit,
I almost laughed.

"You okay, babe? Dizzy? Nauseous? Headache?"

"I'm okay," I murmured in return. "I just need
to scrub myself clean and sleep for a week." I felt
dazed, violated. Familiar scenery went unnoticed
as we sped past. My heart was pounding like a
drum, and that wasn't good. My mind and body
had been invaded by a dead girl; Sammy was back,
and I was afraid. What was happening to me?

What was *going* to happen to me?

Joe seemed determined to look after me, and
I didn't mind. It had been a while since I'd been
looked after, and at the moment, I didn't seem to
be doing a very good job looking after myself.
When we got to my house, he helped me with my
clothes and ran the shower, making sure the water
was hot before helping me step over the edge of
the tub.

"I'll be waiting right here," he said, lowering the
lid of my hot pink fuzzy toilet seat and settling
himself on it.

"You don't need to—"

"Let me know if you feel dizzy or faint," he
said firmly, reaching to twitch the shower curtain
closed. "I'll be right here to catch you." And he sat

there patiently while I went through the motions of washing.

Contaminated. Drained. Crystal's invasion had shaken me to the core. How was it possible for two people to share a body? My body. Bad enough the unpleasant tingling as she'd spread throughout my veins, but I'd felt the malevolent maelstrom of her emotions, as well. Anger, bitterness, rage. What had Crystal Cowart been so angry about?

She'd left me feeling poisoned.

Joe helped me into a soft pair of pajama bottoms and a T-shirt, as though I were a child who needed help getting dressed. I could tell he was still angry by the white lines around his mouth, but his hands couldn't have been more gentle. He pulled back the covers on my bed and ushered me in, tucking them around me.

I felt like I could sleep for a week.

"He really gets to you, doesn't he?"

My eyelids wanted to open, but they were too heavy. The pillow was so soft against my cheek. "What do you mean?" I mumbled, afraid to hear his answer. I was doing my best not to think about Sammy. Joe was the man I wanted—I didn't understand how I could possibly be drawn to someone else, even for an instant.

Joe lay down on top of the covers and spooned against me, tucking his knees beneath mine. "I know what he wants, Nicki," he murmured, kissing the place where my shoulder met my neck, "and I know why he wants it." He nuzzled me there, his warm weight giving me reassurance, his voice soothing despite the words he was saying. "I'm not blind. You're special, in so many ways."

"I don't want to be special," I managed to grump, still not opening my eyes.

He chuckled against my hair, giving the damp strands a quick kiss. "I don't think you have a choice in the matter," he whispered, eerily echoing my thoughts. He kissed my hair again. "You are what you are. Now go to sleep. I'll be here for a few hours, then I have another shift. Evan will be here to check on you later."

I felt a wave of contentment, of safety, and then I drifted into the welcome oblivion of sleep.

Hours later, I felt him leave, and groggily responded to his murmured kiss of farewell. The bed seemed empty without him, but I couldn't seem to stay awake.

Dreams, disjointed but intense, broken by snatches of consciousness that registered Evan's voice, the sound of the evening news coming from the TV in the living room, and even the quick *beep, blip, beep* of the alarm as Evan set it for the evening. Then I heard his car start and the slow rumble of the engine as he drove away, back to his own apartment. I glanced at the clock and saw it was nearly midnight.

I'd slept the day away and wanted only to sleep more. I got up long enough to use the bathroom and get myself something to drink, then I was back in bed. Vaguely, I wondered if I was getting sick, but I knew what the real problem was. Life had just taken a sudden turn, and it was a scary one. The longer I could keep the covers over my head, the better.

But in the end, there was no escape. Somewhere in the night Sammy came to me again, using a much more subtle approach than the one he'd used on the sidewalk. I barely felt it as his fingers skimmed my skin, moving up and down my arm, soothingly, then along a bare hip. A tingle of pleasure as his knuckle brushed my nipple ring. I think I murmured something as his kisses burned my neck, probably moaned as his strong legs spread my own. Then he was inside, and I woke with a start, drenched with sweat, heart pounding.

I lay there in the dark, in the home I'd lived in as a child, and knew real fear. My dad wasn't here anymore to chase the boogeyman from under the bed, and my mom had brought me my last glass of water. They were both gone, lost on a rainy stretch of road eight years earlier.

Trembling and throbbing, I heard again Sammy's voice in my head—the words he'd spoken in my dream. The words he'd said as he slid himself home.

"Come over to the dark side, Nicki." He'd smiled, as only Sammy could, as he'd taken possession of me in his own way. "We have cookies."

CHAPTER 3

"Possession is hardly something to fool around with, Nicki." My sister Kelly's tone did nothing to reassure me.

"Gee, ya think?" I rolled my eyes, though she couldn't see it over the phone. "It's hardly like I *wanted* the skinny skank to do it, you know. It was creepy. It was gross." I shuddered at the memory of Crystal's bony essence, prickling and bubbling in my veins like Drano. "I have to figure out how to keep it from happening again."

"I'll do some research. There must be ways to guard against possession."

I slid into a chair at the kitchen table, breath-

ing a little easier. If anybody could find out anything, it was Kelly. We were twins, though we'd
only known each other less than six months,
and couldn't be more different. My home was
in Atlanta, while she'd had spent the winter in a
haunted house in Savannah, learning how to cope
with the family "knack"—our weird ability to see
and hear the dead.

"Why didn't you call me yesterday, right after
this happened? Are you okay?" The way she fired
questions at me told me how worried she was.
"Any aftereffects? Weird feelings? Hallucinations?
Anything like that?"

"No, but I was really out of it afterward—
completely wiped. Joe brought me home and put
me in bed, and that's the last I remember until I
woke up this morning."

Well, not the last thing I remembered.

But Kelly didn't need to know about the
dream—it was too personal.

"What do you think Sammy wants this time?"
Her voice was somber.

"The same thing he wanted last time, I guess—
he's pretty determined to get me on his side.
Grandma Bijou told me he culls his victims from
the herd the way a wolf does with the sheep—
which is why he played us against each other

when we were in Savannah. I can only assume he's trying to create problems between me and Joe, so I'll fall into his arms or something."

Or something.

"How's Joe taking all this?"

"He's not happy, but he seems to be handling it okay. We really haven't had a lot of time to talk about it—I was practically comatose yesterday, and he's at work now. Life in the E.R. doesn't stop just because you have a weird girlfriend," I joked, knowing Joe and I still needed to talk more. Just because he *seemed* okay didn't mean he was.

There was silence. Then she said, "Savannah is only four hours away, you know. You should come here, to the Blue Dahlia, and be with family."

A pang of guilt hit me. The only family we had was the elderly Bijou Boudreaux, transvestite florist and Southern belle extraordinaire. The sweet old lady who owned the Blue Dahlia was really a man, and either the citizens of Savannah didn't know or didn't care. Our mother—the woman who'd given us up at birth—had been Bijou's daughter, Peaches Boudreaux, who'd died before we had a chance to get to know her.

"Bijou will be worried," she said, still working the guilt angle.

"Don't tell Bijou anything, and she'll have no reason to be worried. Better yet, distract her—

send her shopping for new cushions for the porch swing or something."

The Blue Dahlia was an elegant old house, our family heritage, and Kelly loved it there. If things had turned out differently, we would've grown up together in the rambling old place. But Peaches had given us up for adoption, and we'd been separated, neither of us ever knowing the other twin existed. She'd made her living as a psychic before she died, and I still wasn't quite certain how to feel about her.

Kelly sighed, exasperated. "Grandma Bijou is very sensitive, Nicki. I can't pretend with her; she'll see right through me. She'll know something's wrong."

"I'll tell her myself when I'm ready," I said firmly. "I'll call the flower shop and talk to her when she's Leonard. She's much more reasonable when she's Leonard."

"You're not safe in Atlanta." Kelly changed tack, returning to the original argument.

"I'm not safe in Savannah," I said. I didn't blame her for nagging, but Little Five Points was my home. "Sammy could show up wherever I go. I'm staying here."

Knowing my stubborn streak as well as her own, Kelly finally dropped the argument. "I can't believe you didn't call me yesterday when this happened." Her sigh of frustration came through loud and clear.

"I'm sorry, okay? I'm still new at this 'depending on other people' thing. I've been taking care of myself for almost eight years."

"You depend on Evan all the time."

"I've known Evan since we were kids. He grew up next door."

"You have to let me in, Nicki."

Silence on my part. She was right, and I knew it. I was a bad sister.

So I said the words aloud. "I'm a bad sister."

"You're *the* bad sister," Kelly corrected me, "not *a* bad sister." She giggled a little, and I knew by her teasing that she'd already forgiven me. "I'm the good one, remember?"

I gave a snort. "That's just what you want people to think. There's a bad girl under that good girl exterior. I've seen her peek out once or twice."

She laughed. "People who live in glass houses shouldn't throw stones—I've seen your good girl side pop up more than once."

"That is a bold-faced lie." My outrage was fake, and she knew it. "I'm bad to the bone, and don't you forget it."

"Right. Now go pet a kitten or something while I do my research. I'll call you back."

I hung up feeling better, knowing that Kelly and

I were cool and that whether I was used to it or not, she had my back.

Nicki Styx and Kelly Charon. How ironic that we'd both been adopted by parents with names taken straight from Greek tragedy. Styx was the dark river that separated the living from the dead; Charon, the grim guardian who ferried souls across it. Separating my sister and me at birth hadn't protected us from our strange heritage; death had found us anyway.

The phone rang again as I was putting it back in the cradle. I jumped, nearly dropping the damn thing. Checking the caller ID, I saw it read JOE OFFICE, and let my shoulders ease.

"Hey, baby." He'd only been gone a few hours, and I missed him already.

"You need to come down to the E.R., Nicki." Joe didn't sound nearly as cheerful as I'd hoped he would. "Something weird's going on down here."

I went cold all over.

"What is it?" Visions of floating surgical instruments and electronic equipment gone haywire filled my head.

"The hospital is holding an inquiry into Crystal Cowart's death," Joe answered tersely. "Administration has already scheduled me for a meeting with the staff attorney. They want my statement."

I wasn't sure what to say.

"Sammy got his footage on the eleven o'clock news," Joe said grimly. "The entire city of Atlanta has now seen you publicly accuse me of murder."

"Oh my God!" *Shit.* "I'm so sorry, Joe. You know I wasn't myself!"

You're not supposed to speak ill of the dead, but I couldn't help but think it—Crystal Cowart had stirred up a lot of trouble. I shuddered involuntarily, remembering her icy rage. "I know you'd never just let someone die!"

Joe's voice softened. "I know, Nicki. I know. I'm not mad at you. I just need you to come down and give the lawyer your statement, too."

The back of my neck prickled.

"You mean, like tell some guy in a suit that I was possessed? That the ghost of Crystal Cowart appeared while we were having Mocha Lattes?" Selfish of me to think of myself at a time like this, but I couldn't help it.

I didn't want to be some freak on the eleven o'clock news.

But I didn't want Joe in trouble, either.

"I'm sorry, baby," I took a deep breath, and let it out. "Of course I'll come down." I ran my fingers through my hair, wishing I had time for another shower. "I'll tell the lawyer I was whacked out on 'E' or something."

"You're not going to lie about taking ecstasy," Joe said firmly. "You don't take drugs, and you know it."

"The suit doesn't know it," I grumped back. "And I don't care what some fat-cat lawyer thinks, anyway. Give me a few minutes to pull myself together, and I'll drive over."

"No need to rush. The appointment isn't until two o'clock."

I glanced at the clock on the microwave, relieved to see that it was still early, not even eight thirty. Morning sun streamed through the window over the sink, striking the bottles I kept on the sill and turning them into colorful sun catchers.

"I'm really sorry, Joe." *Poor guy deserves better.* I was trouble with a capital "T."

"I'll let you make it up to me later."

Despite my gloomy thoughts, I couldn't help but smile. The coffee was ready, and I helped myself to it gratefully, cradling the phone between an ear and a shoulder.

"Oh, you will, will you? How generous of you. Maybe you'd like me to rub your feet, get you a newspaper, make you dinner?"

Joe burst out laughing, and it did my heart good to hear it. "That's when I'd *really* worry about you being possessed by somebody else. The Nicki Styx I know isn't nearly so submissive."

"Hey, it could happen," I joked, getting into it. "I could be possessed by the spirit of June Cleaver."

Joe's chuckles died, and after a moment, so did mine, leaving silence on the line.

"I guess that's not really funny, is it?"

"How are you feeling this morning?" Joe answered my question with a few of his own. "Any aftereffects? Headache? You promised to tell me if you had symptoms of any kind."

"I'm okay." Doctor or no doctor, the concern in his voice gave me the warm fuzzies. "I called Kelly, and she's already surfing the Internet for ways to guard against what happened yesterday."

"You should talk to Bijou. Tell her exactly what happened."

I was surprised. He seemed to have more faith in the eccentric old woman than I did.

"I'm going to." I foresaw at least a two-hour phone conversation, including a lecture about family and another guilt trip about not staying in Savannah. "I'll call her, but first I'm going to get cleaned up and head to the store. Evan was there alone all day yesterday."

"Be careful, Nicki." No more teasing—Joe was now dead serious. "Sammy opened that store in

Little Five Points to be near you. He's obviously out to stir up trouble. I wish you'd stay home."

I sighed. "I can't give up my life, Joe. It doesn't matter whether Sammy is across the street, in Savannah, or in the depths of Hell. He could show up anytime, anywhere."

Joe didn't answer, so I went on. "He can't make me do anything I don't want to do, remember?" *Or so I'm told.* "I have to face him down. It's the only way to make him go away. He'll get bored soon—he just wants to scare me." *And doing a good job, too.* But I didn't say that out loud.

"If I wasn't concerned about what he might do to you in retaliation, I'd pay him a visit myself." The cold anger in his tone made me very nervous. I'd seen only a tiny portion of what Sammy was capable of, and I knew he could do much, much worse; Joe losing his job was one thing, Joe losing his life was another.

"Don't do that, please." I'd beg on my knees if I had to. "He's not mortal—you can't deal with him like you would an ordinary man. Please, Joe—for me. Don't go there."

"I can't stand doing nothing," he bit out. "It goes against the grain."

I could picture him now, running ragged fingers through his dark hair, looking tired and worried and sexy as hell. I envisioned him in his cramped little office at the E.R., surrounded by stacks of paperwork: medical charts to be reviewed, test results to be deciphered, life-and-death decisions to be made.

He so didn't need this.

"It's going to be okay." I forced myself to sound cheerful, reassuring. "I've dealt with Sammy before and lived to tell about it." I gave a little laugh. "If I can handle voodoo queens, haunted houses, and hundred-year-old ghosts, I can handle Sammy."

CHAPTER 4

Forty-five minutes later I was out the door and on my way to work. I took extra care to make sure the house was locked and the burglar alarm set.

Not that an alarm system would help against demons from the underworld, but whatever.

The loud thump of bass from a car radio came to my ear as I walked down the driveway toward my little red Honda. The trees on my street were thick with spring growth, so I couldn't see where the music was coming from, but it was way too loud for this quiet neighborhood.

AC/DC's "Highway To Hell," getting louder and louder.

No way. Not possible.

I stood outside my car, listening, as the music got even louder.

And then he was there, pulling into my driveway with a crunch of gravel and a blast of sound, looking wicked cool behind the wheel of a classic black vintage Mustang convertible.

Sammy. In the flesh. Again.

The Mustang came to a halt right behind my Honda, blocking the driveway. Sammy's hand flicked toward the radio dial, and the music died abruptly, leaving only the low rumble of the engine in its wake.

"Care for a ride, little girl?"

Sammy lowered his RayBans enough to peer over, giving me his sexiest grin. Bright blue eyes, full of mischief. The cocky bastard appeared to be truly enjoying himself.

"I'm glad you're here, actually." I wasn't going to let Sammy's commando attack rattle me. *So he knows where I live . . . why expect anything different?* "It gives me the chance to say 'fuck off' in person."

Sammy burst out laughing, tilting his head back and slipping his sunglasses into place.

My knees were shaking, but he didn't know that. Unless he had x-ray vision, which he might, but I didn't care. I was no expert on the powers of

Satan—my time as a goth had been spent exploring the fashion side, not the dark side.

Besides, I was pretty pissed. His little trick with the video footage had been totally uncalled for.

"Oh, Nicki," he said, still smiling. "Do you know how rare it is for someone to say that to me?" He cocked his head to the right, patting the seat next to him with a flourish. "Come, ride with me, and we'll talk."

"No." I took refuge in what I'd learned about Sammy in the basement of an old house in Savannah; he had no power without my consent. If I didn't *want* to go for a ride with him, I didn't *have* to go for a ride with him.

"Don't you want to talk about your boyfriend's little problem? I can fix it, you know."

Dammit.

"Hear me out." Sammy placed a hand over his heart, almost as though he had one. "That's all I ask. I promise I'll be a perfect gentleman." His smile faded, became a rueful grin. "I just want to talk to you, Nicki. One early-morning ride on a beautiful spring day, that's all I ask. If you still want to be a good little girl after that—though I can't imagine why—I'll leave you alone."

"You'll leave me alone." I was highly suspicious of any plan as simple as this.

Sammy nodded, hand still on his heart. "I'll leave you alone."

It was a bad idea. I knew it in my heart, I knew it in my soul.

But I saw Joe's face, the way it looked when I'd opened my eyes that day in the E.R.—concerned, caring, totally hot in a guardian angel kind of way. Joe was meant to be a doctor, and my accusation of murder could well end his career.

"You'll keep your hands to yourself," I said flatly, "and you'll have me back here within one hour."

Sammy grinned, cheerful as a child who'd gotten his own way. "One hour," he said. "Honest to God."

I cringed, literally, half-expecting a lightning bolt to strike Sammy on the head. "Are you kidding me?"

"Lighten up, Nicki." Sammy leaned over the passenger seat and threw open the car door. "Where's your sense of humor?"

Atlanta in the springtime is a beautiful thing; pink and purple azaleas carpet the hillsides, the white dapple of dogwood everywhere you look.

I couldn't enjoy a minute of the passing scenery, even though I adored Atlanta, adored azaleas, and adored vintage cars like the cool old Mustang. To be cruising down Stone Mountain Freeway in one, top down, should've been a real treat, but my stomach was churning. AC/DC was no longer blaring on the radio, but I was on my own private highway to Hell.

"It was a woman, you know," Sammy said casually. He drove one-handed, resting an elbow out the Mustang's open window. The wind whipped his short blond hair. "Women have always been my downfall."

"You're going to blame women for your downfall?" I wasn't buying it. "It takes two, buddy."

Sammy shook his head, smiling a little. "Not all women, Nicki. Just one woman."

"Oh, I see. Some woman broke your heart, and that's when you decided to become evil." I couldn't believe I was talking to the Devil this way. "I've heard this same sob story at goth bars all over Atlanta. Can't you come up with a better line than that?"

There was silence, and for a moment I worried that I'd gone too far.

"She didn't break my heart." Sammy shook his head. He was watching the road, but his thoughts were obviously elsewhere. "Lilith was only doing what she was created to do."

Lilith?

Stone Mountain Freeway was dotted with scenic rest stops overlooking the mountain. Sammy slowed, pulling into one. The Mustang eased to a stop with a sluggish crunch of gravel, and he cut the engine.

"It's been eons since I've felt the need to explain myself." He laughed a little, as though finding such an idea hard to believe, then looked away, toward the trees.

I said nothing, and after a moment, Sammy slipped off his RayBans and turned his head, piercing me with those blue eyes. "Hear me out."

I sighed, resigned to hearing a load of crap, and wanting only to get it over with so I could go home. The front seat seemed a bit cramped all of a sudden, his lean, jeans-clad leg far too close to mine. "Go ahead." I checked my watch. "You've got about forty minutes left on your hour. Tell me your story."

"I was an angel once." Sammy said it simply, as a statement of fact. He lifted a hand—bare of rings today, I noted—and waved it toward the clouds over Stone Mountain. "Long ago, I rode the heights of glory with my celestial brothers, heights you could never imagine." For just a moment, his face was rapt, but the look was fleeting, marred by the sardonic curl of a lip. "Then I made the mistake of looking down, turning my eyes from the heights and letting myself be distracted by the blue-green bauble known as Earth."

How weird to hear the planet referred to as a cosmic marble.

"I saw a woman." Sammy's gaze turned inward now, remembering. "She was gathering fruit"—here he smiled—"just as the legends say, but she . . . she was the real fruit. More delectable than the reddest apple, the ripest peach, sent to tempt mankind with her sweet juices."

I shifted, uncomfortable with the erotic imagery.

"There was no shame," Sammy murmured, almost to himself, "no shame in what we did. Was she not placed in that garden to arouse man's desire? If poor Adam, writhing in his mortal coils, was powerless in her grasp, then how was I, an angel already so attuned to ecstasy, to resist her?"

My mouth fell open.

"You're blaming *Eve*?" It'd been many years since I'd been in Sunday school, but even a bad girl like me was familiar with the story of the Garden of Eden.

"Lilith." He shook his head. "Her name was Lilith. Storytellers always tinker with the facts."

Whatever. "You're blaming Lilith for tempting *you* and getting you kicked out of Heaven?" This was a total reversal of the Bible story, and quite frankly, not one I was buying. "I suppose she waved a couple of palm fronds to get your attention, then took advantage of your delicate angel sensibilities."

Why do guys always blame it on the woman?

Sammy rolled his eyes at my sarcasm. "You don't understand, Nicki. Lilith was no innocent; she'd already known the touch of a man. *I* was the innocent. I knew nothing of the physical—I was an archangel, for heaven's sake! But Lilith wanted much more than a naked ape and his pitiful little banana. She caught me spying on her and seduced me, I swear it."

"Be honest, Sammy. You saw it, you wanted it, you took it." I felt a raw flash of jealousy at the mental image I'd created and hated myself for it. "For all I know, Lilith was happy in her little garden, tending her little plot, being faithful to her man. You talk of being seduced—how in the world was Lilith supposed to resist *you*?"

I could've bitten my tongue, but it was too late.

Sammy smiled. "I'll take that as a compliment."

Now it was my turn to roll my eyes, which gave me a chance to look away. The guy's sex appeal was immense, and I couldn't help but wonder if other parts of him were, too.

"I haven't finished my story yet," he said mildly.

"What's your real name?" If we were going to have this conversation, I felt better leading it than trying to follow it.

"Samael."

I shifted in the seat to face him, shoulder against the car door. "That's it?" I was highly skeptical. "What about Lucifer, Beelzebub, the Great Satan?"

Sammy shrugged. "You asked my name, not what people call me. Besides, flattered as I am at the comparison, I'm not that high in the underworld hierarchy. Satan is much more imposing in person." He flashed me a smile. "Though I'm much better-looking."

Now I was even more skeptical. "Now you're telling me that you're *not* the Devil."

"A minor demon only." Sammy reached between his knees and adjusted his seat, sliding it back. "One among many. We are Legion, after all."

My blood ran cold.

"You're a liar." No one could be more devilishly imposing than he was.

Sammy looked at me intently, bright blue eyes very serious.

"That's true. I'm a liar." He looked very different without his usual sexy smirk. "But I'm not lying now."

I had a flashback to one of my favorite movies

when I was a kid; a fantasy adventure called *Laby-*
rinth. In it, a fantastically costumed and very sexy
David Bowie plays a wicked Goblin King, out to
corrupt an innocent young girl. The sweet young
thing has only her wits to save her as she wends
her way through the labyrinth, her unwanted
attraction to the Goblin King distracting her at
every turn.

But I was no sweet young thing, and this guy
was no David Bowie.

He looked a lot more like Billy Idol, which
made my situation much, much worse. I *loved*
Billy Idol.

"What do you want from me?" I felt panicky
all of a sudden, claustrophobic despite the fact
that we sat in an open convertible. The Mustang
was in full sight of the road and any passing
cars.

"You know what I want from you, Nicki."

"I already told you, back in Savannah, that I
wasn't going to help recruit any souls for your
'army.'" I was beginning to feel desperate. "I don't
need that on my conscience."

"At least you have one," Sammy said quickly,
looking at me curiously. "What does it feel like?"

I was hardly qualified to answer that question.

"Just leave me alone."

"I can't do that."

Now I was getting pissed. "Why not? What did I ever do to you?"

He shook his head, not taking his eyes from me. "Nicki, when I'm in the flesh, I'm 'in the flesh.'"

My throat went dry.

"Your flesh calls to mine, and when that happens, I'm powerless against it."

Holy shit. The Devil had the hots for me.

"Just as I was powerless when I first saw Lilith, there in the garden."

I really didn't know what to say, so I kept quiet. The moment seemed surreal—the *swish* of cars as they passed, the sun beating down on my head, Sammy's voice saying things I didn't want to hear.

"It's part of my *punishment*, you see." His lip curled in a way that was already disturbingly familiar. "Lust is what I chose over Paradise, so lust is now what rules me." He glanced down at his lap, and added, "Even as we speak."

I refused to look. I wasn't going to look. My eyeballs would burn in their sockets before I looked.

I looked.

But just for a second, a split second, before my eyes jerked back to the Mustang's dashboard. *So what if the Devil knows how to fill out a pair of jeans?*

"Gee, that looks painful. You should put some ice on it."

Sammy laughed, low in his throat. But he didn't move any closer, and that was good.

A dragonfly hovered in the grass near the car. I focused on the shimmer of its wings, letting it ground me, but my heart was racing.

"You told me you could fix things for Joe," I said flatly.

"That I can." Sammy sighed. "But I'm not ready to yet."

"That was really crappy, what you did." Anger felt better than panic, so I latched on to the feeling with both hands. "Sending Crystal to creep me out like that"—I shuddered at the memory of the anorexic girl's possession—"and forcing me into saying those things about Joe." I turned my head and glared at him. "And putting it on the news? Joe's never done anything to you! You may have ruined his career!"

"Oh, pish." He waved a hand, obviously not caring.

"'*Pish*'? What the hell kind of word is '*pish*'?"

Sammy laughed at the look on my face. "Sorry, when you've lived as long as I have, you sometimes get the current slang wrong. I believe the modern-day equivalent would be 'whatever.'"

I was not amused.

"Look." He shifted in his seat, lifting a knee to rest partly on the console between us. "I brought you out here to tell you my story, not to talk about your boyfriend."

"Your story doesn't add up, Sammy."

"My point in telling you about Lilith is to explain why I do what I do. Don't you want to hear my side?"

"You go around ruining people's lives because you couldn't keep your pitchfork in your pants? Doesn't make a whole lot of sense to me."

"I was tempted, Nicki. I was deliberately tempted, then punished for making the wrong choice." His voice turned bitter. "Apparently 'sleeping with the daughters of men' was a cosmic no-no, but it would've been nice to know that ahead of time. I didn't ask to be created any more than you asked to be born. Why should I be punished for following the instincts I was given at creation? Should you be punished for being who you are?"

Sammy's argument was making a little more sense than I wanted it to.

"So now I do to others what was done to me. I tempt, then watch as others fall prey to temptation, just as I did. Every time it happens—and it *always* happens—it proves that I was treated unfairly. Perhaps one day the proof will be overwhelming, and I'll be forgiven and allowed back into the celestial fold."

I stared at him, dumbfounded. "You think that what you do is the way to forgiveness? That's really twisted."

For the first time, I saw a hint of impatience in his face. "I've had millennia to become that way. What's your excuse?"

My mouth fell open, but I shut it pretty quickly. *Dissed by the Devil . . . what's a girl to do?*

"Look at it this way." Sammy cocked his head, blond hair gleaming in the sun. His bone structure was beautifully male—cheekbones to die for, big hands, strong chin. "Maybe I don't like being evil . . . did you ever think of that? Maybe I'm wrong, and maybe temptation *can* be resisted." He leaned toward me, leather creaking. His bright blue gaze held me pinned. "But if I'm right, then we're wasting precious time here, Nicki. You and I would be so good together. I know you feel it."

Problem was, I did feel it. I'd felt it the moment I'd first laid eyes on him last Halloween, in a club called the Vortex. Back when I'd thought he was a real person. The attraction had been immediate and intense, but I was committed to Joe then, and I was still committed to him. I hadn't known who Sammy really was until much later, and by then he'd been much easier to resist.

Until now.

A faint whiff of his aftershave reached me. Something subtle, yet spicy, smelling of heat, desire, decadence. I was glad I was sitting down, because my knees were weak. I'd always been a sucker for guys who smelled as great as they looked; it always made me wonder how they tasted.

"Take me home," I said abruptly.

Fine lines crinkled around Sammy's eyes as he smiled. He didn't come any closer, but he didn't pull away, either. "I know you want me, Nicki. Why are you making it so"—he lifted one perfectly arched eyebrow—"hard?"

"Take me home."

My voice was rising, and with good reason. I was *this* far from a panic attack—Sammy was about to have an hysterical woman on his hands.

Or his hands on an hysterical woman.

Either scenario was a distinct possibility.

"You said you'd be a gentleman," I blurted. "I listened to your story, just like we agreed, and the answer is still no. Take me home."

He leaned back, and I breathed a little easier. My heart was pounding like a scared rabbit's. Not a good thing for a woman with a heart murmur.

"You do realize that I can make your life a living hell, don't you?" His tone was conversational, not angry at all.

"You mean you haven't started yet?"

Sammy chuckled as he reached between his knees, readjusting his seat. He slipped on his Ray-Bans and turned the key, bringing the Mustang's engine to life.

"Oh, I've only just begun, Nicki." He turned his head, giving me a wicked grin. "I've only just begun." His hand moved in my direction, and I jumped, but he was only reaching for the gearshift. Gravel crunched as he aimed the car toward the highway. "Buckle up."

"Hey . . . wait a minute." The hair on the back of my neck rose—I hadn't forgotten the terms of our agreement. "You said if I listened to your story and still said 'no', you'd leave me alone."

Sammy barely glanced in his side view mirror as he pulled out onto Stone Mountain Freeway. "Surely you know me better than that by now." The wind whipped his short blond hair, making it spikier than ever.

"I lied."

CHAPTER 5

"You went *where* with *who*?" Evan's voice rose with every syllable. "Are you nuts? What the hell were you thinking?"

I shot him a look over the jewelry counter, in no mood for a lecture.

He quickstepped down from the window display—he'd been dressing our Jayne Mansfield mannequin in a white lace Gunne Sax dress from the seventies. It was too virginal for her, and the ruffles didn't suit her generous curves. "You need to stay far, far away from that guy! Yesterday you were possessed by a dead girl, and today you go for a drive with the Devil?" His face was almost as white as Jayne's dress. "Are you insane?"

"Depends on who you ask."

Evan was not amused. "I can't believe you went off alone with Sammy, Nicki. Promise me you won't do that again."

I looked at him sourly over the bracelets I was sorting. He knew I didn't like being made to promise, because I always did my best to keep my promises.

"Promise me," he insisted.

Familiar with that tone of rising hysteria, I sighed. He was worried, and with good reason. "I promise," I said. It wasn't like I was going to do it again anyway. "But nothing happened, and you need to calm down. I know it's hard to believe, but Sammy just wanted to talk."

Evan clutched the yellow straw hat he was about to put on Jayne a little too tightly. "Talk?" he squeaked.

"You're crumpling that hat, and you've got to be kidding—it's way too much with those ruffles."

Color rushed back into his cheeks, and I was relieved. Seeing him pale as a statue made the situation worse. This was a guy who couldn't watch a scary movie without covering his eyes, yet the poor baby ended up partners with a girl who saw dead people and got hit on by the Devil.

"So you're a critic this morning, is that it?" He

tossed the hat aside, a quick gesture that showed his irritation. "I suppose you don't like *my* outfit, either, Miss I'm-Not-Afraid-Of-Anything," he snipped.

That statement was *so* not true, on both levels, and he knew it; he looked fabulous as ever in loose linen pants and a fitted black tee. His belt was a narrow vintage Gucci, black with a thin silver buckle.

And I *was* afraid. Very afraid. But it wouldn't help to let him see it.

"Love the outfit," I said sincerely. "I can really tell you've been working out." I grinned, doing my best to lighten the mood. "Having a bouncer for a boyfriend obviously agrees with you."

"Hmpf." He allowed himself to be only partially mollified. "Butch is only part of the reason I've buffed up. You know I've always kept an eye on my figure."

"You have." I bobbed my head in total agreement. "And every other man's."

Evan smiled a little at that, and I knew the threat of a hissy fit was over, at least for now.

"Only the cute ones," he amended.

"Only the cute ones," I agreed.

With a sigh, he went back to dressing Jayne. "I know what you're doing, Nicki, so stop trying to change the subject." A floral scarf was held against

Jayne's dress, then discarded. "This is serious. The Devil just moved in right across the street." A nervous glance toward Divinyls through the front window. Bright red banners marked GRAND OPENING fluttered in the morning breeze. "He showed up at your house."

"So he did," I said, keeping my voice steady, "and there's nothing I can do about it."

"You can stay away from him," Evan snapped. The way he was flipping through the scarf rack told me he was more scared than angry.

I didn't blame him.

"Sammy says he's not the Devil," I said, with a vague hope of making Evan feel better. "He says he's only a minor demon."

He threw up his hands. "Does it matter? Oh my God, Nicki!"

I picked a simple pair of faux pearl earrings and an ivory Bakelite bracelet for Jayne to wear with her ruffles, and slid the jewelry cabinet closed. "It's weird," I said thoughtfully. "He's never overtly threatening toward me personally. He really seems to want me to *like* him." I was thinking out loud now. "I mean, he's the Devil, right? He could cast me down into the fiery pit or something if he really wanted to, couldn't he? Why take the time to wine and dine me like this?"

"You *ate* with him?" Evan looked horrified.

"No, no." I shook my head impatiently as I handed him the jewelry. "I meant the way he's showing up and being all charming and everything. Why doesn't he appear as a scaly red demon with a pitchfork and a goatee? I'd be scared shitless. I'd probably do anything he told me to."

"Because that wouldn't be nearly as much fun for him," Evan said sourly. "I knew that first night at the Vortex that he was trouble, but you wouldn't listen."

I sighed, resigned to hearing his rant all over again.

"It's not like I knew who he was, Evan. I thought he was just some guy hitting on me at a Halloween party. Joe was right there. I didn't do anything wrong."

"You were practically drooling over him."

"That's not true," I said irritably, but it kinda was.

"Then you had to go and let him in the store, sell him some clothes, let him chat you up."

"I didn't invite him to the store, he just showed up. What was I supposed to do, turn away a paying customer? He spent over five hundred dollars that day, as I recall."

Evan cut me off with an impatient wave of the hand. "Did I tell you Sammy was bad news, right from the start, or did I tell you?"

I sighed again. "Yes, you told me."

"And did you listen to me?" An eyebrow quirked in my direction.

"How could I help it?" I muttered.

"What's that?"

"Enough with the lecture already. This isn't my fault. I didn't do anything to encourage him, and once I found out who he really was, I told him where to get off."

I'd been pretty proud of that, actually. I could've easily given in to all the things that Sammy had to offer, but I hadn't. Even when I'd been pretty sure that refusing him would cost me, big-time.

And here I was, paying for it again, with interest this time.

A rapping on the glass door got our attention. Handbags and Gladrags wasn't open until ten, and that was twelve minutes away.

A man stood there, waving frantically to catch our eyes.

As if we could miss him. He was three hundred pounds if he was an ounce, sporting a hideous red-and-green Hawaiian shirt and baggy khaki shorts. He had more hair on his legs than he did on his scalp, just a fringe of wispy white curls on top. He looked like a balding, vacationing Santa Claus, minus the beard.

"Nice shirt," Evan muttered, obviously unable to help himself. "A Holiday Inn somewhere is missing a pair of drapes."

"Be nice," I hissed, turning my head to hide my grin. "We're not open yet," I called over my shoulder. "Ten o'clock." I wanted to get Jayne dressed and posed first . . . maybe an umbrella?

"Miss Styx? Miss Styx, my name is Elwood T. Thompson." The old guy ignored my back, raising his voice to be heard through the glass. "Could I talk to you for a minute, please?"

How does he know my name?

I turned, looking at the man again. This time I noticed he had a woman with him. She was small and short, with brown hair and tired eyes.

"Please, Miss Styx." He was persistent. "It's important."

Crap. "I've heard of fashion emergencies, but this is ridiculous." My muttered comment was meant for Evan, who ducked behind Jayne's shoulder to hide his chuckle.

With a sigh, I turned and walked toward the front door, flipping the dead bolts with a practiced hand as I eyed my visitors through the glass.

Elwood had a broad smile on his chubby face, while the woman with him looked bored. Thin where he was fat, wearing a nondescript gray T-shirt and jeans, she glanced around idly as they stepped into the store, but it was Elwood who demanded my attention.

"Thank you. Oh, thank you." He seized my hand in a moist grip, pumping it with enthusiasm. "I can't tell you how glad I am to meet you."

"Uh-huh." I was always friendly with the customers, but Elwood's friendliness seemed a bit excessive. "Is there something I can help you with?"

"Oh, yes," he said, "I really need to talk to my wife."

"Okay . . ." I drawled, uncertain as to what that had to do with me. I shot Evan a curious look as I pulled my hand from Elwood's damp grasp, resisting the urge to wipe it on my pants. "Do you need to use a phone or something?"

The woman beside Elwood met my eyes briefly, then looked away. No help there.

Elwood shook his head. "I saw you on the news last night."

Uh-oh.

"My wife passed away six months ago," Elwood said earnestly. "I really need to talk to her."

Evan was standing behind me now. I was grateful to have him at my back.

"I'm sorry, but I can't help you." I was gonna kill Sammy for this . . . just what I needed, crazies knocking on my door thinking I was one of *them*. "That stuff on the news has nothing to do with me."

Elwood looked confused. "But it was you—I saw you. You said you could help people talk to their lost loved ones; you said you could channel them."

Good Lord. "Look, Mr.—"

"Thompson," he said eagerly, "Elwood T. Thompson."

"Mr. Thompson." I held out a hand, trying to usher his bulk toward the door. "I'm not a psychic, or a 'channeler' or whatever. That stuff on the news was a setup. I can't help you, and I think you should go."

"What do you mean?" Elwood was immovable. "I have money. I'll pay your fee, whatever it is."

Evan spoke up. "Nicki's gift doesn't work that way." He took a step forward, so he was standing right beside me. "And I believe she asked you to leave."

I was proud of him for sticking up for me, because even if Elwood looked like a bald Santa Claus, he was twice Evan's size—but I wished he hadn't used the word "gift."

"I knew it!" Elwood was beaming. "What's it gonna take, Miss Styx? Five hundred? A thousand? I'll pay it."

I sighed. The guy was a lost cause, so I turned to the woman standing beside him, who hadn't said a word.

"You and your friend need to go now," I said. "Take him home. I can't help you."

The woman's eyes went wide; it was the first sign of interest she'd shown since she came in the door.

"You can see me," she gasped. "Oh, Elwood, it's true!"

And that's when I knew I was screwed.

"My friend?" Elwood asked, obviously confused.

I stared at him blankly, then looked back at the woman.

"Tell him it's not his fault," she said rapidly. "Tell him I forgive him."

I glanced at Evan to find him giving me a strange look. "Um . . . Nicki?"

Crap.

Why did these things keep happening to me?

"Tell him it's okay," the woman insisted. "Tell him I'm not mad, and I love him, and I'll be waiting for him."

Further proof that love was blind, I suppose.

The woman looked like a mouse, while Elwood was larger than life.

Literally.

"He has to let me go," the woman continued. "His guilt is keeping me here."

Oy.

The bell over the door tinkled. Two young girls who should've been in school made a beeline for the jeans rack, but I was nobody's mother, and I had a business to run.

With a sigh, I reached out and took Elwood by one damp, chubby hand.

"Come in the back. We'll talk."

Elwood was sobbing like a baby; a big, round, balding baby. His shoulders shook, his belly jiggled, and tears ran down his cheeks as he pressed a wad of tissue to his mouth.

"I should've listened to her," he sobbed. "She told me she had a headache, but I wanted to go to the model train show."

Model trains? Geesh.

"I went off and left her there, all alone. I stopped off for fast food on the way home, and by the time I got back"—Elwood shook his head, a new wave of tears threatening—"she was sitting in her chair with the TV on. Gone." Overcome, Elwood gave in to the flood of tears and sobbed even harder.

"I was watching my soaps," the woman said, sending Elwood a worried look.

I really wasn't sure how to go about this . . . there were no manuals for the "newly psychic" or "newly able-to-see-dead-people." It was hard enough for me to believe I was sitting here talking with a dead woman, much less translate the weirdness for somebody else.

"She was watching her soaps," I said, for lack of anything else to say.

"Yes!" Elwood nodded, mopping at his face with the tissue.

"My head hurt," the woman said. "I closed my eyes, just for a minute, and it was all over." She seemed resigned to her fate, not upset at all.

"It was quick," I told Elwood. "She didn't suffer."

Elwood drew in a deep breath, pulling himself together. He nodded. "An aneurysm, the doc said."

I handed him another couple of tissues from the Kleenex box on the counter, glad we kept some in the storage room.

"I'd like to talk to her," Elwood said. "Can she come through?"

I looked at him blankly for a minute, until I realized what he was asking.

"I'm not a psychic, and I don't 'channel.'" The

word itself was making me testy. Unlike my birth mother, I was no backroom Madame Zelda. "I already told you that."

Elwood heaved his bulk to the side, scrabbling for a rear pocket. "I have money—whatever you want." His chubby face was red from crying, his nose looking even bigger, which was saying a lot.

"Look, it's very simple." It was sad, really, how eager some people were to part with their money. "I'm just going to tell you what your wife has to say; you're going to listen; and then you're going to go away and never come back here again."

Elwood looked slightly hurt at that last part, but I didn't care. I was about to do him a huge favor, and I expected one in return. "And you won't tell anybody, either."

He opened his mouth to speak, but I interrupted. "Ever," I added firmly.

I waited until he nodded, then settled his enormous rear end back in the chair. It gave a creak of protest.

Then I looked at the woman standing quietly beside him.

"What's your name?"

"Darlene," she said. "Darlene Thompson."

"Speak now, Darlene, or forever hold your peace." I couldn't help a bit of sarcasm.

Elwood gasped, but I ignored him as I listened to Darlene's story.

"It wasn't his fault," she said earnestly. "There was nothing he could do—it was that quick." She snapped her fingers to emphasize the point. "I *wanted* him to go to the train show." She looked at him affectionately. "Elwood loves his toys, but I find model trains pretty boring." Then she shrugged. "At least I *did* find them boring." It was amazing how calm she was about being dead. "I had a peach pie cooling on the stove for when he came home." The woman smiled, a sad smile. "I thought we'd have a lot more time together, Elwood and I, but that's just not the way it worked out. I'm being pulled away, but he's hurtin'. He needs to accept I'm gone." Darlene looked away, just for a split second, then turned back to her husband. "I would've stayed by his side forever if I could, but I'm tired. He needs to let me go."

Unexpectedly, my eyes filled with tears. I dashed them away, leaving streaks of black on my knuckles. That's what I got for overdoing it with the eyeliner this morning.

Elwood's chair creaked as he shifted, impatient.

I took a deep breath. "Darlene wants you to know that it wasn't your fault. She wanted you to go to the train show without her, so she could watch her soaps."

Elwood's lower lip trembled, but he stayed quiet.

"There was a peach pie on the stove."

A shuddered breath, more tears, more mopping. Elwood was having a hard time, and I couldn't help but feel sorry for him.

I snagged a Kleenex for myself, dabbing at my mascara and probably making it worse.

"I'm tired," Darlene repeated, and she looked it. She must've been a faded wisp of a woman in life, because in death she held little spark. "He needs to let me go."

"She says you need to let her go," I said to Elwood, keeping my voice even with an effort. "You'll see her again." This last comment was my own contribution. I was no seer, but I knew what I'd *seen*—a place of peace and light and music, where you knew everyone, and they knew you, and all the questions you'd ever had were answered.

"You've been there, haven't you?" Darlene's question drew me back to her. She was looking at me curiously. "You know what's beyond, don't you?"

"Beyond" was a good way to put it. Beyond comprehension, beyond understanding, beyond explaining.

"Yes," I said simply. "I do."

"Should I be afraid?" Darlene was asking me, a total stranger, a very important question.

I didn't hesitate, knowing anyone who inspired this kind of devotion in her husband had to be a good person. "No. You don't need to be afraid."

Darlene smiled, and I was glad to see it. She didn't look quite so mousy when she smiled, and I had a glimpse of how she must have looked to Elwood as a young woman, however many years ago.

"Tell my dear, sweet husband that when we said, 'Till death do us part.' it was truer than we thought. We had twenty-four good years together." She was still smiling. "But death will only part us for a little while. Tell him I said that, just like I said it."

So I repeated it, word for word, as Elwood cried quietly into his tissues.

"Tell him we knew this day would come, and he needs to be strong."

So I said that, too.

"It was supposed to be me," Elwood sobbed. "*I* was the one who was supposed to go first."

"Tough shit," Darlene said simply, shaking her head.

I went with the flow. "Darlene says 'tough shit.'"

The look on Elwood's face was priceless, and then he burst out laughing. Crying. Whatever . . .

it was hard to tell. "That's my Darlene," he finally said, when he could speak.

"Nicki?" Evan's head popped in the door to the storage room. "Are you okay back here?" He gave Elwood the eyeball, obviously unable to decide what was going on. "Are you gonna be much longer? We have customers."

Evan was giving me a way out, and I appreciated it, but I didn't need it. We were done here.

"You have to let Darlene go, Elwood." I rose from an old folding chair, more than ready to leave the cramped little room. "What's done is done, and you have no reason to feel guilty. She loved you, she's not mad at you, and she's ready to move on. Your guilt is keeping her here. That's all I can tell you."

I'd done what I could; I was nobody's afterlife marriage counselor.

"Seriously, Nicki, we have customers." Evan's tone became more insistent.

Elwood heaved himself to his feet, finally getting the message. "I can't thank you enough, Miss Styx."

Yeah, yeah. Enough already. I was anxious to get out of that room, anxious for Elwood and Darlene to leave, and anxious for things to get back to normal.

Whatever normal was.

For just a moment, Darlene poked her head around Elwood's broad back, smiling. "Thank you. I'm glad Elwood finally found somebody who could see me. Most of you people are such fakes." She waved, a mere wiggle of her fingers, looking like the girl she must've been once, and then she was gone.

I couldn't help but smile in return, though I wasn't one of "you people," and the only thing fake about me was my eyelashes.

Darlene was no longer there, and Elwood thought the smile was for him. Before I knew it, he had me in a chubby, moist bear hug.

"You have a true gift," he said. "Thank you."

My face was squished against his Hawaiian shirt, somewhere between a palm tree and a pineapple. "No problem," I mumbled, and extricated myself as quickly as possible. "Good luck."

Evan earned my undying gratitude by ushering Elwood past me through the door and into the hallway. No need for me to follow; their voices got farther and farther away as I slumped against the wall, relieved.

"I'm so disappointed in you, Nicki."

Sammy's voice made me jump.

He was there, in the shadows, leaning against the shelves where we kept cleaning supplies.

"What the hell are you doing here?" I was in no mood for more of Sammy's games, and it made me furious to see him so at ease in my store.

Sammy didn't react other than to spread his hands and say softly, "I am with you always."

The hair rose on the back of my neck—the air in the room seemed electrically charged.

"Get out," I whispered, feeling like a mouse trapped by a cobra.

Sammy smiled, a slow curve of the lip that ended more like a sneer. The way his arms were crossed showed off his biceps, and the way he stood showed his lean hips to advantage. No baggy jeans for this guy. Big silver belt buckle, black leather strap bracelet, studded.

The wall behind me kept me upright. My heart was pounding—small wonder—and I struggled to remind myself to breathe.

Sammy straightened up, still smiling. He came toward me—I'd have to push past him to get out of the storage room.

I opened my mouth to scream for Evan, but something stopped me. Maybe it was his scent, dark and rich; Kahlua and cream, frankincense and myrrh. Or maybe it was his eyes, pale blue and lit from within with something I wasn't sure I wanted to define. I was struck dumb by the breathtaking sensation of being so close to him;

the planes of his chest were right before my eyes, flat belly mere inches from my own. Wide shoulders and big hands that screamed *one-hundred-percent-male*, and ready to prove it.

If the bulge in his jeans was any indication, he was more than ready.

"The next time a spirit comes to you"—Sammy's lips were mere inches from mine, breath warm on my skin—"I want you to turn it *away* from the Light, not toward it."

I closed my eyes, unable to bear being this close to him without screaming, without speaking or without ripping his clothes off. I heard how he referred to a lost soul as "it," and my stomach clenched. My mind screamed "no," while my lips yearned for his breath, and my fingers itched to touch him.

I couldn't believe it—he was evil, but my body had a mind of its own.

"He's putting these thoughts in your head," I told myself sharply.

Black satin, red velvet, neck arched for my tongue . . .

I loved Joe, my sweet Joe. The perfect guy.

Candlelight, incense, rampant ecstasy . . .

I gasped at the flood of images, and that was enough to break the spell. Opening my eyes, I ducked my head and made a dive for the door.

Sammy didn't try to stop me.

"You're wasting your time," I rasped loudly, double-timing it down the hall toward the front of the store. My voice wasn't nearly as shaky as my knees, and I was glad. "Go away. Leave me alone."

CHAPTER 6

"You've gotta do something, Kelly."

I hated how desperate that sounded.

"He's everywhere. He's messing with my head. I know he's evil, and he scares me to death, but every time I see him, my mouth starts to water. I wanna jump his bones."

Cliché, but there it was.

I'd rehearsed this conversation in my imagination several times during the drive to Columbia Memorial Hospital to meet Joe, but I just couldn't quite bring myself to dial Kelly's number.

How was I supposed to confess I was hot for the Devil when I was in love with Joe? What would it mean to my sister to know I was drooling over some other guy?

Joe and Kelly had known each other long before they'd known me. They'd met in college, been married to each other for two years before she'd run off and joined the Peace Corps.

The whole thing was still weird.

I loved them both, and I believed it when they both said it was long over between them. I'd put on my big girl panties and dealt with it.

But it was still weird.

I needed someone to talk to, but I hadn't dared tell Evan that Sammy had shown up in the back room; it would've scared him too much. He had already been traumatized by a spiteful spirit once because of me—if Evan truly knew how deep things had gone with Sammy, I could lose my best friend and my business partner in one fell swoop.

So with a sigh, I punched Bijou's number with my thumb and drove one-handed while it rang, far away in Savannah.

Bijou's way of saying hello was, "I've been so worried about you, dear."

My shoulders eased, just a little bit, at her sweet Southern drawl. I'd interrupted afternoon tea with the Red Hat Club, I was sure; I could hear laughter and clinking china in the background. A former B&B, the Blue Dahlia was the perfect place for many of Bijou's social clubs to meet.

"No need to worry, Bijou." *What a liar I am.* "I'm just calling to let you know everything's okay."

"What a liar you are, dear," she said calmly. "Wait just a moment while I step out on the veranda." The background laughter and tinkling of china grew fainter, then ceased altogether. "Ah, there we are. Now tell me everything."

I could picture Bijou so clearly, sitting in one of the white rockers on the front porch of the Blue Dahlia, wearing one of the floral silks she favored. Probably wearing a flowered hat on top of that carefully coiffed gray wig.

"Samael's here," I blurted, "and he's not going away." Bijou knew who Sammy was—she'd dealt with him before, when her daughter Peaches was alive. "He's trying to seduce me, threaten me, scare me . . ." I made a noise of frustration. "I'm not really sure what he's doing."

"Are you willing to be seduced?" Trust Bijou to home in on that one.

"No," I said instantly. "But he's making it hard." My cheeks flamed at the mental image *that* statement created. "I mean, he's playing dirty. He sent the spirit of a girl who died under Joe's care to possess me—it was totally creepy. She made me say bad things about Joe, on camera, and the footage showed up on the evening news. Then Sammy came to my house this morning and appeared in the store after that. He says he's drawn to me, that he can't leave me alone. Like Lilith in the garden." I kept talking, hoping it would make me feel better. "One minute he's threatening me, the next minute he's trying to get in my pants. What do I do?"

"Keep your legs closed," Bijou said, with a bluntness that surprised me. "Remember, he can't make you do anything you don't want to. The Devil is all about temptation, dear. Forcing you to do anything against your will defeats his purpose."

"Oh, I know his purpose," I said glumly. "He explained that part pretty well."

"He mentioned Lilith?" Bijou was a sharp old bird. She kept her tone neutral, but I knew the question meant something.

"Yes." I waited, anxious to hear what she had to say.

"That's not good."

No shit, Sherlock.

I'd never say that to her, of course—Southern belles did not put up with bad language.

"Having the knack makes you valuable to him, Nicki." Bijou was referring to my ability to see the dead. According to her, our family legacy was getting stronger: Kelly and I had the "knack," Peaches had been a "seeress," while Bijou herself was merely an "intuitive." Each generation stronger than the one before.

"Valuable because he can use your gift for his own evil purposes, and valuable because it makes you different. Being different forces a person to make hard choices." My dear old tranny granny knew of which she spoke. "Some choose to become stronger, to embrace their uniqueness and use it for good. Those who don't—or simply can't—often end up as servants of powers greater than their own."

There was a silence.

"Which one was Peaches?" The question was abrupt, but I really wanted to know. Was my birth mother a good woman who tried to help people, or was she a pawn, used to recruit soldiers for Sammy's "army"?

I was afraid I'd never really know for sure because I'd only met her a few times, briefly.

And by then she was already dead.

"Peaches was a good woman, Nicki." Bijou's voice quivered slightly, as it always did when she spoke of her daughter. "She tried to do right by the people who came to her, but I don't claim to know her mind. I know she made mistakes."

Bijou hesitated. "But you're stronger than she was."

I didn't know what to say.

"I saw it right away, at your mama's funeral. Kelly in her wheelchair and you standing straight and tall beside her, head held high." Bijou's voice broke, then steadied. "Not a tear in your eye. Three strong men flanking you."

I remembered that day, too. Kelly, me, Joe, Evan, and Butch—the only mourners at Peaches Boudreaux's funeral, until Bijou showed up. The smell of early autumn, scattered leaves tumbling over the graves, a kind-eyed preacher whose name I'd forgotten.

"You have to be stronger than he is, Nicki." Bijou's voice turned no-nonsense. "The Devil's fickle; he'll get bored soon enough. Now tell me about this possession. Who was the girl? What did she want? Were you aware of what was taking place?"

"Oh, I was aware, all right." I shuddered inwardly at the memory of Crystal invading my body. "I could hear her voice in my head, feel her inside my veins, you know? She was angry at Joe, said he hadn't done anything to save her." It was sad, really. I would've felt sorry for Crystal if she hadn't been such a bitch. "She was on drugs or something when she died—very thin, not a healthy person." *To put it mildly.* "She took over my body long enough to accuse Joe publicly of murder."

"How was she cast out?"

I winced, uncomfortable with her choice of words. "Demons" were a concept I was becoming all too familiar with, and I didn't like it.

"I just concentrated really hard and kind of pushed her out."

"Ah," Bijou said, with satisfaction. "I'm so proud of you, dear."

Proud of me?

"You need to practice that skill, master your mind as well as your body. You absolutely must spend some time each day meditating, growing stronger. Visualization is the key."

Where had I heard that before? Oh, yeah . . . yesterday morning. Evan's New Age talk show.

"Great." I spoke my thoughts aloud. "Maybe I can reincarnate my way to a new me while I'm at it."

"Don't be silly, dear," Bijou replied. "Reincarnation requires a great deal more effort. Concentrate on the matter at hand."

I sighed, resigned to hearing a lesson on how to meditate properly.

Maybe while I was at it, I'd take up yoga and become a swami, turban and all.

* * *

The legal counsel for Columbia Memorial Hospital was a woman named Lisa Butler. Midthirties, hard-eyed, long brown hair; attractive in a "corporate kick-ass" kind of way. She was sitting in a chair in Joe's office when I came in, the two of them chatting like old friends.

Joe stood up, smiling, which eased my mind considerably. This interview was not something I'd been looking forward to.

Lisa stood up, too, a measuring look in her eye as Joe made introductions.

"Nice to meet you," she said, but I didn't really think she meant it. She was probably only a few years older than I, but we were worlds apart in style. Her dark gray suit was okay—probably Liz Claiborne—but did nothing for her; the color made her brown hair look dull. A little jewelry would've gone a long way, but she wore nothing but a pair of small silver studs in her ears.

Pretty, but plain.

I shook her hand before giving Joe a quick hug of greeting. If Lisa thought our show of affection strange, she didn't show it.

"Thank you for coming, Miss Styx." Lisa took her seat again. When she crossed her legs, I saw her shoes; bombshell pumps, black leather with near-stiletto heels.

They were not the shoes of a conservative attorney, and were my first clue that I should stay on my toes.

"Dr. Bascombe assures me that your accusation against him was meant in jest, but the hospital's board of directors is not amused. A public accusation of murder against one of our staff is a serious matter." Lisa obviously believed in getting straight to the point.

I'd barely settled in my chair, but I wasn't going to let this woman rattle me. "I realize that. I'm sure Joe told you the whole story already." I wasn't sure what Joe had told her, so I was doing a little dancing. "I apologize if what I said made the hospital look bad."

Actually, I didn't give a damn about the hospital, only about Joe's job.

"Yes, I've already taken Dr. Bascombe's statement, but I'll need to take yours, as well."

"My statement?" *An apology wasn't good enough?*

"Nicki's an aspiring actress, Lisa," Joe said.

I am?

"It's called method acting."

Method acting?

"I'd just finished telling Nicki about what a hard night I'd had in the E.R., and she was trying to tap into the emotions involved by pretending to be the mother of one of my patients. Some guy was filming a commercial at the time and caught it on video. That's it."

Lisa shot me a look. "Is that true, Miss Styx?"

She knew Joe was lying, but she'd chosen not to call him on it. Instead, she was going after me.

"I'd had too much to drink," I said flatly, choosing to make the lie simpler. "I didn't know what I was saying."

Across the desk, Joe sighed, but I ignored him.

"It was barely nine thirty in the morning, Miss Styx," Lisa said mildly.

"That's right." I gave her a tight smile. Let her think what she wanted; my all-night party-girl days were long over, but at least I had a few to look back on.

Lisa Butler probably *wished* she had a few to look back on.

"Don't you think it was rather disrespectful to make fun of the deceased? Have you no sympathy for the bereaved?"

My temper started to rise. I didn't need to justify myself to this woman, and I knew more about the "bereaved" than she could ever imagine.

"Like I said, I didn't know what I was saying."

"Well"—Lisa leaned back in her chair, touching a manicured finger to her chin—"judging by the bizarre rant that came after the accusation, I suppose it's a believable excuse. You were impaired by alcohol; if that's the defense we need to use, then we'll use it."

"Bizarre *rant*?" I didn't care for Lisa's tone *or* her choice of words.

"You know, that bit about being fat and how dead people talked to you."

Of course Lisa would've seen the video— probably seen it several times.

Then I realized what else she'd said. "A defense to use against who?"

"The Cowart family, of course." Lisa eyed me coolly. "We've already heard from their attorney."

"The guy's an ambulance chaser." Joe was obviously irritated. "1–800-ASK-TONY is plastered over every bus in town."

"I'm familiar with Tony Danforth," Lisa replied. "He *is* an ambulance chaser, and a real jerk. He's also a bulldog with a nose for fresh meat, Joe, and you're looking like Grade A steak to him right now. We'd be foolish not to take him seriously."

I couldn't help but notice her use of the word "we."

"Wait a minute," I said. "Joe didn't do anything wrong." *Except get involved with me.* "He shouldn't be held responsible for something I said while I was"—I mentally gritted my teeth—"under the influence."

"We're talking malpractice, here, Miss Styx." Lisa leaned forward in her seat. "Negligence, at best. You publicly accused Dr. Bascombe of doing nothing to save a dying woman, and by association, the rest of the hospital staff, as well. While the board has already issued a statement denying culpability, we need to get our ducks in a row."

I was tempted to tell Lisa what she could do with her "ducks," but a quick glance at Joe's face stopped me.

"Fine." I leaned back and crossed my legs, giving Lisa a good look at my boots—Giuseppe Zanotti anklets, pointed toes, buckles and all. My boots could kick her heeled pumps' collective ass any day. "Let's get it over with."

Lisa pretended to hesitate, then said, "I'd be remiss if I didn't point out that what you said goes beyond slander, Miss Styx. It was caught on video and played over the airwaves. Dr. Bascombe is well within his rights to sue you for libel."

Joe spoke up, voice hard. "I already told you that's not going to happen, Lisa." He leaned forward, both hands on his desk. "Let's move on."

"Wait just a minute here." Words like "libel" and "sue" were nothing to toss around lightly. "Are you saying you *recommended* Joe sue me?"

Freaking lawyers . . . Who the hell did this woman think she was?

"The hospital board would be in a much stronger position if he did." Lisa barely glanced at me, giving Joe her attention. "It would bolster our defense if Dr. Bascombe took this as seriously as we do."

I stood up, ready to rip Ms. Butler a new one. "I came down here to apologize and clear things up, not to be threatened with legal action."

Lisa turned a bland, blue-eyed gaze in my direction. "Actions have consequences, Miss Styx."

"Then sue the television station! Don't they have some liability here?"

"We're looking into it," Lisa said coolly.

Furious, I looked at Joe. "Do I need an attorney?"

He rose from his chair, shaking his head. "Not as far as I'm concerned." The look he shot Lisa was extremely unfriendly. "But maybe it wouldn't be a bad idea." He came around the corner of his desk, adding, "In fact, maybe I should hire a private attorney of my own."

"Let's all calm down, shall we?" Lisa hadn't moved from her chair. She crossed her legs for good measure, swinging a stilettoed pump in my direction. "I'm merely laying out all possible options." She shrugged. "If Dr. Bascombe is willing to let bygones be bygones in his personal life, it's hardly any of my business, now is it?"

"Damn right it's none of your business." She was an Ice Queen, this one. "You're making a big deal out of nothing."

"I doubt that the board of directors would agree with you."

"The board of directors can take their opinion and . . ."

"Nicki," Joe said warningly.

It was just my name, but it was enough to make me shut up. I didn't need to get Joe in more trouble than he was already in.

Then I heard it—a giggle, high and shrill, with an edge of mania that raised the hair on my arms.

I jumped, unable to help myself, and looked around to see where it came from.

"Something wrong, Miss Styx?" Lisa raised a plucked eyebrow in my direction.

I ignored her, and looked at Joe. "Did you hear it?"

Before he could answer, the laughter came again, and my blood ran cold.

I didn't like the sound any more than I had yesterday morning on the sidewalk outside Moonbeans. Crystal Cowart was here, somewhere, and unless I missed my guess, all hell was about to break loose.

"Um . . . I'm gonna go," I said, edging toward the door. "I just remembered someplace I need to be."

In bed, with the covers over my head.

Joe, being nobody's fool, caught on immediately, but the fool in the bombshell pumps was clueless.

"Surely I haven't run you off?" Lisa looked somehow pleased at the prospect. "You musn't take what I say personally."

Actually, I'd taken what Ms. Legal Beagle said *very* personally, but now was not the time to argue.

Another evil giggle, and then a stack of paper on Joe's desk went flying.

Too late.

Lisa gasped, uncrossing her legs.

A coffee cup full of pens and pencils tipped over, spilling them all to the floor. Lisa leapt up from her chair.

"What the—" No need for Joe to finish that sentence, as he had a pretty good idea *what*. "Clumsy of me." He scrabbled for a stray pen, but I wasn't sure Lisa was buying it. He'd been standing beside the desk, nowhere near the cup.

Since I already felt like a deer in the headlights, I'm pretty sure I looked like one, too. "I gotta go," I repeated, and bolted for the door.

I had some major meditating to do.

"You're not going anywhere, Chubby Cheeks," said Crystal, and my veins filled with ice. She was just behind and to the right of me—I could see her rail-thin figure from the corner of my eye.

I pulled at the door handle, but it didn't budge. Desperate, I glanced over my shoulder at Joe.

He moved toward me, walking straight through Crystal Cowart, whom he didn't see. Her image wavered like smoke, then steadied.

"Oo," said Crystal, mockingly, "that felt good, baby. Do it again."

Gross.

"The door seems to be locked," I said, trying to speak normally for the benefit of eagle-eyed Lisa.

"Your boyfriend is a real hottie, even if he is a murderer," Crystal said, conversationally. "I'm going to enjoy hanging around him for a while."

I couldn't answer without speaking to thin air, so I said nothing, refusing even to look at her. Joe tried the door handle; it opened easily for him.

"Bye, bye, Chubby Cheeks, and don't you worry about a thing," Crystal said mockingly. "I'll take good care of Dr. Goodbody."

I couldn't help it—I shot her a glare.

It only made her laugh. "I'm going to enjoy driving you both nuts," she said, fading as I watched. "See you around."

"Nicki?" Joe's hand was on my elbow.

I was just standing there, in the open doorway.

"Miss Styx?" Lisa Butler's concern did not sound genuine. "Are you all right?"

"It was nice to meet you, Lisa," I lied, with a tight smile. "But I've got things to do. Joe, I'll see you later."

CHAPTER 7

"What's going on, Nicki?" Joe caught me by the elevator before I had a chance to escape. Luckily, Lisa didn't seem to be with him, but I drew him aside just in case.

"It was Crystal Cowart." I kept my voice low, glancing anxiously at a passing nurse, who was paying us no attention whatsoever. "She was in the room with us, standing right in front of you."

The elevator dinged, and the doors opened. We stepped back to accommodate an orderly pushing an old man in a wheelchair. Once they were out of the way, I ducked inside the elevator, and Joe followed.

As soon as the doors closed behind us, he said, "Sammy's got you really freaked, doesn't he?"

For a moment, the comment made no sense, because we were talking about Crystal. Then I realized what he meant.

"He's using me, and he's using this poor dead girl, who would've died regardless of what anyone did for her." Joe took my hand. "You're afraid."

I hesitated, not wanting him to know how truly terrified I was at the thought of Crystal possessing me again. Or of his dumping me because I was a freak who'd cost him his job.

He smiled, a little ruefully. "I've seen you stand your ground against a voodoo priestess and her entire cult, Nicki. The way you just bolted tells me a lot."

I looked at him, feeling helpless, which was not a feeling I enjoyed.

"She can't hurt you, Nicki," he said gently. "And she can't hurt me, either."

"She's haunting you, Joe. She said she's going to enjoy driving us both nuts."

He shrugged, apparently unconcerned. "Now that I know she's out to cause trouble, I'll be on my guard. What can she do to me? Flip a few papers? Knock over some pens?"

"Famous last words," I said glumly. "Look what she did to *me*. With Sammy's help, there's no telling what she can do to *you*."

For just a second, Joe's eyes gleamed fiercely. "Let him bring it, then," he muttered. "He needs to stop hiding behind the women and fight like a man."

I stared at him, memorizing the fine lines at the corner of his eyes, the way his dark hair curled at his collar. This would never be a fair fight—how was I going to keep Sammy from ruining Joe's life, his career? Today it was an anorexic ghost with an axe to grind; what would it be tomorrow?

I hadn't said a word, but the next thing I knew, Joe had his arms around me, my cheek pressed against his white lab coat.

"You've seen him again, haven't you?" he said.

Feeling vaguely guilty, though I wasn't sure why, I answered honestly. "Yes. He showed up twice this morning." I didn't give Joe all the details—he had enough to worry about today. "Both times I told him to get lost, and he did."

Joe sighed. He unwrapped one arm long enough to push the elevator button for the ground floor. Then he tipped my face up to his.

"You keep telling him that, babe, and don't

forget—I'm right here. Anytime you need me, I'm right here."

His eyes were so green, so intense . . . that was the last thought I had before his lips came down on mine. I clung to him, kissing him back gladly, fiercely, letting my body say everything I needed—wanted—to say.

Here, in Joe's arms, Sammy's image faded.

I wished I could stay here forever.

But the elevator gave a slight jerk, then dinged.

Joe broke the kiss, but kept his arms around me. I buried my face against his chest, just for a moment, then pulled away.

I didn't need to be told that it wouldn't look good for one of the hospital staff to be seen kissing a girl in an elevator, and he was in enough trouble because of me as it was.

"I'll be okay," I said, as the doors opened. A pair of elderly women were waiting to get on. "I'll call you later."

"You'd better," Joe said, very seriously. There was a smudge of pink lipstick on his upper lip, and a smear of makeup on his white coat, which kinda took away from his sternness. But it was so cute.

Take that, Lisa Butler. Miss Tight-Ass Attorney probably *wished* she could make out in an elevator.

Belatedly, I rubbed my hand over my own lip as a signal, but Joe didn't catch it.

"What floor, ladies?" I heard him ask as the elevator door closed.

What a guy. I smiled as I headed toward the parking lot, remembering how safe I'd felt in his arms.

Sammy didn't stand a chance. Good always triumphed over evil.

Didn't it?

"Aside from the obvious—crosses, holy water, that type of thing—the only other references I can find to avoid possession by evil spirits are some arcane references to emeralds and yarrow root." Kelly was on the other end of the line again. "Oh, and some supposed 'spells' that need to be cast under a full moon, but I somehow doubt their effectiveness."

"Oh, my God, Kelly, if you start telling me I need to cast a 'circle of protection' or something like that, I think I'll go stark, raving nuts."

My long, horrible day was finally over, and I was home in my jammies, feet propped on the coffee table while I sipped a glass of merlot. Concrete Blonde was on the CD player, the curtains were drawn and the doors were locked.

I know, because I'd double- and triple-checked them.

"You could try baptism," Kelly said.

"Kelly, this is the Bible Belt. I've already *been* baptized." Calvary Baptist Church, as a child of twelve. I used to attend every Sunday with my parents, until fifteen or so, when I'd declared organized religion to be brainwashing and that forcing me to attend was a violation of my civil rights.

My poor parents had shaken their heads and continued to go without me.

Kelly sounded worried. "There's always exorcism. A priest could bless the house and the store."

I shuddered involuntarily. That movie had given me nightmares for months.

"If my head starts spinning around on my shoulders, or I start vomiting pea soup, a priest will be the first person I call."

"Stop making jokes, Nicki." Kelly sounded irritated. "I know that's how you deal with stress, but this isn't funny."

"Laughing is always better than crying."

"How would you know? I've never seen you cry, not even when Peaches died."

I sighed, because we'd been down this road before. "I didn't know Peaches when she was alive. How was I supposed to grieve for her?"

Plus, I knew she was okay—not only did I know that there was a world beyond this one, I'd known that whatever essence made Peaches who she *was* still existed.

And I didn't like to cry. It made my eyeliner run and my nose swell like a grapefruit.

"Just because I don't cry every time I get upset doesn't mean I don't care."

"You should let it out, Nick." Kelly's voice was somber. "It's unnatural to hold your feelings in—it's not healthy."

Good thing my sister wasn't there to see me roll my eyes. She hated it when I did that.

"You're rolling your eyes, aren't you?"

Damn. "What are you now, a psychic?"

Kelly ignored my sarcasm. "Bijou told me you called her today. Have you tried meditating yet?"

"I'm getting myself relaxed first," I said loftily. "The wine hasn't kicked in."

Kelly made a rude noise, which I ignored.

"Just remember to breathe properly. It's very important."

"Okay, okay, quit nagging. I'll meditate. Let me know if you find out anything else I should be doing."

"Be careful, will you? You think you're a lot tougher than you really are."

You think you're a lot smarter than you really are.

A knee-jerk mental reaction; I didn't say it, or even mean it. Kelly was a first-class egghead, and her mother-hen routine covered a lot of personal insecurities. If nagging me made her feel better, I'd do my best to put up with it.

For now.

"I'll talk to you tomorrow, okay?"

"Okay."

After I hung up, I tried my hardest to settle into what Bijou called a "meditative state." I finished the wine, turned off the music, and settled myself comfortably on the couch. My breathing was regular—in through the nose, out through the mouth—concentrate, concentrate, concentrate.

It was the "clear your mind" part that was hard.

My conversation with Kelly had sparked something, and after about five minutes of useless breathing exercises, I gave up trying not to think about it. I got up from the couch and padded through the quiet house to my bedroom, where I opened the closet and took something down from the top shelf.

My mother's jewelry box.

I ran my hands over the carved cedar, admiring the workmanship. The box was a beauty, elaborately scrolled except for two smooth, painted ovals on the lid. Quaint pastoral cameos of young women picking flowers, the scenes similar but different, the colors faded with time. She'd told me that one of her uncles had given her the box as a child.

Mostly costume jewelry, of course—Dan and Emily Styx had never been wealthy. They'd always valued love and comfort over material things, though they'd been big believers in life insurance. I'd never have been able to open Handbags and Gladrags otherwise. Between that and the house, inherited mortgage-free, my parents had left me well taken care of.

A few rings gleamed up at me from furrows of velvet; Mom's high-school ring, a tiny ruby heart Dad had given her one year for Valentine's Day, and the ring I was looking for—a square-cut emerald she'd inherited from her own mother. I slid it on, but it was loose on my ring finger, so I slipped it on my index finger instead.

Everything else—bracelets, watches, a few necklaces—lay piled in a heap of gold and silver.

From the pile I picked up one other thing; a tiny gold cross my mom used to wear. I'd almost buried her with it, but I was glad I hadn't.

Kelly was wrong about how I never cried.

I let the tears wash over me like a flood, then put the cross around my neck and went to bed.

CHAPTER 8

Some days you're the bug; some days you're the windshield.

The next morning, it became obvious that I was still nothing more than a yellow smear on the front of a black Mustang convertible.

"There she is!"

I'd barely stepped out of the back room at Handbags and Gladrags when I was confronted by a group of women clustered in front of the cash register. They were all plump and middle-aged, either staring at me or shooting each other significant glances.

Evan turned and gave me an eye roll, then said to the woman who'd spoken, "I told you, Nicki is *not* a psychic. We sell clothes and accessories, not snake oil."

The woman gave Evan a dirty look, then ignored him. "Greetings from the Goddess, Nicki Styx. We have come to bask in your bright blessings."

"Look at her aura," another one of the women exclaimed, "such a glorious shade of yellow!"

Further proof of the bug thing, if you ask me.

Evan gave a snort of laughter, covering his mouth quickly with a hand. "Oh, please," he muttered.

The "aura woman" looked at him. "Careful, dear—your rainbow is showing."

"I should hope so," Evan snipped.

I didn't know whether to run or to burst out laughing, so I settled for, "Um . . . can I help you?"

"We're the Sisters of Circe."

I'd heard of the Sisters of *Mercy*—they were one of my favorite goth bands. But since the group of chubby, aging women looked nothing like rockers, nurses, or prostitutes, I asked, "Sisters of what?"

"Circe. *Sir-see.*" The woman who was doing most of the talking looked impatient. "A powerful sorceress of the ancient Greeks."

"The Greeks?" Evan brightened. "Finally, something I know something about."

A third woman spoke up, giving Evan a pointed look. "Could we speak to you privately, Miss Styx?"

"Anything you have to say can be said in front of my partner, ladies." I stepped up and stood next to Evan, shoulder to shoulder, as much to show support as to gain it. "I believe he's already told you that unless you're here to buy something, you're wasting your time."

The women—six in all—shot each other a few anxious looks. Then the woman who seemed to be their leader—fiftysomething, no makeup, long gray hair that could have used a brush—gave a decisive nod. "So mote it be."

"So mote it be," the other five repeated in unison.

Evan and I exchanged a glance of our own.

"My name is Shadow Starhawk," the gray-haired woman said, "and we would like to talk to you about the manyfold benefits of the Wiccan way."

"Shadow Starhawk?" I repeated, uncertain as to whether I'd heard her correctly.

"Shadow is my craft name," she said slowly, as though speaking to an idiot. "To the mundanes I'm known as Sally Smith."

"Of course you are," I said faintly, more convinced than ever that this was *not* my day. "What was I thinking?"

Sally ignored my sarcasm. "Sister Ravenwood saw you on the news the other night and has divined that you would be an excellent addition to our circle. Talents such as yours are hard to find."

Enough was enough.

"I'm sorry to disappoint you, but I have no interest in joining your"—I waved my hand vaguely in the air—"circle, or whatever. I'm a businesswoman, plain and simple, and I have work to do, so if you'll excuse me . . ."

"Ah." Sally smiled. "I applaud your commercial instincts. A woman must survive, after all. Men are so"—she flicked Evan a slightly contemptuous glance—"fickle."

Evan bristled, but I put a hand on his arm. We'd long ago agreed that the customer was always right, even if the customer was a raving lunatic.

"I can't help you," I said bluntly, "and I think you need to leave."

Sally's eyebrows shot sky high, though I found it hard to believe I was the first person ever to reject her. "You don't understand. We're here to help you channel your talents into something much more lucrative than running a secondhand clothing store."

I wasn't sure if it was the word "channel" or the

word "secondhand" that did it, but my temper ignited.

"Get the hell out of here!" I shouted. "And take your broomsticks with you!"

"Well"—Sally took an involuntary step backward, and huffed—"I never!"

"Obviously not," Evan chimed in pointedly. "Now go before I call security on your wrinkled old asses."

There was a collective gasp from the six women, then deathly silence.

"I don't think you know who you're dealing with here." Sally had a mean look in her eye. She glanced around at the women who flanked her, and said shortly, "Let me speak to her alone."

None of them said a word, though I saw a couple of worried looks exchanged. Slowly, they backed away, moving in a small knot toward the clothing racks to give us some privacy.

Evan, however, didn't budge.

Sally ignored him. She kept her voice low, obviously not wanting her friends to overhear. "Opportunity is knocking, girl. There is power to be had in the workings of the craft, yours for the taking. Don't underestimate me, or what I'm offering."

I stared at her for a moment, an extreme sense of dislike snaking its way down my spine.

"Why would you offer anything to me?" I asked her coldly. "I don't even know you."

She gave me a nasty little smile. More like a sneer, really. "Maybe the Devil made me do it."

If this woman and her band of mystical misfits was Sammy's idea of a way to tempt me over to the dark side, he wasn't as smart as I thought he was.

"You're strong," she murmured, "but I can make you stronger. Insult me again, however, and I'll make your life a living hell."

I'd never responded well to threats, and I wasn't about to start now. I leaned over the counter, going toe-to-toe and eye to eye with the old witch.

"Bring it on, Hagatha. Being turned into a toad is the least of my worries."

She tried to stare me down, but I knew I'd won when she turned away, shooing the other five women toward the door. "I won't forget this. You've made enemies of the wrong people."

To which I replied, very succinctly, with one word.

"Ribbit."

As soon as the bell above the door tinkled behind them, I looked at Evan, still steaming. His mouth was open, but he didn't say a word.

Then his lip started to twitch, and before I knew

it, we were both laughing so hard we had to grab on to the counter for support.

"Ribbit?" he gasped, between gales of laughter. "*Ribbit?*"

The day got a little better after a few nice sales; a couple of giggly high-school girls were going to be wearing vintage gowns to their high school's Spring Fling, and a guy with a sparse gray ponytail bought an expensive pair of Tony Lama wingtip boots and a half dozen tie-dye T-shirts.

I did my best to ignore the steady stream of customers who came and went across the street at Divinyls, but I caught Evan glancing anxiously out the front window a time or two when he thought I wasn't looking.

No sign of Sammy, thank goodness. I fingered the tiny gold cross around my neck frequently, not really believing it was having any protective effect, but comforted anyway.

"We should have a vintage lingerie section," I said idly to Evan, when we finally had a lull. "Some of those long slips over in the formal section would make great nightgowns."

Evan wrinkled his nose. "I don't know, Nicki— I've never been crazy about the idea of selling other people's old underwear."

"Under*garments*," I corrected. "No bras or

panties, of course, but slips? I don't see why not. We women know how to take care of our delicates."

"I'll resist the obvious reply to that comment," Evan said archly.

I giggled a little, knowing how hard it was for Evan to resist a chance to say something naughty.

"You not only look like a chipmunk, you sound like one, too." The woman's voice was all too familiar.

I froze, my arms full of clothes and my back to Evan.

"What's the matter, Chubby Cheeks? Cat got your tongue?"

Very slowly, I finished racking some shirts that had been left in one of the dressing rooms, and turned around, scanning the store for Crystal.

I didn't see her.

Not wanting to scare Evan, I kept my mouth shut.

"That skirt makes you look like a whore," Crystal said, "and fishnet stockings with combat boots are *so* last week. Is that the best you could come up with today, Little Miss Goth Wannabe?"

Okay, *now* she was pissing me off.

"Evan, would you mind checking the storeroom and seeing if we have any more tie-dye? That guy with the ponytail pretty much emptied us out."

"Who would've thought a bunch of drugged-out hippies like the Grateful Dead would single-handedly spawn a decades-long fashion trend." Evan gave a disapproving sniff, muttering to himself as he went in the back. "And those ties by Jerry Garcia . . . please. Talk about irony. Turn on and tune out—here's a symbol of corporate America to wear while you're trippin'."

Evan had never been a "Deadhead."

Wish I could say the same.

"Okay, Crystal, where are you?" The store seemed empty, but I knew she was here. "What do you want?"

"I want to be alive again," Crystal said, "but I'll settle for making your boyfriend wish he was dead."

I turned and saw her standing next to the Marilyn Monroe mannequin. Bad choice, because the comparison was startling. Marilyn's generous curves (achieved with the help of a padded bra and overstuffed panty hose) made Crystal's scrawniness even more apparent.

"There was nothing Joe could do." I kept my voice calm, matter-of-fact. "He told me all about it. You were—*"How did one put this?"*—gone before you reached the E.R."

"That's bullshit," Crystal sneered. "I was fully

conscious the whole time. I watched him take one look at me and shake his head, like I wasn't worth saving. He just let me lie there. Then some stupid nurse pulled a sheet over my head, and everything went dark."

A shiver crept down my spine. I'd had a similar experience once, in that same E.R., right down to the sheet being pulled over my head. But there'd been no dark for me. Instead, there'd been a tunnel with a bright light at the end, and an incredible experience that had changed me forever.

As calmly as I could, I tried to help Crystal understand. "You were already dead, Crystal. You saw what was going on because your soul was still there, confused about what was happening to you. There was nothing anyone could have done."

She stared at me, arms at her sides. "You're even more stupid than you look," she said. "My master was right about you."

I didn't know whether to be creeped out or just plain insulted. "Your master said I was stupid?"

Crystal gave me an ugly smile, all bright red gums and yellow teeth. "He said you were stubborn. I'm the one who thinks you're stupid."

Bitch.

"Look, Crystal—"

I'd gotten no further than that when Evan came back, arms full of tie-dye.

"This stuff is hideous," he said, "but it sure sells well."

One look at my face stopped him in his tracks.

"Uh-oh. Maybe I'll just go, um . . ." Evan trailed off, while I nodded an affirmative. He backtracked so quickly I almost laughed, except I didn't feel like laughing.

When I heard the door to the back office close behind him, I breathed a little easier.

But then the front door opened, bell tinkling, and my heart sank.

It was a woman, middle-aged and overweight, lank brown hair drawn into a messy knot on top of her head.

"Mama," Crystal whispered, and my heart sank even further.

The woman's face showed evidence of a hard life. She had the look of someone who'd never had more than two cents to rub together and never expected to. Her clothes were clean, but worn; too-tight jeans and a stretchy pullover top, old sneakers that had seen better days.

"Are you Nicki Styx?" A smoker's voice, raspy and gruff.

"Yes," I said. "And you must be Crystal's mother." No sense beating around the bush.

Her eyes gleamed with suspicion. "How'd you know that?"

Without meaning to, I glanced toward Crystal. The spot where she'd been standing was empty.

"You wouldn't believe me if I told you. Now what can I do for you?"

The woman tightened her grip on the shoulder strap of her purse, bringing a chubby arm across her belly to hold on to the bag with both hands. "I'm Tina Cowart. I wanna know if what you said about my girl was true."

I needed to tread carefully here. "Dr. Bascombe didn't kill your daughter, Ms. Cowart. I was talking crazy, and some guy filming a commercial caught it on tape. That's all."

"That doctor—he's your boyfriend, ain't he?"

"Yes."

"So you'd lie for him, wouldn't you?"

I shook my head in frustration. "I'm not lying, Ms. Cowart. Joe told me what happened, and I believe him."

She looked at me, stone-faced.

"Maybe you should talk to him yourself."

"Lawyer won't let me," she said. "So I'm talkin' to you."

I refrained from pointing out that her lawyer was an ambulance-chasing scumbag. I'd seen his commercials—guys like him preyed on people like Tina Cowart. "Crystal was so thin—and her teeth . . . You had to know she was having problems before she ever went to the hospital."

Tina's lip quivered, just a tiny bit.

I didn't want to hurt anybody's feelings, but the truth needed to be said.

"How would you know? Boyfriend tell you that, too?"

Despite Tina's hostility, I couldn't help but feel sorry for her. She *had* just lost her daughter.

"Look, I know Crystal was anorexic. And I know girls like that usually have deeper problems than how much they weigh."

"*Girls like that?* You don't know nuthin' about my girl! My Crystal was gonna be a model; she was gonna *be* somebody!" Tina was getting angrier by the minute. "She was the prettiest girl in her ninth-grade class! All the boys was after her."

Oh, man. Unless I missed my guess, ninth grade for Crystal Cowart had been a long time ago.

"I'm sorry for your loss, Ms. Cowart." What else was there to say?

She glared at me for a second, then looked away. Her hands flexed uneasily on her purse, as though I were about to snatch it from her. "I come here to find out if what you said about my Crystal was true," she repeated. "Was she talking to you or what?"

I'd thought she wanted support for her lawsuit, but it was apparently more personal than that.

"I . . . I'd been drinking. I didn't know what I was saying."

"I done my share of drinkin'," Tina said flatly. "And you didn't look drunk to me. Didn't sound it, neither." She looked around the store, assessing it with a world-weary eye. "I don't normally hold with no psychic mumbo jumbo, but if my daughter has something to say, I'd sure like to hear it."

I had a hard time meeting her gaze, so I turned and walked away, putting the counter between us.

"It was that 'fatty' thing you said." Tina hadn't budged from her spot by the door. " 'Fatty, fat, fat, fat.' That's what Crystal used to say . . ."

She trailed off, but given her hefty size, I knew the rest of that sentence was ". . . to me."

"I'm sorry. I can't help you." I seemed to be saying that a lot today.

"I loved her, you know." Tina took a step forward. "Her and me didn't always see eye to eye, but she was my child. I want her to know I loved her."

Despite my desire to stay out of it, my heart twisted. "I'm sure she knows, Ms. Cowart."

"*Mama.*" Crystal's whisper swirled in the air, giving me the shivers.

For a moment, I wondered if Tina Cowart had heard her; her eyes narrowed as she stared at me.

"Did you ever meet my Crystal?"

The question took me by surprise. "No," I lied.

She cocked her head. "Then how come you know about her teeth?"

Before I could make up another lie to cover myself, a wave of weakness swept over me, sickeningly familiar.

"You can't win, Chubby Cheeks," Crystal said, from inside my head. *"And no stupid little gold cross is gonna help you."*

Horrified, I tried to turn, to run, before it was too late, but my feet seemed frozen to the floor, and all I could manage was a half turn of my head.

There, in the street outside my display window, stood Sammy.

He was staring right at me, and he was smiling.

"What's the matter with you?" Tina's voice seemed to come from far away.

Concentrate, Styx, concentrate.

But it was no use. Sammy threw back his blond head and laughed, and I was lost.

"You never loved me, Mama," I said, through clenched teeth. "All you ever cared about was where your next drink was coming from." I would normally never say something so mean, but the words kept coming. "Love your beer, don't you? That's one of the reasons you're so fat . . . and why your last loser boyfriend dumped you."

My head jerked to the right, so I was facing Tina Cowart directly. "You make me sick."

Tina's face was white as a sheet. "Crystal?" Her lower lip trembled. "Is that you, baby?"

Oh, man—if insults were what passed for affection between Crystal and her mother, they deserved all the pity they could get.

"Don't feel sorry for me, you little bitch." Crystal was evidently reading my mind while she swirled around in there, and my thoughts made her furious.

I tried to focus, to feel nothing—no pity, no anger, no panic. Only a single-minded effort to get rid of Crystal's invasion. My body was frozen in place, but my mind was still my own.

And I was going to keep it that way.

"I have my master to help me, Chubby Cheeks . . . what do you have?" Crystal's mental taunting was edged with desperation, and I took hope from it.

Tina Cowart took a step closer, throat working. The look on her face was difficult to describe. "Crystal? Are you in there?"

Trying even harder to concentrate, I forced my eyes to close. Almost immediately, I received a mental image of the Light . . . pure, white . . .

blindingly so. I drank it in, bathed in it, and felt my strength returning.

Crystal evidently felt it, too. *No! No, not yet . . .*

My body responded to Crystal's agitation; I began to shake, to tremble. I gritted my teeth, keeping my eyes closed, concentrating on the Light. It pulsed and glowed, drawing me in as it had the first time I'd seen it, many months ago.

A sudden rush of energy swamped me—my body swayed in an effort to withstand it, and then everything went black.

CHAPTER 9

"Do unto others, Nicki, as you would have them do unto you."

It was déjà vu all over again—the Light, the tunnel, the music of the cosmos ringing in my ears like the pure, perfect notes of a celestial choir. The indescribable feelings of love and comfort and *knowing*.

And the Voice. The nameless, faceless Voice that knew and loved and comforted.

I couldn't feel my body—I wasn't sure I *had* a body. All around me floated bright shapes, colors without form or substance. These *beings* radiated warmth and acceptance, and somehow I knew that the shifting kaleidoscope of colors was caused by their emotions—the blues of love and comfort, greens of hope and joy, red and orange for warmth.

"Don't be afraid," the colors whispered, without words. *"Be strong, and embrace who you are. There is purpose in everything, and in everything there is purpose."*

"To those to whom much is given, much will be asked," said the Voice. "Go back, and take comfort in knowing that all is as it should be."

Then I was floating, up and away from the brightness of the Light, watching it recede while my soul cried out in sorrow. Once again I'd been so close, yet I was still so far. The Light became a sparkle, then a pinprick, then disappeared altogether, leaving nothing but darkness.

Oblivion beckoned, but was evidently not to be. My body felt heavy, burdensome. Slowly, I became aware of an unpleasant odor. Oblivion didn't smell like cigarettes, did it?

"Don't die on me, girl," a woman's voice muttered. "I've got enough problems as it is."

I opened my eyes to see a face looming over me. Pudgy cheeks and dirty brown hair, drawn back in a messy bun.

Tina Cowart. Crystal's mother.

"Wha—what happened?" I was lying on the floor, my head in Tina's lap. It was an effort to sit up, but it was better than breathing in the stale fumes rising from Tina's clothes.

"You passed out," she said, sighing in relief. The smell of cigarettes on her breath was worse than her clothes, and enough to push me to my feet. My knees were wobbly, so I grabbed the edge of a nearby counter and held on.

"Do you need me to call somebody?" Tina asked. She struggled to her feet as well, grunting a little with the effort.

I shook my head. "How long—" My throat was dry, so I swallowed hard before finishing. "How long was I out?"

Tina shrugged. "Not long. Less than a minute, maybe."

A minute? I'd been to eternity and back that quickly? Time had no meaning where I'd been, I suppose.

I took a deep breath, already feeling steadier. The last time this happened, I'd awakened in the hospital a day later, stiff and sore. I'd had to take antibiotics for two weeks to clear up the lingering infection that was the source of my heart failure. This time it was different—my heart was pumping away just fine, if a little too fast, and I'd only blacked out, not died.

I think.

Had it been a dream? A hallucination?

"You okay?" Tina's question brought me back to reality.

I nodded, wishing she'd go away. "I'm okay."

"Was that my daughter?" Tina showed no inclination to leave just yet. "Was Crystal . . . you know . . . speaking through you before you passed out?"

Oh, man. Crystal the Mean Meth-head. I turned my head toward the front window, where Sammy had been standing, moments before this ugly little episode had begun, but saw nothing but the usual foot traffic ambling by. The bright red banners across the street at Divinyls flapped in the breeze, mocking me with their cheerful phrases of WELCOME! and GRAND OPENING.

"I'm not feeling too well," I mumbled, not anxious to answer questions. "I'm gonna go lie down, so if you don't mind, I'd like to lock up the store now."

Tina eyed me, obviously debating whether to push harder or back off. "Tell Crystal I love her," she said, evidently making up her mind as to the answer to her own question. "I know she never meant them mean things she said." She turned toward the door, hesitating. "And tell her I'm sorry." A tired, defeated look crept into her eyes. Her rounded shoulders seemed to be set in a permanent slump. "She'll know what for."

I would've felt sorry for Tina Cowart if I hadn't been so busy feeling sorry for myself. As it was, I was barely able to keep from shoving her bodily out the door. When she turned and left, I nearly sagged to my knees in relief, grateful for the counter's support.

The tinkle of the shop bell drew Evan from the back. His look went from apprehensive to concerned the moment he saw me. "Nicki? Are you okay?"

His arm was around my shoulder in moments, familiar and comforting, and I leaned into him, letting my head rest against his shirt.

"No," I said, sounding like a total wimp. "And I don't think I'll ever be okay again."

The light from my lava lamp bathed the top of my dresser, soothing and soft as the lava itself. I watched the gooey shapes rise and fall, tumbling over themselves in their haste to rejoin the gunk at the bottom.

"I'm worried about you," Joe said. We were in bed, his bare chest beneath my cheek. "That's twice now she's possessed you."

I'd told Joe about my visit from Crystal and Tina Cowart, but I hadn't told him about blacking out, because I knew he'd make me go in for testing and scans and X-rays, things I didn't need. If there was anything I'd learned from my two trips to the Light, it was that when your number was up, it was up. And when it wasn't—BAM—back to the real world you'd go.

"Why is she so angry? She has to know I didn't kill her." There was absolute certainty in his voice. "At some level, she knew what she was doing to herself was dangerous. She didn't become that emaciated overnight—surely some doctor somewhere had given her a warning before now."

"She said something about all doctors being stupid," I told him. "I don't think she took warnings very well."

He sighed beneath my palm.

"She was a messed-up person, who died angry at the world, which made her a beacon to Sammy. He's giving her anger an outlet, keeping her alive in a way." I was musing aloud. "But ultimately he'll take her soul."

"Bastard," Joe muttered.

I raised a finger to his lips, not wanting to tempt fate by talking about Sammy any longer, particularly while we were in bed.

"It's sad," I murmured. "I feel sorry for her."

It *was* sad. As creepy as she was, Crystal was dead, and she'd apparently never been happy.

Never *would* be happy.

She'd made a deal with the Devil, and in the end, the Devil always gets his due.

"Maybe it's time to call in a priest," Joe said.

I raised my head to look at him. "I'm not Catholic."

He smoothed the hair away from my face as he answered. "Neither am I, but I don't think it matters."

I put my head back down, cheek warm against his skin. "I don't know. Seems kind of hypocritical to ask for help from the church when I haven't been inside one for years." *Except for Granny Julep's funeral.* But Trinity Baptist Church was Southern Baptist to the core, and I doubted the old black preacher who'd given Granny's eulogy would be interested in crazy talk about demons from a girl he'd never met. Particularly a girl with pink streaks in her hair and a wild story about seeing dead people.

"We have to do something," Joe murmured. His hand stroked my arm, soothing and slow. "I don't want anything to happen to you, Nicki."

Unexpected tears prickled, but I blinked them away. I kissed the warm skin closest to my lips—his chest, just below the right nipple. "It's going to be okay," I said, hoping like hell that it was true. "I'm practicing my meditation techniques, just like Bijou told me. As long as I'm strong, I can kick Crystal out when she tries to take over. If I get strong enough, I might be able to keep her from getting in there to begin with."

"For how long?" Joe asked, effectively shutting down my argument. "How long can you keep that up, Nick?" His hand stopped its stroking, squeezing my arm gently instead. "You've got a weak heart valve, remember? I'm worried about the strain, both emotional and physical, that this puts on your body."

I bit my lip, knowing exactly how close to the mark he was. Another reason not to tell him I'd blacked out. I was fine now, just fine, and I wouldn't have been sent back from the other side a second time without a reason. *"Don't be afraid,"* the colors had said. *"There is purpose in everything, and in everything there is purpose."* My number was obviously not up yet, but I didn't want to argue about it.

Not at the moment.

I kissed him again, right where the fine hair surrounding his nipple started to curl. His chest was mostly hairless, except for a few light swirls I found both endearing and sexy. "I'll be careful," I murmured, stroking the firm skin beneath my fingers. "Don't worry."

Joe's heavy sigh was laced with frustration,

and I couldn't have that. We'd just spent forty-five glorious minutes getting *rid* of frustration.

I let my hand travel down the faint trail of hair that led to his belly button, then flattened it over his already flat stomach. Closing my eyes, I slid it even lower, knowing I'd reached my goal when the hair turned from silky to coarse, from a light dusting to a prickly nest of curls.

Joe stirred against my hand, and I cupped his balls with my palm, hefting their weight. I loved how they felt—tender little sacs of vulnerability, so readily filled with man juice.

I was all set to slide down and pay them some attention when Joe took my wrist, sliding my hand over his hardness instead. It surged beneath my palm, and sent a jolt of heat into my belly. *All this talk of worry when we could be doing something else.* I stroked him, closing my eyes at the sensation of silken skin over hard flesh, velvety and alive beneath my fingertips.

He shifted, rolling me onto my back. His heat was against my thigh and belly now, still hardening. He pressed it against me, deliberately, letting me feel how it surged and thickened.

"Mmmm." I moved my hips, pressing even closer. "You don't seem to be worried about the effect *this* will have on my heart."

"No," he muttered, brushing heated lips against my neck, just below my ear. "I'm only worried about the effect it has on mine."

And then his hand was on my breast, and his lips were on my throat, and rational thought disappeared.

"*This is mine,*" his body was saying, and my body was responding, not even trying to deny it.

I slipped one hand into his dark hair, and slid the other around his back, freeing my arms so he could do whatever he wanted. And then I kissed him with all the love in my heart as, with no further preliminaries, he drove himself home.

Still damp from our earlier lovemaking, I gasped, clutching his shoulders.

"You're mine," Joe confirmed my hazy, pleasure-drenched thoughts, dragging his lips across my cheek and burying his face in my neck. "Mine," he repeated, driving his point home with a well-timed thrust. "He can't have you."

My dazed eyes flew open, but Joe began a steady rhythm that left me breathless. I couldn't speak, and didn't want to anyway. Words seemed so insubstantial, so pale next to the sensations I was experiencing.

"I want you to remember this," Joe whispered,

sliding in and out as I clung to him, not caring if my nails hurt. "I want you to remember what you're fighting for." A slow, deep thrust drew a groan from both of us, then Joe ceased to move at all, holding himself motionless deep within me. He threw back his head, throat muscles working. It was primal, overwhelmingly so. His arms felt like steel bands, shoulders like stone. "What *we're* fighting for." His breathing was ragged, and so was mine. All I could think of was how he felt, right this moment, muscles bunched beneath my fingers, hips pinning me to the bed.

"This is good," he said, pulling out just the teensiest bit before sliding back in. "What we have is good," he gritted, eyes closed, "and I want you to think about it when you need to be strong."

All I could do was moan, overwhelmed by intensity. He didn't expect an answer—what he really wanted was my surrender, and I gave it to him.

He felt it, and ground his hips against mine, circular motions that rasped against my most sensitive spot, an almost unbearable friction that I never wanted to end.

He pushed harder, burying himself even deeper

as I peaked, gasping, losing myself in the *feel* of this man, this moment.

"What we have is good, Nicki," he whispered in my ear, holding himself deep within my body as I throbbed, fireworks exploding behind closed eyelids. "Don't forget what we have."

CHAPTER 10

How the heck was I supposed to clear my mind this morning if I couldn't forget the night before?

Morning sun streamed across the hardwood floors of my dining room. I was practicing meditation again, just like I'd promised, but all I could think about was Joe.

Maybe I really *could* trust a guy to stand by me forever, no matter what.

Commitment had always been a scary thought, but now it was scarier than ever because I had so much to lose.

I stared at my hands, loose in my lap. My mother's emerald ring on the right, the antique silver and marcasite ring Joe'd given me on the left. He'd given it to me on Halloween night—"for the prettiest ghoul I know"—he'd said, sealing his fate.

I smiled a little, remembering. Not that we were engaged or anything, but yes, his fate was sealed, because he'd made me fall in love with him. Which meant I could get my heart broken in a variety of excruciatingly painful, possibly agonizing, and—now that Sammy was back—twistedly brilliant ways.

But I wasn't going to try to do anything stupid to drive him away to keep him out of danger, like I might have done earlier in our relationship.

He knew what he was in for.

Didn't he?

The meditation thing was a lot harder than it seemed. Bijou told me she liked to meditate in her library, in a wing chair by the fireplace. Flames were a good thing to look at while you cleared your head, she'd said.

I didn't have a fireplace, so I'd gone for the stereotypical cross-legged position on a pillow on the floor. Mooning over Joe wasn't helping. I needed to concentrate, so I did my best to remember everything she'd told me.

Keep your head, neck, and back straight but not stiff.
Check.
Put aside all thoughts of the past and the future. Stay in the present.

There were dust bunnies under the dining-room table.

Focus on your breathing. In through your nose, out through your mouth.

Had I brushed my teeth this morning?

In through the nose, out through the mouth.

The oil light had come on in my car yesterday. I needed to make an appointment to get it serviced.

In, out.

Who breathed like this anyway? Breathing was not something I normally had to think about.

Use your breathing as an anchor when your thoughts overwhelm you. Focus on your body, the rise and fall of your chest, the air as it fills your lungs, then empties.

Good thing I'd never been a smoker. I'd seen pictures of what happened to a smoker's lungs—very gross.

A knock on the front door made me jump, destroying my feeble attempts at concentration. But I didn't get up, just called from my pillow on the floor, "Who is it?"

That door had two dead bolts on it—dead bolts I knew were locked.

No answer, which made me nervous.

"Who is it?" I called again.

Out in the street, a car door slammed. The faint sound of an engine, then nothing.

Goose bumps rose on my arms. Apparently, whoever had knocked on my door was gone, so I should have felt safe, but I didn't. Cautiously, I rose and padded toward the door, barefoot in my T-shirt and pajama bottoms. I pressed my eye to the peephole, seeing nothing but my empty front porch.

Not about to open the door yet, I moved to the living-room window, peering through the curtains. The porch was empty except for my potted plants, some of them in dire need of water.

My dad's old rocker was in its customary place by the railing, and in it sat a small white basket with a jaunty pink bow on the handle. It looked like an Easter basket, but Easter was nearly a month past.

A gift basket. From whom?

I peered through the window a couple of seconds longer just to make sure there was no one lurking on the sidewalk before I opened the door and went out to retrieve it.

The basket was filled with fresh greenery. It smelled great, very herbal. One of the bundles had yellow flowers. An assortment of small bottles, hand-labeled, and rolled scraps of paper, each tied with pink ribbon. A note addressed to me lay on top.

It looked harmless enough, cheerful even. I took one last look around my empty front yard before taking the basket inside, wondering why the florist hadn't waited for me to come to the door. But I made sure I engaged both dead bolts behind me before taking it over to the couch.

"ST. JOHN'S WORT," read the label on the first bottle. There were six or eight of them, filled with different-colored powders in shades of yellow, green and gray. "ASHES OF ALFALFA. ESSENCE OF RUE." Homemade labels, in feminine handwriting. Hardly your typical set of spices, and they didn't look or sound like bath salts, either. I opened the note.

"Ms. Styx," (it said, in the same handwriting that was on the bottles) "please accept these in the spirit they are offered. I think you may need them."

That was it. No signature.

FENNEL SEEDS, ANGELICA, DRIED SNAPDRAGON. I picked up one of the little scrolls and slipped off the ribbon. ~Spell To Find Something That's Lost~, it said at the top, and I frowned, disappointed. "Great," I muttered, "I'm getting gift baskets from the loonies now."

Suddenly the basket didn't seem so cute. I didn't care for witchcraft, and I'd already learned the power of carefully prepared herbs from an old voodoo woman named Granny Julep. "No, thank you, Ms. Nutball-Whoever-You-Are," I said aloud. "I don't need your kind of help." I put the basket down on the coffee table a little harder than I needed to and went back to the dining room to pick up my meditation where I'd left off.

"I can't find my keys, Evan," I said into the phone. "I'll be in as soon as I do." Tired of scrabbling through my purse for the umpteenth time, I dumped the entire contents on the counter. I always left my keys in a wooden bowl by the front door, out of habit, but I obviously hadn't last night.

"Did you check the bathroom?" Evan asked.

"Now what would my keys be doing in the bathroom?" I answered, exasperated. I'd been looking for the damn things for five minutes, and I was beginning to get aggravated. I mean, I'd driven

myself home, hadn't I? They had to be here somewhere.

"Don't be snippy," he warned. "I'm not in a good
mood this morning, either."

Lipstick, breath mints, wallet, comb, receipts . . .
no keys. "Sorry," I said, turning my back to the
mess on the counter. "I'm just frustrated."

"So am I," he countered. "Butch hasn't wanted
to cuddle in almost a week."

Oh my. "Trouble in paradise?"

Evan sighed. "He says he's just tired, but even
when I offered to—"

"Too much information!" I interrupted him
before he could finish the sentence.

"—give him a back rub," Evan finished, none
too patiently, "he said he just wanted to sleep."

"Well, he does work nights," I said, my mind
still on my missing keys. "If the man says he's
tired, then he's just tired." People had to give
people they loved the benefit of the doubt, right?
"By the weekend, you two will be making up for
lost time."

"I hope so," Evan said, but he sounded uncon-
vinced.

I was scanning the living room as we talked,
hoping a wider perspective might help me find
the keys. The basket was on the coffee table, right

where I'd left it, the little scrap of paper with its pink ribbon lying loosely on top.

"I'll talk to you when I get in, okay?"

"Bring me a Danish," he said fretfully. "I need to drown my sorrows in some sugar, and that's the only kind I'm getting lately."

"I'm not bringing you a Danish, and you'll thank me for it tomorrow."

"A muffin, then." Evan must be seriously worried to be ignoring both fat *and* carbs. He was usually very careful about his figure.

"A bran muffin," I agreed, "to help you get all this 'Butch is losing interest' crap out of your system." *Where the heck were my keys?*

"Potty mouth," Evan retorted. "Make it blueberry," and hung up.

I put the phone down on the counter and stuffed everything back into my purse, leaving only a crumpled tissue and a few random receipts to throw away. Then I turned back toward the living room, thinking hard.

The wicker basket was directly in my line of sight.

Stupid basket. Stupid charms and powders.

Aggravated enough to do something stupid myself, I muttered, "Why not?" and walked over to snatch up the little scrap of paper.

SPELL TO FIND SOMETHING THAT'S LOST

CONCENTRATE ON THE MISSING ITEM AND
RECITE THREE TIMES:
WHAT IS LOST, MUST NOW BE FOUND
TAKE MY LUCK AND TURN IT AROUND

Sounded simple enough. No magic powders, no full moon, no animal sacrifice.

What could it hurt?

I visualized my key ring, oversized Betty Boop dangle and all, and said, "What is lost, must now be found. Take my luck, and turn it around." Then I said it again, twice.

I waited a couple of seconds and looked around, feeling vaguely guilty. I was the one always harping at people not to mess with the spooky stuff— if my sister Kelly found out, she'd never let me live it down.

No keys in sight.

"Should've known." I tossed the scrap of paper back into the wicker basket, disgusted with myself for even considering that a silly charm might work, and oddly relieved it hadn't. Just to be sure, I turned and looked around the room a final time, seeing a few scattered magazines and a couple of empty wineglasses from last night, but no keys. The couch cushions were messed up from an earlier search, so I bent to straighten them. As I did, the toe of my heeled sandal hit something just under the edge of the couch, and I heard a telltale jingle.

I'll be damned.

But I didn't say it, because you never know—sometimes saying things out loud makes them come true.

CHAPTER 11

Three minutes later I was in my car and on the way to work. Glancing at my watch, I decided that since I was already running so late, I'd get two blueberry muffins at the coffee shop instead of one. Evan could soothe his need for comfort food, and I could have the other for lunch. I briefly considered going to a local Starbucks instead of Moonbeans, but decided against it; I wasn't going to let Sammy affect my regular comings and goings.

I'd almost made it to my regular parking spot behind Handbags and Gladrags when the *whoop* of a police siren made me jump. A check of the rearview mirror revealed an Atlanta police cruiser directly behind me, no lights. He *whooped* at me again, a short burst that apparently meant, *pull over.*

With a sigh, I turned on my blinker and kept moving, flinching as his siren whooped again, longer this time. Heads were turning all up and down Moreland. With the police cruiser right on my tail, I pulled slowly into my reserved parking spot near the service entrance to my store, right next to Evan's little white Volvo.

Then I made the mistake of opening my car door.

"Remain with the vehicle," came a harsh voice from the cruiser's loudspeaker. "Hands where I can see 'em."

I froze. I know I hadn't been speeding, because I'd already slowed down to pull in and park. I hadn't run any red lights or made any improper lane changes; Moreland was a narrow, two-lane street, and I drove it every day.

I looked at the cruiser; the officer behind the wheel was a middle-aged white guy in big black aviator sunglasses. He stared at me, expressionless, then raised the microphone to his lips, and repeated, "Remain with the vehicle."

Gee, maybe you could shout a little louder. I don't think they heard you on the West Coast.

I bit my lip and stayed where I was, hoping he'd hurry up and tell me what I'd done wrong so I could go about my business.

Unfortunately for me, he seemed in no hurry to do so. He fiddled with his dashboard, talking into the microphone again. I couldn't hear what he was saying, but I could hear occasional bursts of static and voices coming through his car radio.

I waited, leaning back into the seat, hands on the steering wheel where he could see them. Every so often I checked the rearview mirror, but all I got was more staring, more static, and more waiting. I wondered if Evan was watching us through the security camera; we'd installed one last year to watch the service entrance after someone tried to break in. If he was, I hoped he had the sense to stay inside—the cop seemed like a hard-ass, and I didn't want Evan involved in this.

Whatever *this* was.

The cop finally opened the door to his cruiser and stepped out. He was pretty fit for an older guy, broad in the shoulders, trim at the waist. The aviator sunglasses were a bit much, though, obviously designed to intimidate, as was the grim line of his mouth.

"What's the problem, Officer?"

"License and registration," was the only answer I got in return.

I leaned over to get my purse, and he was right there, watching every move I made as I rummaged through my bag for my wallet.

Let him watch; I had nothing to hide. He took my license without a word, then put out his hand for my registration, waiting as I popped open the glove box and pulled it out.

He finally took his eyes off me long enough to scan my driver's license, pairing it with the registration.

The silent treatment was getting old. I tried not to let my irritation show, knowing it would probably only make the situation worse. As a businesswoman, I didn't want to rile the local police—Little Five was an eclectic old neighborhood, and not without its share of crime.

Never bite the hand that covers your ass, as Evan always said.

"Sir, may I ask why you pulled me over?" I looked directly up into his face, keeping my tone polite.

"Tag's expired," he said shortly, "and you're burning oil. Left a trail of black smoke all the way down Moreland. Georgia law requires an emissions inspection once a year."

Well, shit. That's what I got for putting it off. Can't renew your tag without an inspection, but I hated waiting in line. "I was just about to make an appointment to get my oil changed," I offered, thinking maybe it would help.

"Tag's expired, Miss." The cop was cutting me no slack. "You're in violation."

"I'll get it taken care of right away, Officer." I smiled at him, hoping he'd smile back.

He didn't.

Instead, he turned and walked back to his cruiser, still carrying my license and registration. The sinking feeling in the pit of my stomach told me I was about to get a ticket.

Sure enough, almost ten boring minutes later, during which Deputy Dawg evidently ran a check on my license and registration, he emerged from the cruiser carrying a fat little notebook.

"Well, did you find out I'm wanted in twelve states?" At this point, I figured a little sarcasm couldn't hurt me. A *lot* of sarcasm maybe, but not a little.

"You'd be in the back of my cruiser now if you were," said Officer A-Hole, flatly. The guy had no sense of humor. He handed me not one slip of paper, but two. "As it is, you're lucky to get away with an expired tag and an overdue emissions inspection." He put both hands on my car and leaned in. "And the next time an officer of the law signals you to pull over, I suggest you do so immediately. Failure to yield the right-of-way can cost you another $100.00."

"What?" I couldn't believe what I was hearing. His face was so close I could see a reflection of myself in his sunglasses, and I didn't look happy. "Failure to yield the right-of-way? When did I do that?"

"Section 40–6–6 of the Georgia code," he said flatly. "When signaled by law enforcement, civilian drivers shall immediately drive to a position parallel to and as close as possible to, the right-hand curb of the roadway." The monotone quality to his voice told me he'd repeated that phrase many times before. "Not take their time searching for a parking place."

"I wasn't searching for a parking space," I said indignantly, still unable to believe what a jerk the guy was being. "This is my *regular* parking spot! I was almost in it when you started blasting your siren at me!"

Sheriff Shithead straightened up, slapping his black notebook against his palm. "I can see you don't take warnings very well, young lady." He whipped out his pen and went to work on ticket number three. "Some people need to learn things the hard way, I guess."

"Oh, come *on* . . ." My whines and protests went unheeded. Thirty seconds later I had my ass handed to me on yet another slip of paper, which I snatched with ill grace. It was only with an effort that I kept my mouth shut, particularly when Officer Numbnuts had the nerve to say "have a nice day" before he walked away.

I tossed all three tickets down on the passenger seat, giving in to the urge to curl four of the fingers of both my hands into an obscene gesture.

But I kept them in my lap where Deputy Douchebag couldn't see them—for all I knew there was a Georgia code against shooting a "*police*" officer the bird, even when they deserved it.

"Where the hell have you *been*, Nicki?" Evan's greeting as I walked in the back door didn't help my mood.

"Where do you think I've been," I snipped, slamming the door behind me. "You won't believe what just—"

"Grab some paper towels and come help me." His voice came from the store bathroom; the door was open, and he sounded a little frantic.

"What are you doing in there?"

"I'm ruining my favorite pair of Prada loafers," he yelled. "The toilet overflowed."

Lovely. Just lovely.

I tossed my purse on the battered old desk we used in the back office and headed toward the storage room for a mop and paper towels.

"Yoohoo," came a female voice from the front of the store. "Anybody here?"

"Be right there," I called out, snatching up a roll of paper towels and looking around for the mop. It wasn't in its usual spot, so I just took the towels and darted toward the bathroom. "Just a minute!"

Evan barely glanced up—he had the mop and was busy using it, slopping at the wet floor while trying to keep his feet dry. He was standing on a pile of clothes that looked vaguely familiar.

"Not the stuff from the Junior League thrift sale," I said, groaning. "There was designer stuff in there."

"Then you shouldn't have left it piled on the chair in the back room," Evan snapped. "This was an emergency."

"I was taking it to the dry cleaner," I snapped back.

"Then you should've taken it yesterday! Or last week!"

It was on the tip of my tongue to say something

nasty, but I bit it instead. We were both obviously having a bad day.

"We have a customer out front," I said shortly, handing him the paper towels. "I'll be back."

He gave me a look, but kept his mouth shut. That was one of the good things about our friendship—we both usually knew when to shut up.

I hurried down the hall to the front of the store, feeling harried and hassled and more than just a little cranky.

"There you are, dear," said my grandma Bijou. She was standing on the other side of the cash register, looking her fastidiously feminine self in a lavender print dress with a matching hat. I was so stunned to see her that I did a double take. What convinced me I wasn't seeing things was the very stout black woman with a frown on her face who stood beside her.

"Odessa and I decided to pay you a surprise visit!" Bijou said, opening her arms for a hug. She was beaming. "Just imagine, a spur-of-the-moment road trip to Atlanta, at our age. Isn't it wonderful?"

"Wonderful," I mumbled, face pressed against a plump lavender shoulder. She smelled like hairspray and roses. I lifted my head and looked at Odessa, who had yet to crack a smile.

"Just wonderful."

CHAPTER 12

"Lord have mercy," Odessa said sourly. "It's a good thing we used the restroom at Cracker Barrel on the way here."

We were standing in the hall outside the flooded bathroom. I'd tried to excuse myself for a minute so I could help Evan clean up, but my visitors insisted on seeing the damage for themselves.

"Evan," I said, so sweetly my teeth hurt, "you remember my grandmother, don't you? She and her friend Odessa have come for a surprise visit."

Evan gaped at us from atop his pile of soggy clothes, mop in hand. "Ms. Boudreaux," he exclaimed, pinning a smile on his face that was as fake as the one on mine. He stepped calmly over to join us in the hallway, as if greeting little old ladies while cleaning the toilet was an everyday occurrence. "How nice to see you again!" He started to extend a hand, but glanced at the wet mop he was holding and obviously thought the better of it. "What a surprise!"

"Lovely to see you, too, dear," Bijou said. "And do call me Bijou."

"You always keep a pile of good clothes on the floor of your bathroom?" Odessa asked him bluntly. "Those don't hardly look like rags to me."

"Evan," I said, smiling a little more genuinely this time—it was a rare occasion for Odessa and I to agree on anything, even if she didn't know she was agreeing—"meet Odessa."

"Nice to meet you, Odessa." He looked a little wary, and I didn't blame him. "Nicki's told me all about you."

I watched as they sized each other up—an older black woman with a bad attitude, and a young, fashionable, gay guy who never took attitude from anybody. I was curious to see what sparks might fly.

"Hand me that mop," Odessa said, "and go visit with Miz Bijou and your girlfriend."

Evan's brows shot to the ceiling.

Odessa rolled her eyes, fairly snatching the mop from his hand. "Don't get your panties in a wad, honeybunch. Go on now, go visit. I'll clean this up."

Ordinarily, I'd pay big money to see Evan speechless, so it was a real treat to see it for free.

He tried to rally. "Thank you, but—"

Odessa brushed him out of the way as if he were a gnat, heading into the bathroom with mop in hand. She still had her purse over an arm. "Lord have mercy," she said again. "Don't nobody ever clean this place?"

"Every night," he said, trying to sound indignant but failing miserably. "After we close."

"Huh," came Odessa's skeptical reply.

I caught him by the arm and led him away, knowing that once Odessa was set on a course, it would take a hurricane to blow her off it.

Besides, it would keep her scowl centered on something other than me for a change.

A few minutes later, Evan and I had my grandmother Bijou comfortably ensconced on the couch in the back office. She took in the room, eyes faded but sharp. The battered old file cabinet and mostly neat desk, the posters of the Pretenders and Elvis Costello on the wall. I sank down in an old leather arm chair, letting her look, while Evan washed his hands in the utility sink and made us all tea. Her eye fell on the pictures of my parents I kept on the bookshelf, and she made a small noise, pleasure and sorrow combined.

"Your parents?"

I nodded. "Dan and Emily Styx."

"They look like lovely people," she said.

"They were."

One of the pictures was of us on a camping trip when I was about twelve. My dad was laughing at something my mom had just said, while I sat between them, elbows on the picnic table, frosting on my face from one of Mom's cupcakes. She always made cupcakes before we went camping.

"It would've made Peaches happy to know you were so well loved," Bijou said.

"She knew."

A carefully drawn eyebrow arched in question.

"Peaches came to see me, at home, after she"—*after she died*—"and we talked about my parents. She knew I was okay with her giving me up for adoption. She knew I had a happy childhood."

"Ah," Bijou said softly. Her gaze turned inward for a moment. "I'm glad."

Odessa could be heard muttering to herself down the hall.

"I do hope you'll forgive an old woman her

whims," she said briskly, changing the subject. "I know this is quite sudden, Odessa and me showing up like this, but we promise not to be a bother—"

A clatter from the bathroom made Odessa's opinion on the matter quite clear, but Bijou ignored her.

"We absolutely promise not to be a bit of trouble."

I had to smile a little at that, knowing blatant bullshit when I heard it. Still, I felt a surge of affection for this odd elderly person who'd recently come into my life; a true Southern lady, who wasn't a lady at all.

"And you don't have to worry about putting us up, because we've already taken a room at the Embassy Suites." Bijou made it clear that everything had been decided. She patted her white patent leather purse with gloved fingers, lavender to match her hat. "We've come to see you, of course, but we've also come for a bit of sightseeing in the big city; I understand the new aquarium is quite impressive."

"I'm glad you're here," I said, surprised to find it true. She was lying, of course; she was here because she was worried about me, but I found it sweet that she'd bother to lie about it. "As soon as Odessa's through in the bathroom, I'll show you both around the store, then we can meet up later for dinner at my house . . . say, seven? I'll write down the directions."

Bijou smiled, relaxing. Her dress had a girlish frill of ruffles at the hem. White sandals, pink polish on the toes. "That would be lovely."

"How's Kelly? Why didn't she come with you?" My sister was going to get an earful for not giving me a heads-up about Bijou and Odessa's visit.

"She's fine"—a smile of affection creased the old woman's face—"just fine. She and her young man had a date this weekend, so she preferred to stay in Savannah."

"She and Spider seem to have really hit it off," I said. "Do you like him?"

"Very much so. Never judge a book by its cover, I always say."

Spider's "cover" was one of earrings, tattoos, and piercings, as well as a deep and abiding fascination with the paranormal. I liked him, too.

"Good." I smiled, glad all the small talk was out of the way. "Now tell me the real reason you're here."

She didn't bother to lie this time. "I just had a feeling you were going to need me, dear," she said simply. Rhinestones gleamed on her hatpin—a beautiful piece of vintage jewelry I wouldn't mind having in my display case. "When I said the same to Odessa, she insisted we come right away."

I somehow doubted that.

Bijou shot a glance toward the hallway, lowering her voice a little. "It was suggested we not call, because you'd tell us not to come."

Got that right.

"And we didn't want *him* to know we were coming." She said this so matter-of-factly that it gave me pause. "If *you* knew we were coming, *he'd* know we were coming, and we'd lose the element of surprise."

I knew exactly to whom she was referring, of course, though I'd prefer not to. She wasn't saying Sammy's name aloud, so neither would I.

"Here we go," Evan said, a little too gaily. "Tea's ready."

"Ah, thank you." Bijou beamed at him as he handed her a cup—his favorite blue-and-white one, I noted. "That smells heavenly. Chamomile, is it? Steeped with lemon?"

Never able to resist a compliment, Evan preened a little as he handed me my mug. "It is. I add a little honey to the mix."

"You certainly do," said my grandmother, decisively. "I'm so glad Nicki has you as her friend." She lifted her tea briefly in his direction, then took a sip, smiling.

Evan surprised me by actually tearing up a little. He looked at Bijou for a moment, then he looked at me, and said, "I'm sorry I snapped at you for being late."

"I'm sorry I snapped at you over the clothes on the floor."

"You still owe me a Danish."

"I don't owe you a Danish, I owe you a muffin."

"Danish."

"Okay, a Danish." I smiled at him, unable to resist adding, "But don't ask me later if your butt looks big."

"Deal." We clinked mugs on it, and life was back to normal.

Kind of.

CHAPTER 13

"Simple Wiccan magic," Bijou said. "Herbs and charms. Benign, for the most part."

It was after dinner, around nine o'clock. Joe was helping Odessa in the kitchen, Evan had just gone home to be with Butch, and my grandmother and I were enjoying a well-deserved glass of red wine in the living room. I say "well-deserved" because my bad day had continued throughout the *whole freakin' day*. The phone line for the credit-card machine had gone down, the plumber had never shown up, and I'd snagged my favorite black sweater beyond repair—vintage Pierre Cardin, hand-knit. Some low-life skank managed to shop-lift a three-hundred-dollar Judith Lieber bag I'd left on the counter while I was distracted with other customers, and I'd spent twenty minutes scrubbing profanities off the wall in one of the dressing rooms. I'd rushed by the grocery store on the way home to pick up some frozen lasagna, only to find my microwave blinking "666" instead of the time, completely useless no matter how many buttons I pushed. I'd stuck the lasagna in the oven instead, only to set off the smoke detector when it broiled instead of baked. If Joe hadn't stopped at Papa Donatello's for stuffed shells and cannoli on the way over, I'd have been screwed.

"*Mostly* benign?" Bijou's comfortable acceptance of the gift basket I'd found on my doorstep that morning should've reassured me, but it didn't. She'd been fascinated with it, poking through it while I'd poured the wine. Quite frankly, I'd forgotten it was still sitting on the coffee table.

Once she brought it up, though, I couldn't stop thinking about my very bad day and the silly little charm that had helped me find my missing keys this morning.

I picked up the small envelope addressed to me and read the note again. "*Please accept these in the spirit in which they are offered. I have a feeling you may need them.*"

Whoever left it better be wrong.

"The first rule of Wicca is 'And it harm none, do what ye will'," Bijou said. "It's an old, earth-based theology, one that promotes harmony with nature. Wiccans believe any good or any ill you do someone will come back to you three times over, so most coven members are quiet, gentle types." She smiled and took a polite sip of her wine. "You'd be surprised how many are in the Savannah Garden Club."

I wasn't surprised by anything anymore, at least not at the moment.

"The women who came into my shop calling themselves the Sisters of Circe didn't seem like garden-club types." I remembered the mean look in the eye of Sally Smith, or Shadow Starhawk, or whatever she called herself. "The one who did the most talking was downright nasty. Do you think one of them left the basket?"

I guess I sounded worried, because Bijou *tsked* at me. "You mustn't let yourself be intimidated, Nicki. Chin up. Shoulders back."

My body responded to her drill-sergeant tone without thinking, and she was right. I immediately felt better. Stronger.

"Whoever left the basket, it seems their intentions were for good, not ill; all the herbs are beneficial. Open the other scrolls," she said, "and let's see what the remedies are for."

I reached for a scroll and opened it to find a purification and relaxation spell that was mostly about candles and a hot bath—I could've figured that remedy out myself. Another scroll held the words to a spell to free yourself of anger, and the third was a ritual to reverse a curse. The fourth one I didn't like at all, because it was a spell to summon spirits.

But the last one was the worst, because it was a spell to mend a broken heart.

"Great," I said to my grandmother, "I'm evidently expected to be angry, dirty, and brokenhearted. But if somebody out there thinks I'm going to summon spirits, they're sadly mistaken." No need to call any spiritual attention to myself, that's for sure.

"What's all this?" Joe came into the living room, leaving Odessa to clatter my dishes to her heart's content. From the sound of it, she was poking her nose into every single one of my cabinets, but I didn't care.

I handed him the wine I'd already poured for him, and said, "It's a basket of stuff somebody left on my front porch this morning."

He frowned. "What kind of stuff?"

"Herbs and charms," Bijou said placidly, still apparently unconcerned.

Not so Joe. He shot me a look. "Why didn't you tell me about this, Nicki?"

"I didn't know it was a requirement," I snapped irritably.

His brows shot skyward, and so did Bijou's, which left me scrabbling for an apology. "I'm sorry, Joe, I've had such a bad day"—I patted the couch next to me, shaking my head at my own stupidity—"I didn't mean it. Please, I'm sorry."

A loud crash came from the kitchen, making all three of us jump.

"Odessa?" Grandma Bijou rose from her seat, alarmed. "Are you all right?"

"Broke a dish," came the reply.

"Oh, dear." Bijou gave me a worried look, then took the opportunity to beat a graceful retreat, heading for the kitchen.

"But don't worry," Odessa added, loud enough for everyone to hear. "It was an ugly one anyway. Don't that child got no dishes that *match*?"

Bijou was shushing her, obviously embarrassed.

"I'm just sayin'," Odessa was saying. Quieter now, but still "sayin'." "Bad enough we got to eat Eye-talian takeout . . ."

A particularly loud "shush" was the end of that particular diatribe, thankfully.

"I'm sorry I snapped at you, babe, really I am." I

patted the couch again, invitingly. "Come sit with me."

Joe gave me a rueful shake of the head from the other side of the coffee table. "Bad day?" he asked, and plopped down next to me.

"Was it ever," I said glumly.

"I had a bad one, too," he said. "Another round of grilling by the hospital administrator, and another meeting with Lisa Butler. I'm really beginning to think I need to hire my own attorney."

My heart sank to my toes. Here I was feeling sorry for myself over an oil leak, three tickets, and an overflowing toilet, when Joe had *real* problems.

Caused by me.

I slipped an arm through his and leaned my head against his shoulder.

"The worst part of the day was the look on the lab tech's face after I 'accidentally' managed to knock three separate trays of sterile instruments on the floor. I didn't do it, of course—it must've been Crystal—but I couldn't deny it, either. There's no excuse for clumsiness in the E.R."

Oh, no.

"If the staff thinks I'm shaken by this inquiry over Crystal Cowart's death, they'll lose confidence in me. I can't have that." He gave a tired sigh, resting his head against mine. "She's obviously still hanging around, playing tricks. My office was a mess when I got in this morning—everything on my desk had been dumped on the floor. I picked it up before someone saw it; didn't want anyone to think I'd trashed it myself and start rumors about my cracking under pressure."

"This is all my fault," I started to say, but Joe did some shushing of his own.

"It's not your fault, babe," he said, into my hair. "We'll get through it."

The clatter of broken china hitting the garbage can came from the kitchen. Despite the din, Joe and I just stayed where we were, and I slowly felt myself begin to relax for the first time all day.

"I'm sorry you had a bad day," I murmured.

"I'm sorry you had one, too."

"Yours was worse," I conceded. "Tickets and plumbing problems don't compare to truly scary things, like meetings with lawyers."

He laughed, which made me smile.

"I hate meetings," he said.

"I think Ms. Legal Beagle Butler has the hots for you," I said, teasingly. "I would, if I were her."

Joe stretched out his legs, putting his feet on my coffee table. "Yeah," he said, with a sigh and a satisfied smile, "I think you're right. She wants me."

I jerked upright, laughing, and gave him a playful shove. "You're unbelievable." At least he knew the truth when he heard it. "Pretty sure of yourself, aren't you?"

Joe gave me the grin that never failed to set my heart tripping, reaching out to drag me back down against him. "You make me feel good about myself, Nicki." He tucked my head back to its place on his shoulder and kissed my hair again. "But the only thing I'm sure of is that I want to be with you. Lisa is out of luck."

What could I do then but kiss him? And then I kissed him again, just for good measure, before leaning back and putting my feet up, too.

"It's been such a lovely evening"—Bijou came out of the kitchen a few moments later, dragging Odessa by the hand—"but it's time for us to turn in." She picked up her purse and gloves, then held out her arms for a good-bye hug, which I was happy to provide. "The Embassy Suites awaits, as does a long day of sightseeing tomorrow."

"Huh," Odessa said, tucking her purse under her arm. "You won't be up before noon and you know it. Why we needs to go see some stupid fishes anyway . . ."

"Thanks for cleaning up the kitchen, Odessa," I said, interrupting. "I appreciate it."

She eyed me keenly to see if I was being sarcastic. Not much got past those molasses-colored eyes, but since I was telling the truth, I wasn't worried. I was bone-tired, and cleaning up the kitchen after dinner for five was a chore I was happy to avoid. Apparently satisfied as to my sincerity, she gave a grudging nod. "You welcome."

"I guess I should be going, too," Joe said. He accepted a hug from Bijou, speaking to me over her plump shoulder. "Long day today, another long one tomorrow. I've got early rounds."

"Do you have to go?" I was disappointed—we hadn't spent much time alone together.

"Let the man go on home and get some rest," Odessa said, opening my front door. "He a doctor."

As if I didn't know.

Out of patience, I asked, "Is it my imagination or have you gotten crankier since the last time I saw you?"

"Is it my imagination, or has you gotten sassier?"

"Both," said Bijou and Joe, at the same time.

To which I had no reply but a roll of the eyes.

I was in a garden, green with plants and damp with dew. The air smelled of flowers, of earth and growing things. A breeze touched my hair, and I lifted my face to the sun, blinking, and saw clouds flitting across the cobalt sky, high and fast.

A storm was coming. It would drown out the sun's brilliance, leave the garden wet and dripping. But for now it was peaceful. Beautiful, beyond belief.

"Take my hand," came a voice, and I turned.

A man with golden hair, nearly to his shoulders. He stepped from the trees, smiling, holding out his hand. Familiar, so familiar, though I couldn't remember ever seeing him before. "I want you to see it with me," he said, bright blue eyes looking directly into mine. He was wearing white, all white.

"Jesus," I whispered, knowing I had to be dreaming.

"Not exactly," said the blond man, with a wry grin. "Just the opposite, in fact."

It was the sardonic curl of the lip that did it— otherwise I might not have recognized him. He looked so innocent and pure; his face was that of an angel, lit from within. His fingers, devoid of rings, reached for mine, and in the dream, I took them.

"Yes, it's a dream," Sammy said, tucking my hand into the curve of his elbow. "And when you wake, you will resist me again, as you always do." The sideways smile he gave me as we began to walk through the garden was a rueful one. "But for now we will walk, and we will talk, and you will see a side of me that few have seen. You will see what was"—here he stopped, and looked me in the eye—"and what will be."

And when I woke, some unknown time later, I was crying, with no memory of why I cried.

CHAPTER 14

"How exciting to be present at the birth of a new phobia," Evan said sourly.

"It's not a phobia," I retorted. "You don't like spiders, either. Anyway, I'm not going into the storage room by myself until you've replaced the lightbulb. You're the man"—I waved him on with my fingertips—"go do your manly thing."

I couldn't tell him the real reason, of course—if I admitted that Satan himself had been lurking next to the cleaning supplies a couple of days before, he'd never set foot in there again. As it was, I needed plenty of light before I braved it again. "I'll finish dressing Audrey."

We'd been fitting our Audrey Hepburn mannequin into a floaty little cream-colored chiffon from the early seventies. It was elegant and supercute, with sequined straps and glittering beadwork on the bodice. "The shoes I want are in a box on the top shelf next to the water heater—strappy gold sandals, three-inch heels."

"No, duh," Evan said, heading toward the storage room with ill grace. "She'll need the height to balance out all that beadwork. She needs a new ribbon, too. And some work on her hair."

I stepped back and eyed her critically. Audrey's beehive wig could use a little freshening, and a cream-colored ribbon for a headband would be just the thing.

The shop bell jingled, and I glanced over to see a man with dark hair, dressed in a suit and tie. He was carrying a big black book, clutched tight to his chest.

He saw me, too. "Ms. Styx?"

"Can I help you?" A salesman of some kind, I was sure. We got them all the time in Little Five; everybody had a product to sell, and everybody wanted your store to sell it.

"My name is Jimmy Boyd," the man said, coming toward me, "and I am here to save your soul." He held up the book so I could see the title. GOD'S HOLY WORD, it said. Big gold letters, two inches high.

"My soul is quite safe, thank you," I said, without missing a beat. "Evan? Could you come back out here?"

He stopped several feet away. "Don't be afraid, Ms. Styx," the man said, "I have been sent to you by God above, to be your guardian angel upon this earth." He smiled at me, the practiced smile of a snake-oil salesman (I knew "slick" when I saw it). "Praise ye Him, and all His angels," he recited, shaking the Bible in my direction. "Praise ye Him, and all His hosts."

Then he had the nerve to give me a wink.

Right.

I made sure to keep the Audrey mannequin between me and the loony du jour. *Today's special: religious fanatic, served with a side dish of bullshit.* I called, "Evan?" much more loudly this time.

"No need to be concerned. I'm not here to hurt you." The man lowered the book, holding it against his belly with both hands, title side out. "I'm here to set you free." His eyes glowed with excitement, and he stared at me as though I should be excited, too. Late forties, thinning hair, carefully combed. "I'm here to set you free from Crystal Cowart."

"Look, buddy." I backed up, and keeping multiple racks of clothes between us, made a beeline for the register, where I kept a perfectly legal can of pepper spray below the counter. "I am *not* interested in anything you have to sell, so you need to *get out.*" I pointed the pepper spray at him, glad to see my hand was only shaking a teeny bit.

He looked shocked, but I saw no need to beat around the bush.

"You don't understand," he said. "Crystal was a very troubled girl, and I want to make sure she's put to rest."

That got my wary attention. "You knew Crystal?"

"Very well," he said, pinning a mournful look on his face. "Her mother is heartbroken, and her sister . . ."

"She had a sister?" It had never occurred to me that Crystal had a sister.

"Amber Marie," the man said. "Twelve years old and pretty as a picture." He gave me the bullshit smile again, obviously trying to put me at ease. "I'd like to give the family some closure."

Twelve years old. Poor kid.

"I can't help you," I said flatly. "You need to leave." I didn't put down my pepper spray, either.

"Crystal's mother told me about her visit with you the other day," he said, just as flatly. "I think we can help one another, you and I. The Lord works in mysterious ways, and all you need to do is trust me."

Yeah, like that was gonna happen.

The shop bell jingled behind him, and in walked Sammy, larger than life. I gripped the pepper spray tighter. He was wearing blue today, a pale blue T-shirt that matched his eyes.

Eyes, I noted, that were narrowed on my unwelcome visitor, Jimmy Boyd.

"Is there a problem here, Nicki?" I'd never seen Sammy so grim. Always, even when he was being threatening, there was a wicked twinkle in his eyes, like he was having fun. Not so today.

Mr. Slick wheeled around to face him, practiced smile already in place. "No problem. We were just talking." He held up the Bible. "The Lord moveth me to speak the truth to all who will listen."

"Maybe the Lord should moveth you to get your ass out of this store," Sammy said quietly, never taking his eyes from Boyd. "I don't think the lady is interested."

I should've spoken up, but I didn't. Quite frankly, Jimmy Boyd's snake-oil extremism creeped me out, and I wanted him gone.

Sammy was the devil I knew, and Boyd the one I didn't.

There was a brief stare down between the two men, but never any doubt as to the outcome. Boyd flashed me a dissatisfied look over his shoulder, lips thin, and said, "I'll keep you in my prayers, Ms. Styx." Then he left, tucking his Bible under an arm.

Sammy shifted only enough to let the larger man through the door.

As soon as the door closed behind Boyd, I relaxed. Which was weird, considering I was alone with Sammy again, a place I swore I'd never be.

"Thanks." I lowered the can of pepper spray, but didn't let go of it. "Now go away."

Sammy smiled, though it didn't quite reach his eyes. "You're welcome," he said, and stayed where he was.

An awkward silence ensued, at least on my part. I kept hoping Evan would show up, anytime, but he didn't.

"Off you go." I wiggled the fingers of my free hand to shoo Sammy on his way. "Good deed finished."

"Ah, Nicki." He shook his head. "You wound me."

He was uncharacteristically somber today, and I couldn't help but wonder why.

"As if *I*, of all people, would do anyone a good deed."

Even his jokes were off, missing their usual wry tone.

"Then what are you doing here?" I asked.

He shrugged. "The stench of that one carried all the way across the street."

The back of my neck tingled.

"Ah," I said, with a gleam of understanding. "Don't care for the religious types, do you?"

His response surprised me. "I have no problem with true men of faith. God has His army, and I have mine." He crossed his arms over his chest, showing great biceps and a taut belly. "I would hardly put that creature in the same class."

I eyed him warily, not sure what to make of that.

"We all have our hot buttons, and mine is hypocrisy," he said shortly.

"I would think hypocrites would be right up your alley." I had no idea why I was being so bold with him. "Seems like that would make him one of yours."

"Oh, he's mine, all right," Sammy said, grimly. "He just doesn't know it yet."

I had no answer for that. My nervousness increased at the reminder of who I was talking to.

"You look pretty today," he said, for all the world as if he meant it. "Paradise is missing a flower."

Paradise. Last night I'd dreamed of Paradise.

"Stay out of my dreams," I said bluntly, glad of the reminder. "I need my beauty sleep."

A genuine smile, the first since he'd walked in. "You've been dreaming of me?" He stood taller, looking very pleased with himself all of a sudden. "Dare I hope we were naked?"

"No, we weren't naked," I said heatedly. *Not this time.* "But you would know that as well as I."

He just grinned like the Cheshire cat, neither confirming nor denying. The thick leather strap watch suited him, as did the narrow black braided bracelet he wore with it. His rings were back; a heavy silver one on the finger he hooked in the front pocket of his jeans, a smaller one on his pinky.

"We're always naked in my dreams," he said wickedly. "Tell me about yours."

Warning bells went off in my brain. Or maybe it was the smoke alarm in my pants. Whatever it was, it was enough to jar some sense into me.

"That guy was a friend of *your* friend, Crystal," I said coldly. "He wanted to help put her to rest."

Sammy's flirtatiousness vanished. "How ironic," he said. "Since he's the one who killed her."

My jaw dropped. "Are you *serious*?" Totally confused now, I blurted, "Joe said Crystal died because she was anorexic . . . are you saying she was murdered?"

A murderer? Here, in my store?

Sammy looked at me for a long minute, considering. "I didn't say he murdered her, Nicki. I said he killed her." He turned to go. "I'll leave you to figure out the difference."

"And if I do?"

He froze, then turned his head in my direction. The movement reminded me of a snake whose attention had just been caught by a mouse—a slow, sinuous movement designed not to frighten. "If you do what? Figure out why poor little Crystal Cowart was so messed up that she starved and purged herself to death?" His coldness was chilling. "Why should I care? Why should you?"

"I just do." I'd sent more than my share of spirits into the Light. Most were easy—*do me a favor, and I'll rest in peace*—but not all were willing, or able, to go. Crystal wasn't able, yet she needed to be at peace so she'd leave Joe and me alone.

It was hard to meet his gaze, but I refused to look away.

"Why don't I just tell you what happened to Crystal," he said, blue eyes burning into mine, "and save us both some time. She was sexually molested when she was thirteen by the one man she thought she could trust the most—her mother's new Bible-thumping boyfriend, the man you just met, Jimmy Boyd."

I felt nauseous, sick to my stomach.

"Nobody believed her, you see. Who would take

the word of a flighty, attention-seeking girl against such a devout and upright man of God?" A sardonic curl of the lip. "Crystal didn't stand a chance. Her own mother didn't believe her, not even after Boyd dumped her, claiming scandal wasn't 'good for the church.' Stupid woman continues to turn to him for spiritual guidance." A slow blink, conveying either contempt or boredom, I wasn't sure which. "Imagine . . . the man who molested her daughter."

"You sorry bastard," I said, furious at the calmness with which he spoke of Crystal's very tragic life.

"Don't blame me." Sammy raised his palms in my direction. "Contrary to popular belief, I'm not responsible for child molesters. I didn't create them any more than I created rapists or serial killers or psychopaths. Mankind creates more than enough cruelty and chaos to destroy itself, with little help from me."

I had no idea whether he was telling me the truth or not—about any of it—but it didn't matter.

"What's truly sad is that there is no shortage of victims for people like Boyd—the weak, the stupid, the helpless." He sighed pensively, almost as though he cared. "Is it any wonder that so many of those poor souls choose revenge over oblivion?"

"You took advantage of Crystal," I said, my voice shaky. "She was angry when she died, delirious, not thinking clearly." It was true, it had to be true. "She couldn't have had a fair choice in the matter."

Sammy shook his head. "You're wrong. I always give them a choice."

"I think she would've chosen otherwise if she'd been thinking clearly," I said recklessly. "I think you cheated her." I waited for some fire and brimstone. "I think you cheated her out of her soul because she was confused and disoriented when she died."

He shrugged, and the sight of it infuriated me.

"You claim contempt for men like Boyd, but you're as big a hypocrite as he is." That earned me a look I didn't care for. "You claim you were thrown out of Heaven for doing what came naturally; you said you tempt others as you were once tempted, just to prove some things are impossible to resist. Where does Crystal Cowart figure into all that?"

In a flash, faster than I would've believed possible, Sammy had me pinned against the wall behind the counter. His body was hard against mine, male and imposing, his face inches away. "Listen to me, little girl," he said, and his breath smelled of cloves, "I could hurt you. I could hurt you, and those you love"—his nose touched mine, briefly—"very, very badly." He rested his forehead on my cheek, while I stood frozen, not daring to struggle. The hands that gripped my shoulders were hard, but not hurting. My heart was beating against my ribs, breasts pressed firmly to Sammy's chest. "Do as I ask, and become mine," he rasped, sending tendrils of heat from my ear to my belly, "and I will let Crystal's soul go free."

"No," I whispered. Evil held me in his arms, yet fear was fading. "You don't want to hurt me." I would never have believed it, didn't understand it. Just knew it.

He went still as stone. I wanted to touch him, just once, of my own volition, but didn't dare. I splayed my fingers against the wall instead, hearing the can of pepper spray clatter to the floor. My hands stayed flattened against the pebbly surface of the drywall, while the rest of me throbbed with an awareness of *him*.

"Let me offer Crystal peace, and see what she chooses. Let me offer her a way to resolve her anger." I didn't even know where the words were coming from anymore—it just seemed important to say them. "If I do that, and she still chooses you, then you win."

He took a deep breath, and I felt it in every inch of me—his chest, his belly, the thigh pressed hard against the vee of my legs.

"And my prize?"

I couldn't answer. I knew what he wanted went much deeper than the physical. He wanted me to give in to the teeny little bit of dark that lurked inside me, to use it, to flaunt it, like my makeup and my clothes. *If you got it, haunt it, Nicki.*

But I couldn't. I wouldn't.

He seemed to know he wasn't going to get an answer. Moving his head ever so slightly, lips millimeters from my skin, he murmured, "And if I lose?"

My voice was shaky. "If you lose, and she chooses the Light, then you go away and leave me alone." I couldn't seem to draw breath enough to speak above a whisper.

"Is that what you want?" His lips brushed my ear, and my knees weakened.

"Yes."

"What's to stop me from taking what *I* want, little Nicki?" His voice curled into my ears like smoke—I closed my eyes at the sensation.

"Because you want me to want it, too," I murmured, at the limits of my endurance. It must've been the dream, had to have been the dream, that made me so sure of myself.

A growl, very close to my ear, brought my eyes open.

To nothing.

Sammy was gone, and I was standing alone, pinned to the wall by nothing but my own adrenaline. The store was empty.

"Oh, my goodness me," Bijou said, face pale. Splotches of rouge stood out on her cheeks. "You actually made an agreement with him? Have I taught you nothing?" She rose from her chair, beginning to pace.

"I . . ." I fumbled with words, feeling awkward and stupid. Shell-shocked, even. "We . . . he . . . didn't actually *agree* to anything." Shock at what I'd done had driven me straight to the Embassy Suites to see my grandmother. I wanted to tell Joe, I wanted to tell Evan, but I *needed* to tell my grandmother, clinging to a vague hope she might know what to do.

Odessa, thankfully, had her own room, so I didn't have to put up with her glare of disapproval, but it did me no good since Bijou was giving me one of her own.

She reached up and snatched the gray wig off her head, startling me. Rubbing her bald scalp in an obvious gesture of absorbed frustration, my grandmother became Leonard Ledbetter,

Savannah florist extraordinaire. My grandfather. In a dress.

He'd chosen a pink floral today, loose and flowing for comfort. Orthopedic sandals, big white bag. It really did look like there was some Atlanta sightseeing on the agenda.

"Tell me everything he said, every word." Leonard sank back down in the chair, wig in his lap. He was wearing pearl clip-ons, which I found distracting. "I want to hear everything," he said.

So I did my best to tell him, from Sammy's strange reaction to Jimmy Boyd, to the way I'd asked for Crystal to be given another chance to choose between the Darkness and the Light. I even told him about the dream, though there wasn't much to tell—I didn't remember anything except the garden. What I didn't tell him—what I didn't want to talk about—was the heat that flared between Sammy and me, white-hot, though I'd resisted. How my heart nearly beat from my chest at the feel of his breath on my cheek. How guilt and turmoil over it was eating me up inside.

If I loved Joe—and I was sure I did—how could I get so weak in the knees over anyone else?

"Why would I ever, even for a second, believe I could trust him enough to ask him for anything?" I said the words aloud, still stunned at the enormity of what I'd done. I'd asked the Devil for a favor, and I wasn't naive enough to think he'd settle for *nothing* in return.

But I was still hoping. It had something to do with the dream . . .

"It's the curse," Leonard said, sighing. "The curse is affecting your judgment."

"What curse?" I sat bolt upright on the edge of the bed.

My grandfather's eyes were on me, but his mind was somewhere else. "Odessa was right. Someone has put the Evil Eye upon you. It will weaken you, drag you down."

"What?" The word came out as a squawk. "You don't really believe in that stuff, do you?"

"We must negate the spell. It will require the entire coven." He was still talking, but more to himself than me. "Thank goodness I listened to her."

The moment seemed surreal. Here I was, in the middle of the afternoon, sitting on the bed in an Embassy Suites hotel room, listening to a bald man in makeup and a dress talk about curses and covens.

I stood up. "Excuse me, but what the hell are you talking about?"

Leonard frowned, lips thinning. "Language, dear." He stood up, too, moving to the mirror by the dresser. "The basket that was left on your doorstep." The wig was set in place with one quick gesture, adjusted as he continued to talk. "It contained a ritual to reverse a curse, which the giver of the basket quite plainly believed you would need." A final twitch, one more pat to his battle helmet of gray hair, and Grandma Bijou was back. "You had a terrible run of bad luck yesterday, didn't you?"

I did a quick run-through of yesterday in my mind: missing keys, three traffic tickets, a broken toilet, uninvited guests, burned lasagna. *No, no bad luck here.*

"Negative forces are obviously at work, and negativity often draws more of the same," Bijou said. "We can't let someone's malicious use of magic distract you from the battle at hand. The curse must be lifted."

Funny thing was, I didn't believe for a minute that my weakness over Sammy had anything to do with a curse, unless it was the curse of an overactive libido.

I sank back down on the bed, overwhelmed. I could see myself in the mirror over the dresser, and focused on my reflection to calm my racing thoughts. Indigo Blue eyeliner instead of the usual black, to go with the blue shirt I was wearing. It was a shiny rayon blend, pure seventies disco glam, and I'd paired it with a pair of black capris and some cute heeled sandals.

Apparently my *"look like a million bucks, feel like a million bucks"* theory wasn't working for me today.

"Are you saying that someone besides Sammy, and besides Crystal, is out to get me?" I needed her to clarify. "Who? Why?"

"There now, dear." Bijou's arm went around my shoulder. The bed sagged as she sat next to me. "We'll get this all straightened out."

That almost made me laugh, but recognizing how close I was to hysteria, I kept my mouth shut.

"When you called me in Savannah and told me of Crystal Cowart's possession, I was concerned, of course, but felt—with some guidance—you were up to the task of withstanding her. You did so well casting her out that first time, and without any practice." She patted my shoulder approvingly. "The spirit is willing, but the flesh is weak; in this case the spirit is the weak one. You're strong, Nicki. Stronger than you know."

Her confidence in me made me feel a little better, though I still hated phrases like "possession" and "casting out."

"I was doubly concerned, of course, to learn of *his* persistence in pursuing you, but you've

fought him before, Nicki, and won." Her continued avoidance of Sammy's name spoke volumes.
"He cannot be compelled by mortal means—he
will only leave you alone if, and when, he believes
he can't win." She shook her head, frowning. "But
something felt wrong. Something I couldn't put
my finger on. When Odessa came to me with one
of her feelings—"

"Odessa has feelings?" I couldn't resist the
snark.

"Rarely," she said, not missing a beat. "But
when she does, I listen, and that's when I knew
we could no longer remain in Savannah. Trouble
comes in threes, and no sense to sit and wait for
it. He's obviously decided on a three-pronged
attack." She held up her hand, counting them off
with a pudgy finger. "A direct assault, through
Crystal. The more trouble she causes, the more
distracted you'll be. Attack number two is more
subtle—seduction and lies, designed to tempt
and confuse. Never forget that he's a master at
this."

Her use of the word "master" made me uncomfortable.

"The last attack is a hidden one, designed to
wear down your defenses and weaken your resolve—the use of the dark arts by someone you've
angered. Odessa and I came to help you, dear, and

though we can't remove his pitchfork, I think we can blunt one of his prongs."

I was intrigued to learn that Odessa might actually care whether I lived or died, but far more interested in the immediate offer of help.

"I hesitated to say so last night," Bijou went on, "but it's obvious that the woman who came into your store—what was her name?"

"Sally Starhawk. No, Shadow Something-or-other." I shook my head. "I don't remember exactly."

"Huh." For a moment, Bijou sounded eerily like Odessa. "Anyway, it appears she took your rejection of her and her coven very personally, and decided to teach you a lesson, quite probably at his urging. Your reaction to her was no doubt exactly what he was hoping for. From the basket someone left on your doorstep, it is also quite obvious that at least one member of her coven does not agree with her methods."

Wonderful. I had enough to worry about without the Wicked Witch of the West on my ass. "And you can fix this, how?"

Bijou smiled and patted me on the shoulder. "The hag that did this had best recite her Rede and cower by her cauldron, for I do believe the Savannah Garden Club is about to invade the city of Atlanta." She rose from the bed in a brisk flurry of floral fabric. "Now where is my cell phone?" Scooping it up from the bedside table, she hit a number on speed dial. "Estelle, it's Bijou. Two words for you, dear"—she smiled, giving me a wink—"road trip!"

CHAPTER 15

I drove back to the shop in a daze, wondering if life would ever get back to anything *approaching* normal. Was it so much to ask, really?

A nice house, a nice business, a nice boyfriend . . .

"Holy crap," I said, out loud. "When did I turn into little Polly Purebred?"

At the next red light, I flipped down my visor and checked myself in the mirror. The girl who stared back at me wore hip vintage Carreras and plum-colored lipstick. Her hair was dark, short, with a few random streaks of pink. She didn't look like the type of girl who would be craving *normalcy*, for heaven's sake.

Never judge a book by its cover, Grandma Bijou had said, and she was right.

Ah, well. I looked pretty darn good, if I did say so myself. At least I could continue to fool the world into thinking I had it all together, even if I couldn't fool myself. Expressing my not-so-normal side through fashion was second nature, and luckily, I had no urge yet to start wearing pearls and sweater sets.

My wild days seemed to be behind me, though, and I was a little surprised to find that I didn't really miss them. I'd given up drinking everything except red wine after my heart valve wimped out on me. I'd stopped the partying and the all-nighters. I'd had the same boyfriend for over six months, and he wasn't exactly the wild type. Smiling, I amended that thought to exclude the bedroom.

That, of course, got me thinking about Joe again, and how he'd held me and promised me that we'd get through things together. How, when we last made love, he'd told me to remember what we had between us when I needed to be strong.

And corny as it sounds, life became a little easier, just like that.

I took another quick glance in the mirror before

the light changed, then flipped the visor out of the way.

The Polly Purebred side of me wanted normal, but the Nicki Styx side of me knew normal wasn't going to happen. As long as I had Joe beside me, I was okay with it.

"He's dead to me!" Evan raged, tears running down his cheeks. "Dead to me, I say!" He was sitting behind the desk in the back office, a fistful of tissues in one hand and a cell phone in the other.

There'd been a lovers' spat, that much was clear.

I'd come in the store to find it empty of customers, the register unmanned, and my partner nowhere to be seen until I found him in the back—sobbing and furious. "What happened? What's wrong?"

"Butch is cheating on me, that's what's wrong! He can't deny it anymore—I heard the voice mail his loverboy left him!" His face crumpled, and my heart sank. "How could he do it to me?"

"Aw, honey." I hurried around the desk to give my poor friend a much-needed hug.

"I don't understand," he sobbed into my shoulder. "He told me he loved me. He said I was the one. We were supposed to be together forever, he said."

I made murmuring noises of comfort because, honestly, I didn't know what to say. This was why it was so hard to believe in true love because, well . . . because things like this happened to people who did.

Right then I got that skittery feeling up my back that my mom used to call "somebody walking on your grave". But I shook it off (literally), and focused on Evan.

"What happened? Tell me."

"He left his cell phone behind this morning." Evan waved the phone in his hand. "There was a voice mail message from some guy named Jared. They were going to meet up, and this guy promised to make him *very* happy!" Sarcasm and tears distorted his features. Poor guy was crying so hard that I started to cry, too. "He denied it, can you imagine? And *then* he had the nerve to get mad at me for listening to his voice mail—called me nosy!" His look turned to outrage. "Me? Nosy? Do you think I'm nosy?"

Of course you are. "Of course you're not," I said.

"I loved him, Nicki." His face crumpled again, bravado gone.

"I know," I said, squeezing his shoulder. "I'm sorry."

I'd be mad at Butch later, but for now I just

parked myself on the arm of Evan's chair, keeping my arm around him.

The cell phone in his hand rang, startling us both. He checked the caller ID. "No," he said sharply, then pressed his thumb to one of the buttons, turning it off. Tossing the phone onto the desk, he leaned forward and put his head down. In a voice thick with tears, he murmured, "How could he do it?"

I had no answer for him.

Another phone rang, this time the store phone on the desk. Evan reached for it but I stopped him. "Handbags and Gladrags," I said in a clipped tone, fully expecting to hear Butch's deep baritone.

"Could I speak to Nicki Styx, please?" The man's voice was unfamiliar.

"Speaking."

"My name is Tony Danforth. I represent the Cowart family in the matter of Crystal Cowart's unlawful death. I'd like to ask you a few questions."

My heart dropped to my stomach.

"I don't know anything about it," I lied.

"I have video that says otherwise, Ms. Styx."

"If you saw the video, then you know I was just babbling nonsense."

Evan lifted his head. He wiped his eyes with a tissue, only half-listening.

"Nevertheless, I'd like to take your statement."

"Look, I'm very busy right now, but just for the record, I was drunk."

"None of this is on record yet, Ms. Styx." The guy didn't give up easily. "I'm very interested in what Dr. Bascombe had to say to you before that video was filmed. Did he confess to the murder of Crystal Cowart?"

For the first time in my life, I quite literally saw red. "No, he didn't! He didn't murder anybody, you fucking asshole!"

Evan's eyes went wide, but I was on a roll. It was all too much suddenly—no matter how hard I, or the people I loved—tried to do the right thing, there were so many other people out there who either couldn't care less or actively did the *wrong* thing, and I'd had enough.

"Joe Bascombe spends his days saving people's lives, but does he get any thanks for it? No! Scumbags like you look at him and see nothing but dollar signs. You're the reason malpractice premiums are driving doctors out of business!" I related to this particular issue myself—as a business owner, I had to pay through the nose for liability insurance. "You should be ashamed of yourself. Those ambulances you're always chasing have real, live people in them, too, you know. People whose careers get ruined over frivolous lawsuits like this one."

"I can always subpoena you as a hostile witness, Ms. Styx." The jerk was unrattled. "Is that what you want?"

I slammed the phone down as hard as I could, wishing it was the lawyer's fat head. It rang immediately, startling Evan and me both. We let it ring twice, eyeing each other, before I snatched it up.

"Handbags and Gladrags."

"Nicki, I need to talk to Evan." Butch sounded frantic.

I looked at Evan, who shook his head a fast negative. "He doesn't want to talk to you."

"I didn't *do* anything, Nicki!" Butch wasn't giving up easily, either. "He's got the wrong idea! Let me talk to him. We can work this out."

"Sorry, not my call. He says he doesn't want to talk to you." And then I hung up on him, too.

And for the fourth freaking time, a phone rang again. This time it was *my* cell phone, which I wore clipped to my belt. I wouldn't have answered it, except the caller ID read COLUMBIA MEMORIAL HOSPITAL. "Hello?"

Silence, broken by a brief crackle. Then a woman's laughter in the background, flirty and light. "You're so funny, Joe. I sure hope your girlfriend appreciates you." A chair creaked as someone shifted. "But if there ever comes a time when she doesn't, you just let me know."

What the hell was this? "Hello?"

Nobody heard me. "Hello?"

"Nicki and I are just fine, Lisa, thank you."

Joe's voice sounded tinny and distant, though the words were reassuring.

"Joe?" I raised my voice, practically yelling. "Hello, Joe?" He didn't hear me, so he obviously hadn't called me on purpose—more likely just hit the wrong button on his desk phone. He usually called on his cell.

"I understand," Lisa said. "I hope you don't think I'm being forward. It's just that I'm single, you're single—no harm in letting someone know you're attracted to them, is there?

"Hey!" At this point I wasn't sure I wanted anybody to hear me, but I made the effort anyway; the phone was glued to my ear. It crackled, hissing as though about to lose the connection, then blessedly cleared.

"I'm flattered, Lisa, but I'm in a committed relationship."

Relief swept through me.

"I hope it's worth it." Lisa kept her voice light. "We could make your legal problems go away if your little 'wild child' was out of the picture."

She laughed again, like she'd made a joke, but she wasn't joking.

I'd been right about those stilettoed pumps. Lisa was a first-class bitch, and she was playing hard-ball.

To his credit, Joe didn't laugh. But he did ask, "How so?" which made me nervous. "You've seen the emergency-room records. You assured me the board would make their decision based on the facts, not rumors and accusations."

Yeah.

I could almost hear Lisa shrug. "Let's be realistic, Joe. The hospital doesn't like to be associated with anything"—there was a pause— "distasteful. A threatened lawsuit, a possible settlement, the chief of E.R. appearing on the evening news with a self-professed psychic . . ." Another pause. "I have some influence over the board, you know. I could use it on your behalf if I felt you'd left all that distastefulness behind you."

Distastefulness?

"You bitch!" I shouted into the phone, scaring poor Evan to death. "You fucking bitch!"

Evan eyed me as if I'd gone crazy, and he wasn't far off.

The phone crackled, and I was afraid it'd gone dead. Then another voice spoke, a different one this time; an eerie electronic voice that raised the hair on my arms.

"I thought you might enjoy hearing what I'm hearing, Chubby Cheeks," said Crystal Cowart, on the other end of the phone. "Your boyfriend is going to lose his job unless he dumps you." She laughed, and it came through as an ugly, hissing chuckle. "I really hope he dumps you. The Master would be so pleased."

For a moment, I was too shocked to think.

She'd set me up. She'd actually *set me up* to overhear this conversation between Joe and Lisa, knowing how it would upset me.

A maelstrom of emotion made my hands tremble: anger, frustration, jealousy. All that topped with the spiteful trick of a vindictive spirit, it was just too much.

"Why are you doing this to me?" I wailed into the phone, nearly at my wits' end. I couldn't take much more of this—I really couldn't. "I never did anything to you. Joe never did anything to you— he's a good man!" I took a desperate shot. "Let me help you, Crystal. I can help you."

Evan's eyes went wide, and I thought he was going to bolt. He had the picture by now; I was on the phone with a ghost, and even *that* was too close for comfort as far as my poor partner was concerned.

A hissing in my ear, vaguely resembling laughter.

"Crystal, listen to me—I know about Jimmy Boyd." I tried to pull myself together, grasping at straws. "I know what he did to you."

Her screech of rage took the form of static, nearly shattering my eardrums.

Evan heard it. "What is going *on*?" he whispered, tearful and frightened.

I grabbed his arm and shook my head, returning the phone to my ear. "It was wrong what he did to you—it wasn't your fault."

"Damn right it wasn't my fault," she shrieked, while the line hissed and crackled. "I was just a kid! And she didn't believe me!"

The pain in Crystal's voice made me wince, like shards of ice to my heart.

Evan put his hand over mine, and I grabbed it like a lifeline, letting his warm flesh ground me.

"I'll talk to your mother for you." Frantic and overwhelmed, I made her an offer. "I'll tell your mother what he did, and I'll make her believe me. She thinks I'm a psychic—I'll tell her you came to me and told me what happened—she'll believe me."

Silence, but for static. It went on so long I was afraid she was gone.

And then it stopped. Just her voice, full of angry

resignation, like that of a sullen teenager. "She won't believe you. She's in love with him, even though he treats her like shit."

"What about your little sister?" I challenged. "Amber Marie? Do you want him to get his hands on her? I can get Boyd away from your sister—I'll do it if you just leave Joe and me alone."

What the hell am I doing?

"What the hell are you doing?" Evan asked, echoing my thoughts exactly. He snatched at the phone in my hand, but I was quicker, and jerked it out of the way.

"Just think about it," I said, into the phone. "I do you a favor, you do me a favor." Shaking my head at Evan, I moved back a few steps so he couldn't snatch at me again. This was the only thing I could think of doing to put Crystal to rest. Joe didn't need to be the target in some twisted psychic triangle; Sammy was using Crystal to pressure me, Crystal was using me to pressure Joe, and it was high time I started using *something* to press back.

"I . . ." her voice faltered, fading, "I made a bargain. I can't do you any favors."

There was a *click*, and she was gone.

I lowered the phone.

Evan was staring at me, tear-stained and shell-shocked. I stared back, just as shell-shocked, though for different reasons.

"Let's go," I said, giving myself a mental shake. "It's gotta be five o'clock somewhere."

CHAPTER 16

Luckily, in Little Five, you never had to look far to find an open bar. We locked up the store, and ten minutes later Evan and I were sitting in a back booth at Marley's, an ancient dive that reeked of spilled beer and cigarettes no matter what time of day it was.

We were uncharacteristically silent until after the first shot; vodka for Evan, Jack Daniel's for me. I hadn't had whiskey in a while, and it went down like fire.

"What are we going to do?" Evan looked miserable, and despite my own drama, my heart went out to him.

"Why don't you call Butch," I suggested gently. "Talk to him."

He shook his head, getting teary again. "No." Blinking them back, he picked up his second shot glass. "First Rule of Evan—someone cheats on me, it's over. Talking just prolongs the agony." A second shot of vodka followed this statement, making him gasp.

I was familiar with the Five Rules of Evan, though at the moment I could only think of three. No cheating, no drugs, no white socks with dark pants. He'd dumped more than one guy in the past for cheating, and a few for displaying poor fashion sense, but I had the feeling that Butch was the first guy who really *mattered.*

"Maybe it was a mistake," I said, wondering if it could possibly be true. They seemed so good together. "Maybe you just took the message the wrong way." A misunderstanding would be nice; Butch's muscle-bound exterior and teddy-bear personality were the perfect fit for a high-strung drama queen with a heart of gold.

Evan picked up Butch's cell phone, which he still carried, and punched in some numbers without saying a word. Then he handed it to me and looked around for the waitress, signaling her for more drinks.

Listening, I heard a man's say, "Butch, it's

Jared. Great to chat with you yesterday, and I've got fabulous news!" The voice was obviously that of a gay male; straight men lack inflection. "Stop by at lunchtime, and I am going to make you the happiest man alive. You're going to be thrilled," he gushed, "I promise." And then he hung up.

My heart sank, but I tried to be optimistic anyway. "Well, so he knows a guy named Jared. Big deal."

Evan gave me a deadpan stare. "In the eight months we've been together, he's never once mentioned anyone named Jared. It's a date, Nicki. He changed the password on his computer, being secretive about his calls—I think he's been chatting up guys on the Internet and made a date with one." Rubbing his hand over his face, he went on, "He's been keeping secrets from me. I told you he was losing interest."

"But—"

"No buts." *Poor Evan.* "When I asked him about it, he got all nervous and defensive, and he *yelled* at me." No yelling was the Fourth Rule of Evan. His chin trembled. "He's never raised his voice to me, not ever. He's lying, and that's all there is to it."

I didn't know what else to say, so after a moment, I reached for my second shot and downed it, letting the burn take me. By the time I could breathe again, the waitress was putting down two more apiece for each of us.

"Let's talk about something else," he said. "Tell me what happened back there in the office. What was that phone call all about?"

I closed my eyes briefly, wishing I didn't have to tell him. Wishing I didn't have to throw myself into a big, muddy puddle of emotional issues that had nothing to do with me.

But I knew I had to. Crystal Cowart's dysfunctional family dynamics were not only standing in the way of *my* happiness, they were sucking Crystal's soul into the darkness, and risking the same fate for her little sister.

Do unto others as you would have them do unto you, Styx. "I have to get rid of the ghost who's been possessing me. I have to put her to rest. She's causing trouble for Joe at the hospital, and I just can't have that. He could lose his job." I shook my head, fingering my shot glass. An image of the first time I'd seen Joe—serious, intent, focused on the crisis at hand—flashed into my brain. "I mean, he's a *doctor*, you know? He saved my life! I wouldn't be here if it weren't for him . . . and how many others will he save? *Has* he saved? What if he hadn't been there that night?"

Evan reached across the table and took my hand, squeezing it. He hated to talk about that night. Poor guy had been the one who found me, unconscious, and the one who'd been pacing the hospital waiting room when I died.

Luckily, by the time he found out about it, I was alive again. Same old Nicki, only different.

"You don't have to tell me what a great guy Joe is." His chin trembled. He looked away, briefly, and I knew he was thinking of Butch. "How are you going to put this girl to rest? What's this about a sister?"

"Crystal was molested when she was thirteen by a jumped-up preacher named Jimmy Boyd," I said flatly. "Her mother didn't believe her, and still looks to this guy for spiritual guidance. He came to see me, if you can believe it. He's the one who told me about Amber Marie."

Evan's eyes widened in horror.

"You were talking to a child molester?"

"I didn't know it at the time."

"How did you find out?"

Ooo, now came the hard part. "Sammy told me."

All color drained from Evan's face. I expected him to explode or pitch a hissy fit or maybe even faint, but all he did was pick up his third shot and down it, fast.

"Oh, my God," he wheezed. "He's not going to go away, is he?" He looked dazed, by more than just the vodka. "We're screwed."

"Not yet." I answered automatically, thinking of Sammy's seduction attempts.

"What else could possibly go wrong?" He leaned back in the booth, bracing both hands on the table. "This has been like the worst week *ever.*" He took a deep breath, listing lightly to the right; the vodka was kicking in. Evan had never been good with hard liquor—he usually stuck with a glass or two of white wine. "My dearest friend in the world has been dealing with ghosts, devils and child molesters, and my heart"—his face crumpled in on itself—"my heart has been *broken.*"

"Aw, honey," I murmured, reaching across the table to squeeze his fingers. Then I was struck by a memory.

No, no, no . . . how stupid was I to even think it?

"I'll never get over him, never," Evan declared, crying openly now.

Pretty stupid, apparently. Caution reared its ugly head, but I remedied that problem by reaching for my own shot glass.

Candy is dandy, but liquor is quicker.

It hit my stomach in a spread of warmth. "I may have a solution for you," I said, wanting only to help him feel better. "But it will require a couple more drinks, and a taxi home."

"You don't need a pink candle, you need a blue one," I insisted, shaking my head and immediately wishing I hadn't. The room was already spinning without extra help from me. "You're a boy, Butch is a boy, and there's no pink in that equation."

"The spell says we need a pink one and a blue one," Evan whined. "I want to do this right."

I looked at him blearily, pulling two blue candles from a drawer in the kitchen. "Trust me. I know what I'm doing."

We both burst into laughter at that, because it was such a lie and we both knew it. That's what made it funny.

Of course, just then, *everything* was funny.

Evan staggered toward the couch, giggling and clutching the scrap of paper that held the "mend a broken heart" spell. "Do we have angelica root and dandelion powder? I don't have to drink it, do I?" He plopped down, scanning the instructions in more detail. "Oh no," he groaned, "it says we need clay. We don't have any clay."

A momentary setback, until I remembered the bag of stuff I'd bought at the discount store for the children's corner at Handbags and Gladrags the week before; moms shopped longer when the kidlets were occupied. With a flourish, I whipped out a can of Play-Doh. "Ta-da!"

His eyes got big. "It's like it was meant to be or something," he breathed.

"Good Lord," I said, coming toward him with the blue candles and Play-Doh. "You're drunk."

"So are you."

"Am not."

"Are too."

"Liar."

"Meanie."

"Okay, then," I said, glad to have that settled. "Now let's see what we've got here." I sat next to him on the couch, leaning over to read the paper in his hand. His warm, comfortable shoulder kept me from falling over.

"Create a sacred space and light two candles," I recited, "one pink, and one blue."

"See?" Evan whined again. "I told you so. And how do we create a sacred space?"

I rolled my eyes, then reached out and pushed a stack of magazines off the coffee table and onto the floor. "Voilà," I said, and plunked the two blue candles down right where they'd been. "Sacred space."

Evan made a sound of impatience, but I ignored him, pulling open the little drawer on the coffee table where I always kept a lighter; candlelight was flattering, and scented ones kept the house smelling good, so the lighter got a lot of use.

"Knead the clay into the shape of a heart," I read, and looked at him. "I think that's your job."

He opened the can of Play-Doh and peered inside. "It's green," he said, frowning. "Hearts aren't green."

I gave an exaggerated sigh of frustration. "Work with me, would you?"

"You know I never like to do things half-assed," he grumbled, dumping the Play-Doh into his palm.

"I know, I know. You always prefer the whole one."

"Always." Within a few moments, a chunky green heart began to take shape between Evan's fingers. "Don't rush me," he said, reading my mind. "It's *my* heart, not yours."

True. *Thank goodness.* A teeny part of me was relieved; Joe and I were still good (as far as I knew), and I hoped to keep it that way.

So I waited, watching as he shaped the lump into nearly perfect symmetry. He laid it down on the table and shaped it some more, using his thumbs to smooth and his palm to flatten. And there it was, a little green heart, flanked by the flicker of two blue candles.

"Should we turn out the lights?" he asked, eyeing the arrangement doubtfully.

I gave him a look. "If you think I'm going to do this in the dark, you're nuts."

"Yeah," he said nervously. "You're right. Lights are good. We like lights."

Evan's nervousness defeated the purpose of this ridiculous little exercise, which was to keep him occupied and maybe even make him feel better.

"Okay," I said briskly. "Next step." I checked the paper. "You have to read this out loud."

He took the spell from me and started to read. "What once was whole has now been broken, words of pain have now been spoken." His voice quivered a little on that one. "It says I need to tear the clay heart into two pieces," he whispered, as though someone besides me could hear.

"Do it," I said grimly, on a mission.

A drunken, stupid mission, but whatever.

He picked up the heart and tore it into two chunks, then laid the pieces back down on the table, next to each other. Consulting the paper again, he asked, "Where's the dandelion powder and angelica root?"

I dug around in the stupid basket that some stupid person had left on my stupid doorstep, and handed Evan the stupid bottles full of stupid herbs. He uncorked one and sprinkled it on the left half of the broken heart, then did the same with the other bottle and the other half. Dandelion powder on the left, angelica root on the right.

Somewhere along the way we'd both become solemn—neither of us was laughing anymore.

"Let the earth relieve my pain, and make my poor heart whole again." Evan picked up the two pieces of the heart and mashed them together, herbs and all. In less time than it took him the first time, he kneaded and shaped until the heart was back in one piece, looking only a little worse for wear.

"Now what?"

"It says to let the candles burn down all the way, and to keep the heart in a safe place." He put it back on the table.

I eyed the lumpy, splotchy bit of green Play-Doh doubtfully. "Where are you going to keep it?"

"Where I should have kept my *real* heart," he answered morosely. "Locked up tight. Maybe I'll put it in my safe-deposit box at the bank, where nobody can ever touch it again except me."

"And me," I said. "I have a key."

Evan slumped backward into the couch. "You're the only person I trust with a key to my heart, Nicki." He was slurring a little, but that was okay—poor guy had been through the emotional wringer. "Fifth Rule of Evan," he mumbled, closing his eyes. "Never trust anyone but Nicki."

I smiled, though he couldn't see it. "That's not the Fifth Rule of Evan."

He sighed, without opening his eyes. "It is now."

A knock at the door brought us both upright. We looked at each other.

"Crap," I said. "You get it."

He shook his head. "I'm not getting it. You get it."

I wasn't up for visitors. It was barely dark outside, but I'd been hoping for a nap; I wasn't used to drinking in the afternoon.

"Go see who it is." He nudged me. "Look through the peephole."

I slipped off my sandals and padded to the door, not wanting whoever was there to know I was home. Luckily for me, my car wasn't in the driveway, and neither was Evan's—I'd been serious about that cab.

To my relief, it was Joe's handsome face I saw through the peephole. He knocked again, just as I opened the door.

"Hi, baby!" I smiled, thrilled to see him, but my smile faded when I saw who stood beside him.

"Where's Evan?" Butch asked, shouldering his way into the house.

I stumbled back a little, grabbing for the door, but he was already in.

"Evan? You have to listen to me—"

"Get away from me!" Evan's frantic tone should've warned Butch away, but it didn't. He kept coming, even when Evan shot from the couch and stood behind it, hands raised. "I have nothing to say to you, ever!"

"You've got the wrong idea, Ev," Butch's pleading sounded sincere. "Jared was doing me a favor—"

"I'll bet he was!"

"—he was taking care of something for me—"

"Exactly!"

"—don't be like this, baby. Give me a chance to explain."

I turned to Joe, stunned to see a second man standing there, a man I'd never seen before.

"Hi," he said, all bright red cheeks and awkward grin. Chubby, dark hair, midthirties. "I'm Jared."

Oh, great.

"Where've you been, Nicki?" Joe stepped in, bringing Jared with him. "Your cell phone isn't turned on, and the store was closed." He was frowning. "I've been trying to get hold of you for hours." He shut the door behind him with a click.

It sunk in that I might be in trouble. "I—"

"You brought him *here*?" Evan's tone had progressed to a shriek. He spun on his heel, headed for the back of the house, but Butch darted forward, grabbing his arm.

"Listen to me, sweetheart," Butch was still pleading. "He's just a friend—he'll tell you himself." He shot a desperate look in our direction. "Won't you, Jared?"

"Please," Evan said, trying to snatch his arm from Butch's brawny hand and failing miserably. "Take your little twink and go."

"Stop this." Butch towered over Evan by a good three inches, but I noted how gentle he was, despite not letting go of Evan's arm. He propelled him firmly toward the couch. "You are going to sit down on this couch, and you are going to listen to what I have to say."

The teddy bear had a stern side, it seemed. Which might not be a bad thing for a drama queen softie.

Good feng shui.

"Have you been drinking?" Joe's question brought me back to him. "Butch has been calling me all afternoon—worried sick, I might add—and you've been out drinking? You know the added stress that too much alcohol can put on your heart, Nicki."

Guilt hit me. "I—"

"Jared works at Bridgerton's," Butch said, settling Evan on the couch as he spoke.

"Lah-dee-dah," snipped Evan, poised to flee.

"Sit," Butch said, his voice deepening, "and listen. I mean it."

Evan subsided, reluctantly, onto the couch.

On the one hand, I was surprised to see him so docile, on the other, not so much.

"I've had something on order, and Jared was just leaving a message on my cell phone to let me know it was in."

Beside me, Joe sighed with impatience. I hadn't given him any answers to his questions, but I couldn't seem to focus on anything but the drama at hand.

Jared stepped up, stammering, "It's true—I hardly know him."

Evan shot him a filthy look, and I almost felt sorry for him.

"He's just a customer. A friend of a friend." Ill at ease and blushing, Jared glanced our way and shrugged, obviously in search of some support. "I already have a boyfriend."

Butch ignored all of us. He got down on one knee in front of Evan, clasping both of my friend's delicately boned hands in one of his big, brawny ones.

"Evan Alexander Owenby," he said, not wasting a moment more on explanations, "I have done nothing wrong. You have my heart, and have since the moment I met you."

Evan's eyes were big and locked on Butch's.

"I have never lied to you, although I admit to keeping a secret." Butch's other hand came up, and in it was a small box. "This is what Jared ordered for me, and this is why I got angry when you spoiled the surprise."

Evan's eyes filled with tears, but he was silent. For once.

"So if you take this box"—*nice how Butch made it seem like Evan would choose otherwise*—"you have to be willing to believe me when I tell you that you are the one for me, and that I will never, ever leave you."

My insides melted like butter, even more so when Joe's warm fingers laced with mine. I glanced up to see his eyes soft, and knew that however stupid I'd been today, I'd been forgiven, at least temporarily.

Evan took a deep breath, looked at the box, then back at Butch. "You mean it?"

"I mean it."

Only I knew how hard this was on my nearest and dearest buddy; only I knew the deep-seated insecurity behind the fashionable, clever façade he presented to the world. And only I knew how very, very much he wanted to take that box.

And then everybody knew, because—hand shaking visibly—he reached out and took it.

It was a ring box, of course, and when Evan opened it, his expression told me and everyone else exactly what he thought of what was inside.

"I know we can't get married," Butch said, very low. He and Evan were the only people in the room as far as he was concerned. "But we can commit ourselves to each other. I had two of these made; one for you and one for me."

"Butch's ring will be in tomorrow," Jared piped in, beaming at Evan. He was a lot less nervous now, I noticed. "We had to add more platinum to the band." Ignored by the happy couple, he looked again at Joe and me. "Big fingers, you know."

I wanted to laugh, to dance, to shriek with happiness, but didn't dare.

Evan was having a moment, and it wasn't over yet.

He swiped tears from his cheeks with his free hand, staring at the ring. "Would . . . would you put it on me?" he asked, voice wobbly.

And before my eyes, a broken heart was mended as my Queen Supreme allowed Butch to be his Prince Charming. Never moving from his bent-knee position, Butchie made Evan's fairy tale come true by slipping a platinum band onto his finger.

"I have to go call my boyfriend," Jared murmured, tearing up.

And that's when I allowed myself to shriek with happiness—I couldn't hold it in anymore anyway—and rushed to the couch to give my oldest friend and my brand-new kinda sorta brother-in-law a hug.

CHAPTER 17

"Are you going to tell me why Evan left here clutching a lump of Play-Doh," Joe murmured, "or do I not want to know?"

I smiled as I gave a final wave to Evan, Butch, and the hapless Jared, closing the door. They were gone now, off to focus on their own lives, and leaving me free to focus on mine. I took Joe by the hand and started leading him down the hall toward my bedroom. "I'll tell you all about it," I promised, "right after I show you how much I love you."

Joe stopped. "Is that the liquor talking?"

"No," I teased, tugging at his hand, "I'm pretty sure Jack Daniel's would have a deeper voice."

He didn't respond to my teasing. "That's the first time you've ever volunteered that you love me."

I frowned, confused. I'd told him so before, hadn't I? Of course I had.

"I usually have to say it first," he clarified, squeezing my fingers.

With a sigh at my own stupidity, I moved closer to him, letting go of his hand to wrap both arms around his neck. "I love you," I said softly, looking into his eyes. "You are the man for me, Joe Bascombe."

A slow grin split his face. He locked hands behind my waist, pulling me tight against him. "Say it again."

So I did, happily, elated to find that it wasn't nearly as hard as I thought to finally give my heart to someone, despite the fact that hearts were sometimes broken.

As I'd just learned, as long as a broken heart still beat, there was a chance it could be mended. Life was full of second chances, and in my case, death was full of them, too.

Which reminded me of Crystal, and the mess I was going to have to get myself into to earn her a second chance. *Tomorrow.* I didn't need to worry about it tonight, which was a good thing, because Joe's lips drove all other thought right out of my head.

A vibration against my hip interrupted the kiss. "Is that a beeper in your pocket, or are you just happy to see me?" I murmured, kissing him again.

"It's the hospital," he muttered, kissing me back. "I have to take it." But it was a couple of kisses later before he did, reaching into his pocket with a free hand while keeping the other around my waist. "Damn," he said, craning his neck around more of my kisses. "It's Lisa."

Those two words had pretty much the same effect as a splash of cold water. I hadn't forgotten what that stilettoed shark had said to Joe in his office earlier today. I knew what she was up to.

"I need to tell you something," I said, drawing back.

"What is it?" To his credit, Joe gave my sudden stiffness more attention than he did Lisa's page. "Is everything okay?"

His pager beeped again.

"I overheard what Lisa said to you in your office today." Nothing like being blunt. "I know she wants you to dump me over this Crystal Cowart thing."

His eyebrows lowered.

"I heard her flirting with you, hitting on you."

"Then you heard me turn her down." He was still frowning, obviously waiting to learn how I knew.

I smiled at him, relaxing as I leaned into him again. "I did. You were a very good boy."

Joe made an exasperated noise, shoving the pager back in his pocket. "How did you hear all this? Better yet, when were you going to tell me?"

"It's not like we've spent a lot of time together today, is it?"

"That's not my fault. I tried to reach you all afternoon, remember?"

"Evan was having a crisis!"

"*I* was having a crisis!"

That took the wind out of my sails. "You were?" *I am the worst girlfriend in the world.*

"Yes." Joe's green eyes were serious. "I came to a realization today, and I wanted to tell my girlfriend about it, but I couldn't find her." He put both hands on my waist and pulled me firmly against him, hip to hip. "She has this really bad habit of disappearing on me, particularly when there's ghosts involved. Now tell me how you overheard my conversation with Lisa."

A realization? "It was Crystal," I told him. "She tapped into your office phone somehow, turned on the speaker or something." *What realization?* "She wanted me to hear how"—I hesitated—"how you might lose your job over me."

He sighed, tipping his head to the side. We were

a perfect fit, he and I; no neck-craning or arm-stretching or tiptoes, just hard meeting soft in all the right places.

"I can always get another job," he said softly. "But there's nobody else like you."

I teared up. I couldn't help it.

"You make me happy. You make me laugh. You make me nuts." Joe's lopsided grin made my heart flutter. "You're unique. You're fascinating. I can't imagine my life without you."

My heart fluttered again. "You're just saying that because you're about to get lucky," I said shakily, swiping tears from my cheek with one hand.

He shook his head, still smiling. "You never give yourself enough credit, Nicki. The dark-eyed goth girl with a tough exterior and kind heart; not everyone could deal with the changes in her life the way you do."

I shook my head, burying it against his chest. "You make it sound like I'm some kind of saint."

"Absolutely not." Joe's tone turned a little wicked. "Thank heaven for that."

That was actually true; if I hadn't been kicked out of Heaven because it wasn't my time, I'd still be the shallow, selfish version of myself that existed a year ago.

Before I met Joe. Before life had become truly worth living. Savored. Not to be wasted.

"Let's go into the bedroom," I whispered, pulling his face down to mine. "And find heaven together."

The smell of coffee and a clatter of dishes brought me awake the next morning. I rolled over and cracked open an eye to find Joe standing by the bed with a tray. He was wearing nothing but a smile and his boxer briefs, Calvin Klein sports I'd picked out myself.

"Rise and shine, sleepyhead," he said, cheerfully. "How's your head this morning?"

"Not too bad," I murmured, lying my ass off. It hurt, but that's what you get when you drink too much whiskey on an empty stomach.

"A big glass of water and some ibuprofen first," he said, "then some coffee. Doctor's orders."

The bed dipped as Joe got back into it, balancing the tray with ease. I dragged myself up against the headboard and ran my fingers through my hair, knowing it had to look pretty wild after the night we'd had. "That's quite the bedside manner you've got there." An achy head couldn't keep me from appreciating the sight of a gorgeous man in his underwear. "If you'd done this in the hospital, I would've woken up a lot sooner." My mouth was dry, but I was smiling.

He laughed, handing me a glass of water. "Now

why didn't I think of that?" He watched me down the pills and gulp the water. "Truth be told," he said, a devilish glint in his eye, "I did think of it. You looked pretty cute lying there with your hair all messed up, just like it is now. I had a fleeting thought about waking up with you someday, just like this."

Awwwwwww. Feeling better already, I closed my eyes just for a moment, resting my head against the headboard.

"Coffee and toast when you're ready." He shifted, getting comfortable. "Didn't see any jam, so I sprinkled it with a little cinnamon."

I opened my eyes and gave him my full attention. "Are you for real, or am I just having an incredibly erotic dream?" I was only teasing, of course—but having a half-naked man serve me breakfast in bed was hardly an everyday occurrence.

His eyes crinkled. "I know my way around a toaster," he said, taking a sip of coffee. He wagged an eyebrow. "It's all in the hands."

Laughing, I threw back the covers and slipped from the bed, heading for the bathroom. "Hold that thought. I'll be right back."

I was in there longer than I'd thought, in large part because my skin felt as dry as my mouth, so I washed up and took the time to moisturize. And then, because vanity is sanity, I dabbed on a little pink lip gloss and brushed my hair before coming out.

Joe was still lying on the bed, but he didn't look as happy as he had a few minutes earlier. He had a cell phone to his ear, and he was frowning. "You've got to be kidding me, Lisa."

Crap.

He sat up, moving the tray aside. I had no doubt that if Lisa could see him now, flat-bellied and taut, moving with unconscious athletic grace, nothing would come between her and his Calvins.

"This is bullshit." The bitterness in Joe's voice startled me. "You can tell the board I'm getting my own lawyer." He hung up, flipping his cell phone shut with a definite *click.*

"What's happened?" Whatever it was, it had to be bad.

"I've been temporarily suspended," Joe said, flatly. He was sitting on the edge of the bed, hands gripping the mattress, "with pay. The board of directors thinks it's a good idea for me to keep a low profile until a settlement is reached with the Cowart family." His eyes were bleak. "A settlement, can you imagine?"

The breath left my body in a rush. This was all my fault—all mine.

"Baby, I'm so sorry." Words weren't enough.

"A settlement means an admission of guilt." He

shook his head, eyes turned inward. "There was nothing I could've done for her. Nothing. She coded in the ambulance. By the time they wheeled her in, she'd already been unofficially declared. It's all in the emergency-response records." His eyes refocused, and he was back in the now. "How could those idiots ignore the facts when they're right in front of them?"

Because facts could be twisted, particularly when lawyers were the ones twisting them. Manipulative, bitchy lawyers who wanted their clients to lie down and play doctor.

"What can I do?" I asked miserably, sitting on the bed beside him. His shoulder was tense beneath my palm.

Joe's mouth was a grim line. "Don't worry about it, Nicki. I'll handle it."

But that was the problem—Joe *couldn't* handle it because it involved a pissed-off spirit and a horny devil. The only one who could make it all go away was me.

"I know what to do," I blurted, before I could lose my nerve. "But you won't like it."

CHAPTER 18

Tina Cowart lived in a trailer park on the outskirts of Dullsville, at the intersection of Nowhere and Nothing. If Google maps was to be
believed, it was actually the tiny community of
Bryantville, just northwest of Atlanta. The town's
biggest natural resource seemed to be empty
pastureland, dotted with scrub.

"You have to stay in the car," I said to Joe, for the
third time. "She'll be more open to what I have to
say without an audience."

"I'm not staying in the car," he replied grimly,
steering us past a broken-down mailbox and
a dusty blue pickup truck. An old swing set sat
rusting in the sun, almost as orange as the clay

dirt beneath it. "And for the record, I still think this is a bad idea. You're basing your assumption that Crystal was molested on the word of the biggest liar who ever existed." His lip curled—he'd been pretty pissed to find out Sammy'd been stopping by the store.

I hadn't wanted to tell him, but knew the time for secrets was past. The only thing I kept to myself was the dark little corner of my heart that responded to Sammy's overwhelming sexuality— *I'd resisted, hadn't I*? No need to plant any seeds that might grow into problems later.

I sighed, staring out the window at the squat little trailer I was pretty sure was Tina's. "I know. It could be a giant load of crap, although Crystal pretty much confirmed it."

He shot me a look, and said sourly, "And Crystal works for who?"

He was right. I couldn't trust Sammy *or* Crystal, but I had to do *something*. "I know, I know. Tina Cowart isn't going to like hearing it, whether it's true or not. It's a long shot, and probably a stupid plan, but I can't think of a better one." Turning my head to look out the window, I said softly, "You shouldn't have come with me. You should've let me do this myself. I don't want you to get into any more trouble than you're already in."

Joe let the car roll to a stop a few yards from the trailer and put it in PARK a little harder than was necessary. "Get over it. I'm not used to having my girlfriend fight my battles for me." His eyes were hidden behind his sunglasses, but I knew what I'd see in them: frustration and anger, to hide the sense of helplessness I knew he must have been feeling.

Dr. Joseph P. Bascombe did not like feeling helpless.

I put a hand on his arm. "Just give me ten minutes alone with her. If her ambulance-chasing lawyer finds out you came all the way out here, he could accuse you of harassment or something. It could hurt your case."

A near growl came from Joe's throat. His hands were gripping the steering wheel so tightly the knuckles were white. "What if Crystal's ghost shows up, Nicki? What if she possesses you again?" Worry over me obviously added to his frustration. "I shouldn't have brought you here. Your heart can't take this."

I leaned over and kissed him, quickly, on the cheek. "You let me worry about my heart," I said, and slid from the car. "I'll be right back."

Despite my apparent calmness, my pain-in-the-ass heart was beating a mile a minute. I walked toward the trailer, careful to skirt a muddy patch of red clay—I was wearing tennis shoes, but they were a pair of my favorite Skechers, and I didn't want them ruined. There was no grass to speak of, just dirt and patches of weeds. The lattice surrounding the base of the trailer was rotting and full of holes. Something moved in the dimness there, and I was startled when a little face appeared, all wide eyes and pointy ears, until I realized it was just a cat, watching me.

"Hi, kitty," I said, and it vanished.

The steps leading to the front door of the trailer were rickety enough to make me nervous, and I held on to the railing as I knocked on the door. A dog started barking inside, a deep bark that told me it was a big dog.

"Be quiet, Pete." A female voice, the vibration of footsteps, coming my way. "Quiet!" The door opened, just a crack, and the barking got louder.

I'd expected Tina Cowart, but it was a little girl who peered at me from inside the trailer. Blond hair, unbrushed, in shorts and bare feet. She looked about twelve, with blue eyes and high cheekbones just barely emerging from her baby fat. She could only be Amber Marie Cowart, Crystal's sister.

"Hi." I gave her a big smile, not wanting to frighten her by staring. "Is your mom home?"

She shook her head, not answering. The dog was still barking, and she turned, shoving him back from the door. "Sit," she ordered. Surprisingly enough, the barking stopped. "Stay."

The door cracked open a little wider while she was dealing with the dog, releasing the powerful smell of stale cigarettes from inside the trailer. I could see the dog now, a hairy brown mutt with a face only a mother could love. He was sitting, as ordered, but growled at me low in his throat.

"Pete don't like strangers," the girl said, eyeing me warily. "I can sic him on you anytime I want."

"Don't do that," I said hastily. The dog was obviously a great source of protection, but I couldn't help but wonder what she was doing here alone. It was a Friday morning, and she should've been in school. "Do you know when Tina might be back?"

The girl shrugged, and said, "She's at work," as if that were the answer to my question.

"Isn't she pretty?" A woman's whisper in my ear made me jump. I jerked my head to see who was standing beside me, but there was no one there. "Mama lets her stay home from school if she does the laundry and cleans the kitchen. Keeps her fat ass from having to do it when she gets home."

I didn't need to see Crystal to know she was there, and neither did the dog. It stood up, eyes intent on the empty space to my right.

Amber Marie was oblivious. She eyed me curiously, looking at the necklace of black beads I was never without, checking out the silver crucifix and the peace sign on a leather cord I'd worn along with it. "My sister put pink dye in her hair once. She was going to do it to me, too, when I was old enough." Her lower lip quivered, then steadied. She lifted her chin and squared her shoulders, an oddly mature gesture for such a young girl.

A keening sound, very faint, reached my ears. The dog cocked his head, whining.

"I'm very sorry about Crystal," I said, doing my best to ignore everything but the little girl in front of me. "You must be Amber Marie."

Crystal was crying. I could feel her grief like a cold gust of wind, seeping into my soul.

Amber's face brightened. "You knew my sister?"

I hesitated. "Yes." And then I realized, I didn't need to speak to Tina—the person I needed to speak to was right in front of me. "She wanted me to tell you something."

"Who is it, Amber Marie?" A man's voice. Heavy footsteps shook the trailer, and to my shock, Jimmy

Boyd appeared in the doorway behind Amber. "Ah, Miss Styx. I had a feeling we'd meet again."

A shriek of rage filled the air, but no one heard it but me—and the dog—who cringed and slunk away into the shadows. Grief turned to rage, just like that, and just as quickly, Crystal swooped into my mind with the force of a hurricane, making me stagger. I grabbed the rickety wooden railing for support, fighting for balance, both inside and out.

Kill him, she screamed, inside my mind. *Kill him, before it's too late!* A swirling maelstrom of hate, despair, and desperation gripped me. *He's a liar, a cheat, a fraud! Kill him!*

To my horror, I felt my fingers curl into claws, and felt an urge to launch them straight toward Jimmy Boyd's lying, smiling eyes. Instead, I gripped the railing tighter, refusing to let go. I tried to speak, but couldn't, the force of Crystal's possession stronger than it had ever been.

Focus, Styx, focus. I shut my eyes, gritting my teeth against the shrieking still going on in my mind.

"Miss Styx? Are you all right?" Boyd's voice came from far away. I could only hope he had the sense to stay back—if he touched me with those creepy child-molester hands I'd never be able to stop myself from going for his throat.

"Migraines," I ground out, keeping my eyes closed. *Light, focus on the light.*

A car door slammed, and I knew Joe had noticed my odd behavior.

Let go! Crystal screamed, inside my head, but I wouldn't. The wooden railing beneath my hands was the only stable thing in my world right now. And then, to my horror, I heard a sharp *crack*, and stability was a thing of the past. My eyes flew open, and I stumbled backward, my hands still clutching wood. I staggered, fighting for balance, but there was no need—my body was no longer my own. My legs planted themselves, and without conscious volition, my right hand rose high in the air, holding a piece of broken railing. I was about to bash Jimmy Boyd over the head with it.

"Nicki!" Joe's shout made me pause, though the muscles in my arm shook with strain. He grabbed me from behind, wrenching the wood from my hand.

Noooooo . . . Crystal's shriek of rage made my head hurt, but it was the shocked look on Amber Marie's face that truly brought me to my senses. She was pressed against Jimmy Boyd's side, seeking protection, his arm around her shoulders, pulling her closer.

It terrified me. It made me want to throw up.

And it gave me the strength to focus on Crystal's rage.

Squeezing my eyes shut so Amber Marie couldn't see the crazy look I was sure was there, I spoke to Crystal, who was still inside my head. *Look at what you're doing*, I said silently, without moving my lips, *look!*

Joe's hands steadied me, while I leaned against him and kept up the internal dialogue with Crystal's spirit. *You're scaring Amber*, I screamed, forcing her to hear me. *You're giving him an excuse to touch her, to hold her. Get out of my body and let me handle this my own way.*

"I promised," I said out loud, without meaning to. "I promised I'd take care of it."

"You've done enough, Nicki," Joe said grimly, obviously thinking I was talking to him. "Let's go."

But my feet weren't moving, and for the time being, that was okay with me. I hadn't yet done what I came here for. *Get out*, I told Crystal silently, *you're making things worse.*

Her hold on me was weakening. I could feel it.

"Close the door, Amber Marie," said Jimmy Boyd, pulling the girl backward into the trailer. "You people get out of here before I call the police."

I opened my eyes, clutching Joe's arm.

"Do that," Joe said harshly. "Maybe the police would like to know what you're doing here alone with a little girl who should be in school."

Yes! I'd never loved Joe more than I did in that moment.

Boyd froze, eyes narrowing. "I'm a friend of the family," he said warily, shooting glances between Joe and me.

"Is that so?" The sarcasm in Joe's voice would've been apparent to anybody.

I let the men engage in a stare down while I focused my attention on Amber Marie. As long as I looked at her, Crystal would see what I saw—a scared, vulnerable little girl about to be drawn in to something very, very ugly. She was afraid of the wrong people, and I had to make her see it.

There was a tightness in my chest, a squeezing like a fist around my heart, and for the first time, I was really afraid.

If you kill me, he'll get her for sure, I thought, directing all my brainpower toward Crystal. *If I'm dead, there'll be no one to save her.*

Desperate, I took a deep, shuddering breath, doing my best to ignore the pain in my chest. *Let me help, Crystal. Let me help.*

It was the dog that tipped the scales. His ugly brown face appeared, just by Boyd's left knee. He stared at me, silent and unmoving, eyes intent on my face.

He knows. I couldn't explain it, but the dog wasn't really looking at me. He was looking at Crystal, almost as though he were adding a silent plea to mine. He whined, a thin whine, barely heard.

"Shut up, Pete," Boyd snapped.

Amber Marie frowned, obviously not liking how he spoke to her dog. She straightened, pulling away from him a bit.

Unbelievably enough, the pressure on my chest began to ease. I took another deep breath, easier this time. The swirling storm of rage and anguish inside my head slowed, faltered.

And then, as abruptly as she'd come, Crystal left me.

If Joe hadn't been holding me up, I would've fallen. As it was, my knees buckled, and he braced himself at the weight of my body. "Nick? You okay?"

"I'm okay," I lied. "Just a little light-headed for a second. Lost my balance."

The dog helped me out again, pushing past Boyd to nose my hand. I scratched the ugly mutt under the chin gratefully, murmuring, "Good boy. Nice doggy." He wagged his tail, nosing me even harder.

Amber relaxed visibly, moving forward to grab Pete by the collar. "He likes you," she said, sounding surprised. "He don't normally like people he don't know."

Her diction was atrocious. Small wonder, if she stayed home all the time instead of going to school.

"Get back inside, Amber Marie." Boyd talked to her like he owned her. He was glaring at Joe, his face a mask of hostility.

"Crystal wanted me to tell you something, Amber," I said quickly.

"She did, did she?" Boyd spoke for the girl, narrowing his eyes at me. "When I talked to you yesterday, you didn't seem to know anything about Crystal."

Creep.

I ignored him, looking down at Amber. "Your sister told me a secret."

Her face lit up. "A secret?"

Nodding, I kept petting the dog. "A secret she wanted me to tell you." I risked a hostile glance at Boyd, glad Joe was still there.

Boyd's face flushed, and I saw his fists clench, just once, before he opened them again. "Get inside, Amber," he repeated. "These people are not your friends."

"And you ain't my daddy," she told him flip-pantly, over her shoulder.

The girl had spunk. I was glad, because I had a feeling she was going to need it.

"Now, Amber, honey . . ." His tone turned con-ciliatory, but she ignored him.

"What did Crystal say?" Amber's resemblance to her older sister was obvious, despite the fact that she weighed more at twelve than Crystal had when she died. The high cheekbones, the blond hair—it made me sad to see the little girl Crystal might have been as compared to the bony, angry person she'd become.

It wouldn't do for Amber to see me sad, though. Not if I wanted to be her new best friend. I arched an eyebrow playfully, and said, "Secret. Remember?"

She looked pointedly at Joe, who still had his arm around me.

He sighed, knowing when he was beaten. "I'll wait in the car," he said. The glare he gave Boyd was scorching. "I won't be far."

"Amber Marie . . ." Boyd said warningly, but the little girl cut him off.

"I just want to talk to her!" She turned partway in his direction, still holding on to Pete's collar. "I'll take Pete. We'll be right over there on the swing set."

Jimmy Boyd obviously wasn't used to being thwarted. His face turned red, and the look he gave me was black. But, short of grabbing Amber and physically dragging her back into the trailer, he had no other options.

Besides, Joe was still right there, and so was the dog. Either one looked willing and able to bite his head off if he laid a hand on her. "I'm calling your mama," he said. "She's not going to be happy about you talking to strangers."

Yeah, like Amber Marie needs to worry about strangers with you around.

The swing set was rusty, and the seat was hard. My butt was a tight fit, causing me mentally to swear off the blueberry muffins from Moonbeans for a while. Pete snuffled around the broken lattice at the bottom of the trailer, obviously hoping to find the cat, while Joe sat none too patiently in the car. I could see his fingers drumming the steering wheel.

Amber Marie scuffed the toe of a dirty tennis shoe into the red clay beneath our feet. "What's your name?"

"Nicki Styx."

She eyed me sideways. "How come I never seen you before?"

If anybody needed to be in school, this kid did.

I shrugged. "I didn't know Crystal for very long."

She nodded, as if this made perfect sense. "Crystal didn't have many friends. She spent most of her time in her room."

Unsure what to say about that, I said nothing.

"She said most people were stupid, and pretty girls were all bitches." Another look from beneath her lashes.

Talk about your backhanded compliment. "I imagine some of them are," I said lightly, resisting the urge to react to her use of profanity.

Silence for a moment. Pete snuffled and growled at something behind the lattice.

"You must miss her," I said.

Amber's eyes filled with tears, a couple of them spilling over onto her cheeks. She swiped them away with hands that looked surprisingly clean, though the nails were bitten to the quick. "Yep. But Mama and Mr. Boyd say she's with the angels now, so it's okay."

No, it wasn't.

"Does Mr. Boyd come around here often?" I was glad she'd given me an opening.

She shrugged. "He used to, but mostly we just see him at prayer meetings and church. Wednesday nights, Saturdays, and Sundays."

Tina Cowart was certainly devout. "What's he doing here now?"

She shrugged again. "I dunno. Just came by to see how I was doin', he said."

I'll bet he did.

Still, I had to be delicate. I couldn't just blurt out the ugly truth to a twelve-year-old.

"What did Crystal think of Mr. Boyd?"

Amber gave an unladylike snort of laughter. "She used to call him Asswipe."

I couldn't help my answering smile.

She shot me a mischievous look. "Sometimes she called him Dickhead."

That one was a little too close to home.

"So Crystal didn't like him."

Amber shook her head, blond hair swinging. "Nope. Her and Mama used to get into fights about him all the time. Mama wanted her to go to church with us, but Crystal never would."

"Do you like him?"

Her smile faded. "He's okay, I guess. He brought me a stuffed bunny when Crystal died."

A movement from the trailer caught my eye. Jimmy Boyd had moved aside a curtain and stood watching us through a window.

"I don't like him." There, I'd said it.

"He and Mama used to be engaged or something, back when I was a baby." Amber pushed herself backward in the swing, kicking off. She swung back and forth while she talked. "She says I have to be nice to him, no matter what Crystal said, 'cuz he's a man of God and all that."

Uh-oh.

"What if he wanted you to do something you didn't want to do?" I was trying to go at this sideways. "Would you do it?"

She looked at me curiously. "What's it to you?"

Her directness took me aback. I wasn't used to smart-mouthed twelve-year-olds. Or twelve-year-olds of any kind, for that matter.

"There's a reason Crystal didn't like him, Amber." Taking a deep breath, I started to tell her. "He—"

A burst of frantic barking interrupted me. Pete was going nuts over by the trailer, clawing at the already broken lattice. An unearthly yowl told me that the cat he was after didn't appreciate his efforts.

"Pete!" Amber Marie let the swing's momentum carry her forward, then jumped out. "Get over here! Leave Shadow alone!"

With a sigh, I got up from the swing, too.

"Shadow had kittens last week," the little girl said, over her shoulder. She grabbed Pete by the collar and dragged him backward, showing no fear despite the dog's continued growls. "Five of 'em. Mama won't let me bring 'em into the house, so I made her a bed under here. Wanna see?"

The idea of crawling beneath that trailer was not something I'd even *consider*.

"Not right now," I said hastily. "It would probably upset the mama kitty to have strangers around her babies."

"Yeah," she answered, nodding. "That's why Pete's so riled. He wants to see 'em, and she won't let him."

Smart kitty. Keep the big bad wolf away from your babies.

Too bad Tina Cowart wasn't as smart as the cat.

The sound of a car made me turn around. A battered old Saturn was making its way up the road toward the trailer.

"Mama's home," Amber said brightly.

I sighed, glancing nervously at Joe, where he sat behind the wheel of his own car. The windows were tinted, and he was wearing his sunglasses, so maybe if Tina didn't look too closely, she wouldn't recognize him.

She parked the car beside the trailer and cut the engine, getting out. "Go in the house, Amber Marie," she said, by way of greeting.

"But Mama—"

"Get in that house before I tan your bottom, girl," she said, walking toward us, cigarette in one hand and purse in the other. "Take Pete with you."

To my surprise, Amber did as she was told without any further argument, though the look on her face was sullen. Tina's threat of a whipping was obviously one she took seriously.

"What are you doing here?"

My greeting from Tina was just as blunt as Amber's had been.

"I need to talk to you." No sense beating around the bush. "About Jimmy Boyd."

"He called me," she said, eyes narrowed, "and told me you and your boyfriend was out here causing trouble." She glanced toward Joe, sitting in the car, then back at me. "He says you broke my porch, tried to hit him with a piece of railing."

I could hardly deny it—the broken railing was right there for anyone to see—but I *could* set the record straight. "That wasn't me. It was Crystal, just like in the store," I said, reminding her what happened when she came to see me at Handbags and Gladrags. "She doesn't like his being alone with her sister."

Tina stared at me, taking a drag from her cigarette. I couldn't help but notice that her hand was shaking, just a little. "That ain't none of your business."

"You're right. It isn't. Except Crystal has made it my business."

She swallowed, hard. "You sayin' what I think you're sayin'? 'Cuz that ain't what you said to me the other day."

It was my turn to swallow hard. I didn't like admitting to anyone that I saw ghosts, much less that I was getting possessed by one on a regular basis. Squaring my shoulders and lifting my chin, I said baldly, "I didn't want to tell you the truth, but now I have to. Crystal's spirit won't leave me alone. She's not at peace."

Tina's face flushed. "If she ain't at peace, it's because of that damned hospital," she hissed. "They won't release her body to the funeral home until there's been an autopsy." Her lip quivered, but she covered it by taking another drag off her cigarette. "My baby should've been cremated and put to rest by now. Damn doctors."

It would hardly do to point out that Tina's lawsuit was the reason for an autopsy to begin with. "That's not it, Tina, and you know it." I had to be blunt. "It's because of Jimmy Boyd, and what he did to her when she was thirteen. What he might do to Amber Marie, if you don't stop him."

She went dead still. All color left her face, leaving it white as a sheet.

"Get off my property," she said, so low I could barely hear her.

"It's true." I wasn't going anywhere until I'd made her listen. "Crystal told you what happened, but you didn't believe her."

Color came rushing back into her cheeks. "It *isn't* true," she said, throwing the cigarette to the ground. "Crystal came on to *him*. Jimmy and me were datin'. She was so used to gettin' attention from all the boys that she couldn't stand it when somebody else got some. She got mad when Jimmy didn't take her up on it, that's all." Her voice quivered—rage or grief, I couldn't tell. "She made it all up."

"Is that what he told you?" *Of course it was.* "She was thirteen, Tina! *Thirteen!* Why would a thirteen-year-old girl hit on a grown man?"

She sneered at me. "Don't know much about girls these days, do ya? Crystal knew how to wrap men around her finger from the day she was born." Her look turned fierce. "I ain't gonna let that happen to Amber Marie. She's gonna grow up righteous in the Lord. Pure. Jimmy Boyd is a modern-day apostle. He's gonna help me keep her on the straight and narrow."

I flicked a glance at Jimmy Boyd's pickup. "Apostle, huh? Is that what they call child molesters these days?"

For a second I thought she was going to hit me. Her free hand clenched and unclenched as though she were considering it.

"Jimmy was right about you," she said, after a moment. "You are a lost soul. Empty inside. That's why Crystal can fill your head with lies—because there was nothing there to begin with."

I didn't give her the favor of a reaction.

"You need to get yourself to church, girl." She brushed past me on her way to the trailer. "Now get off my property. You ain't wanted here."

CHAPTER 19

"You might not care about the danger you put yourself in to help others, Nicki, but I do. Does the way I feel mean less to you than the needs of total strangers?" Joe was pissed, and I didn't really blame him. We'd left Bryantville behind us, the Georgia countryside speeding past as we headed back to Atlanta.

"What was I supposed to do, Joe? Let that creep molest that little girl the way he did her older sister?"

"You don't know that he molested anyone," he said grimly, eyes on the road.

"Yes, I do," I said stubbornly. "Crystal told me."

"And you just assume she's telling the truth.

Why would you believe anything she said? She claims I killed her, she claims some guy molested her—she's caused nothing but trouble since the day she died. She's sold her soul to the Devil, for God's sake!" His voice was rising. "How do you know this wasn't just some twisted plan to torment somebody else? Somebody she didn't have access to any other way?"

I bit my lip, staring out the window. "She didn't know Boyd was going to be at the trailer."

"How do you know? Are you a psychic now?"

That comment earned him a look that would've sent Evan running for cover, but Joe wasn't Evan. Not by a long shot.

"She took you over again, didn't she? On the porch."

Reluctantly, I nodded, not trusting my voice at the moment. I didn't want to fight with him.

"You were about to hit that guy with a board."

"But I didn't," I said quickly. "I shoved her out, got control of myself. No harm done."

"This time," he said darkly. "He could've snatched that board away and smashed *you* over the head with it, or me. Maybe that's what Crystal wanted all along—did you think about that?"

"I didn't know what was going to happen," I began, but Joe cut me off.

"Exactly. But you still thought that showing up

out of the blue to tell a grieving mother that her daughter had been sexually molested was the way to go. Has it ever occurred to you that your efforts to do good in the world could actually make things worse?"

I sighed, internally admitting that he might have a point. No matter which way you looked at it, it hadn't been a good plan. I'd risked possession, heart failure, and his career by rushing off into the boondocks with some stupid idea about confronting a grieving mother with something no mother would want to hear.

We were both quiet for a little while as he drove. I knew his anger was mainly due to his fear for my safety, and though he hadn't said anything about his job, guilt over the position I'd put him in gnawed at me. What if Tina Cowart called her lawyer and told him Joe and I had been out to her trailer and threatened her pastor? I'm sure Lisa Butler and the board of directors at the hospital would be thrilled to hear *that*. His temporary suspension could easily become permanent.

It didn't matter that I'd tried to keep him from going. I shouldn't have gone there to begin with, period. Putting my health at risk and ignoring his concerns could be taken as selfish instead of selfless—but I didn't know what to do about it.

It was confusing, and frustrating. Worse, I'd had a chance to save a little girl's life from getting ruined, and I'd totally blown it.

Now Joe was mad at me, and I was no closer to getting rid of Crystal than I was before.

We reached the Little Five Points area in record time, although the silence between us made it seem like an eternity. It wasn't that we weren't speaking so much as it seemed there wasn't a whole lot left to say. I could only hope that the tension would ease once we'd gone on about our usual routines.

And then, with a pang of guilt, I realized that Joe's regular routine wasn't available to him. He was on suspension.

"Look, I'm really sorry," I murmured, as he pulled up in front of Handbags and Gladrags, ready to drop me off. "I never meant to drag you into anything."

He turned his head in my direction, face expressionless. I couldn't see his eyes behind his sunglasses. "I know you didn't."

Hardly the reassurance I craved, but at least he didn't seem angry anymore.

"You're not just risking another heart attack, Nicki," he said quietly. "You're risking our future together."

At that point, I didn't have the nerve to ask him what our future entailed—I was having a hard enough time just dealing with the present.

So I leaned over and gave him a quick kiss good-bye, which he returned. "Call me later?"

He nodded, and I decided to be satisfied with that. Then I got out of the car and went to work.

"Way to go, genius."

The girl in the mirror didn't answer me, but that was okay—I knew what she was going to say before she said it. With a sigh, I finished washing my hands and snagged a paper towel to dry them.

I wasn't used to feeling like a failure, but at the moment I couldn't help it. I knew Joe would forgive my latest fiasco, but what if one day I went too far, and he didn't?

A knock on the bathroom door made me jump. "Nicki? We've got a bunch of customers out here. I need help."

Despite Evan's impatience, his tone was chipper. And why not? He was sporting a ring the size of Texas today, while *my* boyfriend was ticked because I kept sticking my nose in where it didn't belong.

I opened the bathroom door to the sound of women's laughter. "Oh, look," someone said, "I wore an eyelet dress like this to a USO party back in 1945. Ralph always loved me in blue."

"Ralph loved you in anything, dear." That voice sounded familiar.

"Actually, he loved me in nothing even more."

Another burst of laughter hit me as I walked from the hallway into the front of the store. At least a dozen older women were having a good time browsing the racks, and two of them I recognized.

"There you are, dear," said Grandma Bijou. She came toward me, arms open for a hug. The now-familiar scent of roses surrounded me, oddly comforting after the morning I'd had. "Let me introduce you to my friends."

A dizzying round of introductions followed: Estelle, Betty, Lorraine, Pearl, a couple of Marys and at least one Helen—I lost track after that. Telling them apart was going to be a problem, as they were all gray-haired, smiling, and very sweet. Except for Odessa, who was glowering, as usual.

"I told you the Savannah Garden Club was going to invade Atlanta," Bijou said proudly, "didn't I?"

"Oh," I said stupidly, suddenly realizing what was going on, "you did."

Looking around the group, I found it very hard to believe these little old ladies knew anything about witchcraft or Wicca or whatever.

But then, I still found it hard to believe half the things that were going on in my life, so I kept my mouth shut.

"Can I offer you ladies some tea? Coffee?" Evan bustled in, carrying a tray full of yummies and looking very pleased with himself. "You must try the cherry tarts," he said, offering the tray to the woman nearest him. "And the cheese biscuits are to dic for."

He'd obviously gotten a heads-up on our influx of customers; I recognized the baked goods as coming from A Little Taste of Heaven, an upscale bake shop in Buckhead. He even had little specialty napkins.

"Mmm," said one of the women, taking a tart without hesitation, "what a darling young man you are."

I wasn't surprised; little old ladies always loved Evan, and vice versa.

"Isn't he, though?" Bijou beamed at Evan as if he were her own, while Odessa picked up a cheese biscuit and sniffed it suspiciously.

The next hour was a blur of laughter, conversation, and shopping assistance, as Evan and I did everything we could to improve our bottom line while making Bijou's friends feel at home.

"You and Butchie all 'kissed and made up'?" I whispered to him when I had the chance.

The satisfied grin he gave me was enough of an answer for now. I knew I'd hear the details later, when the Garden Club was gone.

The jewelry counter was a big hit, as one of the ladies, Estelle, was a total turquoise lover and another, one of the Marys, adored anything with carved coral. We had some quality Victorian pieces that went like hotcakes—brooches, hair combs, necklaces, and bracelets. Rings were argued over and tried on gnarled, ancient hands that were quick to whip out checkbooks and credit cards. All in all, a great afternoon.

Until it was over.

"Well, dear," said Grandma Bijou finally, looking tired but happy. "I'll expect to see you later this evening at the Embassy Suites. We can all meet in my room at eight o'clock for the cleansing ceremony."

"Cleansing ceremony?" I squeaked.

"To remove the Evil Eye," said Lorraine, eagerly.

"It works best during a new moon," put in Betty, "but we'll make do."

Twelve gray heads nodded in unison, while Odessa gave her trademark, "Huh."

"Great," I said, resigned. "Can I bring anything? Hemlock? Wolfbane?"

Bijou *tsked* at me. "Now is not the time to be flip,

dear. The Lord helps those who help themselves, you know, Wicca notwithstanding."

I looked at Evan to see him nodding along with all the little old ladies. Should've known he'd be a convert after the broken-heart experiment.

"Lord help me" was right.

I hadn't heard from Joe all day, but I figured we had time to grab a quick dinner before I met up with the little old ladies from La-La Land, so I called him around five that afternoon to see if he wanted to meet me at Nellie Belle's for some soul food after Evan and I closed up shop.

Disappointed when he didn't answer, I left him a message and went back to work. When I hadn't heard from him by six, I tried again, but this time his phone went straight to voice mail.

"Wanna grab a bite?" I asked Evan, as I tallied the day's receipts. He'd already locked the front door and was sweeping up.

"Sorry, no can do. I'm cooking chicken stir-fry for Butch tonight. It's his favorite dish." He smirked a little as he added, "Besides me, of course."

"Oh, how the worm has turned," I answered, smiling. "Yesterday the sky was falling, and today Chicken Little is having stir-fry with Foxy Loxy."

"I know," he said, grinning from ear to ear. "Isn't it wonderful?"

He held up his hand to admire his ring for the umpteenth time that day. "Platinum. Can you believe it?"

I could, actually. My best bud was worth his weight in gold, but platinum was even better.

"Are you two lovebirds having the bands engraved?"

Shaking his head, he gave a little shrug. "Butchie doesn't want to. Says by the time we get both of our names on there, it would be too hard to read, and he's right."

I gave him a puzzled look.

"His real name's Bartholomew," he said, trying hard not to laugh.

"Bartholomew?" I was already giggling, having no such compunctions.

"Bartholomew Andreas Bernaducci." Despite his best efforts, Evan burst out laughing. "Why do you think he goes by Butch?"

"It's better than Nicholette Nadine." I laughed, having always hated my middle name, even though I was named after my mom's sister. "Why do parents *do* that to their kids? When I have kids they're going to have normal names like Dave or Susie."

Evan arched a brow in my direction. "Anything you want to tell me?"

I wadded up a used sticky note and threw it at

him. "Bite your tongue. Kids are not on the agenda just yet."

He smirked at me. "Just wait until Joe pops the question. Your biological clock is ticking, you know."

Shamelessly, I gave him the finger. "Tick this."

He *tsked* absently and went back to sweeping. "Naughty, naughty. What would Dave and Susie say?"

I shook my head, knowing better than to encourage him. Pretty soon he'd be arranging play dates for my nonexistent offspring, and ordering baby T-shirts that said, "I only cry when ugly people hold me."

Which would be kind of cute, actually.

A few minutes later I sent Evan home to be with his big bald Italian bouncer, and found myself alone and very, very hungry. Breakfast had been a piece of toast, and lunch a single cheese biscuit I'd managed to snag before they were all gone. I tried one more time to reach Joe, with no success, then left by the front door, resigned to eating dinner by myself.

Nellie Belle's was a hole-in-the-wall, like so many places in Little Five, but they had the best barbecued ribs and corn on the cob in Atlanta. I slid into a booth near the back, glad to find one empty. It was a Friday night, and the place did a steady business, luckily most of it takeout. The red-checkered tablecloth was standard barbecue chic, as was the big jar of dill pickles in the middle of the table.

"What'll it be?" A dreadlocked black teenager slapped some napkins and silverware down in front of me as I got settled. There were no menus at Nellie's, just a chalkboard over the counter.

"Rib basket," I said, "and a Diet Coke. Large." My mouth was already watering—the smell of hickory smoke and baked beans permeated the place.

I could see Lou, the owner, flipping meat on the giant grill, his ever-present blue-and-white bandanna keeping the sweat from his eyes. Every now and then, he'd wipe his face with a napkin he kept stuck in his back pocket. Cleanliness was not next to godliness in a place like this, but I figured the heat took care of most of the germs.

Five minutes later I was chowing down on some falling-off-the-bone tender pork ribs. I had to close my eyes for a second, just to savor the tangy flavor of Lou's homemade barbecue sauce. When I opened them, there was an elderly black woman sitting across the table from me.

"Good, ain't they?" she said. Smiling and plump, she was watching me eat, and obviously enjoying my enjoyment.

I nodded, my mouth full of ribs.

"You need you some molasses corn bread to sop up that sauce." She was wearing a blue-and-white bandanna over her nappy hair, just like Lou, and a pair of horn-rimmed glasses. "Waste not, want not."

Swallowing, I reached for a napkin with fingers already sticky with barbecue sauce. "Don't worry," I said, wondering where she'd come from, "I won't waste any of it. I'm starving."

"Good," she said, nodding, "If you hungry, you come to the right place."

The guy who'd waited on me came up and slid a basket of corn bread on the table without saying a word, then walked away. The place was busy, and so was he, but I was surprised he hadn't asked the old woman what she wanted.

"Did you order already?" I was only trying to be polite. There was no place else for her to sit, and I wasn't going to begrudge an old woman a seat at my booth.

She waved a hand negligently in my direction. "Don't you worry about me none. I don't eat much."

Considering her girth, I somehow doubted that, but I wasn't going to argue—I just pushed the basket of bread toward her instead. "Have some corn bread while you wait. There's plenty."

Taking another bite of ribs, I looked around while I chewed, hoping she'd take the hint that I'd rather eat than chat.

She didn't. "Them ribs is smoked for eighteen hours—that's what makes 'em so tender. You tried the sausage yet? Mmm-mmm. You won't never eat sausage again without wishing it was Nellie Belle's sausage."

I was watching Lou cook while she talked. He was a master at work, moving meat around on the grill, rolling corncobs in butter and wrapping them in aluminum foil, stirring huge pots of baked beans and collard greens, all in a well-timed choreography of motion. On the wall over the grill was a bunch of plaques, some certificates, his business license and a framed dollar bill. But it was the picture in the middle of all those things that made me freeze, rib halfway to my mouth.

IN MEMORIAM—NELLIE BELLE BAYLESS 1923–1999—FOUNDER, LOVING MOTHER, AND BEST DAMN COOK ON THE PLANET. The woman in the picture was elderly, plump, black and wore a blue-and-white bandanna over horn-rimmed glasses.

"What's the matter, chile?" asked Nellie Belle. "You look like you seen a ghost." She laughed out loud, but there was no malice in her laughter.

I stared at her, not knowing what to say.

"Now, now, don't you fret none. I ain't going to hurt you. I just like seeing people enjoy they food, that's all. I seen you in here befo', haven't I?"

I nodded, still speechless.

"They's something different about you now, though. You got a light shinin' on you that wasn't there befo', and when I seen it, I says to myself, 'Nellie Belle, she understand. She gone be able to talk to you without running screamin' out the door.'" She sighed, leaning back in the booth. "It gets lonely sometimes with nobody to talk to." She looked over at Lou and gave him a fond smile. "My boy know I'm here, but he cain't talk to me, and I don't want to scare him none."

My brain hadn't made it past her first couple of sentences. "A light? I've got a light shining on me?"

She gave me her attention again, pushing her glasses up on her nose. "Sure enough. Don't you know about the Light?"

Confused, I nodded. If Nellie Belle knew about the Light, then what was she still doing here? "Yes, but I didn't know it was shining on me."

Chuckling, she crossed her arms over an ample belly. "Oh, it shinin' on you all right. You lit up like a star in a spotlight. You somethin' special."

Special?

"And I tell you somethin' else. That Light a sign that no matter what happens to you in this world, you're going to be all right in the next one, you know?"

I wanted to cry. How nice to hear those words, particularly after the week I'd had.

"Thanks," I said, in a voice barely above a whisper. "I needed to hear that."

" 'Course you did." Nellie Belle sat up straighter, putting her arms on the table. "Everybody need a little reassurance now and then."

"Can I"—I hesitated, having been burned before—"is there anything I can do for you?"

She tilted her head, looking puzzled at the question.

"I mean, is there anything I can do to help you find peace? You don't have to stay here, you know."

Nellie Belle laughed again, gesturing at the basket of corn bread. "Honey chile', as far as I'm concerned, this is Heaven—right here with my boy and my kitchen. I'll go when I'm ready, but I ain't ready yet."

I smiled, relieved. No life-altering task needed to be done today—yay!

"Now eat up," she said, "before it gets cold."

I took another bite of ribs, a big one.

"Good?" she asked.

Nodding, I wiped a dribble of barbecue sauce off my chin.

"That's all I need to hear," she said, and faded away before my eyes.

Shaking my head, I kept eating, knowing it made Nellie Belle happy. Made my stomach happy, too.

CHAPTER 20

I was halfway to my car when I realized that I didn't *have* a car—Joe had dropped me off, and I'd planned on getting a ride home with Evan. But Evan was long gone, and even though I could call him, I wasn't about to interrupt his romantic evening with Butch. I'd already left Joe a message, and he hadn't called me back, so I could only assume he was tied up or something.

Ooo, nice image. We'd have to try that sometime.

For now, since the waist on my jeans felt too tight and the day was mild, I decided to walk home. It was one of the advantages of living in the Little Five Points area—the neighborhoods were older but nice, plenty of sidewalks and shade. A half hour walk would be good for me and bring me home before full dark set in. Then I could freshen up, get in my car, and drive to the Embassy Suites for an evening of Wicca wackiness with the ladies of the Savannah Garden Club.

It didn't take long to leave the shopping district behind and get into the residential part of Little Five. The shadows were long beneath the oaks, but I wasn't worried—most of the crime occurred near the MARTA stations, just like in any big city with rapid transit. There were plenty of kids playing in their yards in the gathering dusk and plenty of people watching them. I knew these streets like the back of my hand, having ridden my bike up and down each and every one when I was kid.

One shadow, darker than all the others, ran right across the sidewalk in front of me and disappeared into some bushes. A black cat. *Crap.*

"That's a sign of bad luck, you know."

I spun around, knowing that sardonic tone all too well.

"What the hell? Are you *following* me now?"

"What the hell, indeed," Sammy said, strolling up as though he didn't have a care in the world. He was wearing dark red today, a long-sleeve T-shirt shoved up to the elbows, with a black logo of some kind on the front. Skinny black jeans and a low-slung belt. "I saw you through the front window as you were passing Divinyls and couldn't help but wonder where you were going." He grinned, completely unrepentant about practically stalking me. "After that, I simply became mesmerized by the sway of your hips. I had no idea I'd walked this far."

I gave him a disgusted look, letting him know I wasn't buying it. "Well, toddle on back to the Devil's playground, hot stuff. Surely you've got some CDs to sell." Spinning on my heel, I proceeded to walk on, ignoring him.

"Where's your boyfriend?" he asked, speeding up to walk alongside me. "Is the saintly doctor off saving lives? Finding a cure for cancer? Donating blood, perhaps?"

The way he asked told me he already knew the answer, damn him.

I kept my mouth shut and kept walking, refusing to play.

"He seems to like playing the hero, doesn't he?" Sammy admired the trees as he walked. "Particularly when there's a lovely damsel in distress involved. And Lisa certainly is lovely, in a smart-but-sexy-librarian kind of way."

That got my attention, as he knew it would.

"Why must you be such an asshole?" I asked him bluntly.

He shrugged, raising his hands, palms up. "It's what I do."

Fuming, I made up my mind to keep walking, faster now. *What was Joe doing with Lisa?*

Before I'd gotten three steps, he was beside me again. "Don't you want to know where they are?"

They? "No."

"Don't you care if she's trying to steal him away from you?"

"No."

"Don't you think I know when you're lying?" He laughed, an ironic chuckle that raised the hair on the back of my neck. "Hello . . . Father of Lies here."

"If that's the case, I pity your children," I bit out, still walking.

"Oh, Nicki," he said, shaking his head. "You're so fiery. Such spirit. It's hard to resist."

"Try, would you?" I was shouting now, not caring who heard. "Would you just *try*?"

He stopped, and I couldn't resist glancing over my shoulder at him—just to give him a dirty look, of course.

Why did he have to be so damned hot, *and* so damned cool at the same time?

"And don't think I don't know about your good buddy Sally Starshine or whatever her name is,"

I said, aggravated beyond reason. "She can send me all the bad-luck mojo she wants. It's not going to change a thing."

He burst out laughing. "I had nothing to do with that," he lied, the big liar.

"But you're not denying you know who she is."

He shook his head. "I'd be foolish to look a gift horse in the mouth, even when the horse looks more like a donkey."

I just glared at him, wishing I had the nerve to smack him, just once.

"But let's not change the subject," he said, smiling. Standing in the middle of the sidewalk, he shoved both hands in his pockets. "They're at the Blue Heron, on Piedmont. A life-or-death emergency requiring copious amounts of alcohol, I'm sure." He shrugged. "I do hope Lisa doesn't require mouth-to-mouth." And then he turned and walked back the way he came.

"Bastard," I muttered, but I wasn't sure, even in my heart of hearts, if I was talking about Sammy or Joe.

"Joe is not that kind of guy, Nicki."

I'd called my sister Kelly before I'd gone half a block.

"Then why is he at a bar with another woman,

and why is he not answering his phone?" I was whining, and I knew it, but I couldn't seem to help it.

"I don't know. Why *is* he at a bar with another woman and not answering his phone?" Kelly had that tone in her voice that reminded me of my mother. *Calm down, Nicki, and think about this rationally.* "Did you have a fight or something?"

"Not a fight exactly, but he did get mad over the Tina Cowart thing earlier today." I'd given her a brief rundown of the events at Tina's trailer already. "And by getting suspended from his job—which is my fault, no matter how you look at it."

"It's not your fault. It's the hospital's fault," she said, dismissing my feelings of guilt over that issue completely. "Who's the woman?"

My lip curled automatically. "She's the lawyer who represents the hospital. She claims she's on his side, but she really just wants to get in his pants."

Kelly laughed. "You're jealous."

"Am not."

She just laughed again, harder this time.

"Gee, Kelly, thanks a lot. I call you up for emotional support, and you just laugh at me." I was ready to hang up on her.

"Oh, c'mon, Nick. Joe's crazy about you. He's not

going to cheat on you with some woman lawyer. He hates lawyers."

"You haven't seen her," I said morosely. "She's not bad-looking." *In a smart-but-sexy-librarian kind of way, dammit.* "And she told Joe point-blank that she was attracted to him and that he should break up with me because I was bad for his career. I heard her myself."

"She said that in front of you?" Kelly was aghast.

"No, not really." I really didn't want to go into the eavesdropping session that Crystal had so nastily arranged. "It's complicated. But I heard her. She also told Joe that he should sue me for libel or slander or something like that, and the hospital would be more supportive over the inquiry into Crystal Cowart's death if he did. *That* part she said right in front of me." *The bitch.*

"Okay, it's official. We hate her guts."

I smiled for the first time since I'd started walking. That "we" made me feel better, even if Kelly was in Savannah, and I was in Atlanta. Having a sister might actually have some advantages, after all.

"Thank you. Now what do 'we' do about it?"

"Hmm . . . you could drive to the bar and pour a drink on her head."

I laughed out loud. "Not my style."

"You could go home, put on some sexy lingerie, and leave a very naughty message on Joe's voice mail that you're waiting for him with some whipped cream."

Much more my style, but the timing was bad.

"I can't. I have to go meet Bijou and the ladies of the Savannah Garden Club at their hotel for a cleansing ceremony or some such nonsense."

"Oh, it's not nonsense, Nicki," she said seriously. Should've known she'd be on Bijou's side when it came to the psychic mumbo-jumbo stuff. "Those women know what they're talking about. Wicca is meant to be used for good, but there's obviously a wicked witch somewhere. Let them help you. What could it hurt?"

I rolled my eyes.

"You're rolling your eyes, aren't you?"

"No."

"You're such a liar."

"So I've been told." I couldn't help but glance over my shoulder, just to make sure Sammy wasn't still following me.

"It'll be okay, I promise." She had no basis for promises like that, but it was sweet of her to make it, nonetheless.

Belatedly I realized that I'd been so busy whining about my life that I hadn't even asked her about hers. "So what are you doing tonight? It's a

Friday night—you shouldn't be rambling around The Blue Dahlia all by yourself."

"Spider's coming over any minute. We're going to have a picnic on the lawn and do some stargazing. He's got a really big telescope."

I burst out laughing. "Is that what he calls it?"

She burst out laughing, too. "No! It's an actual telescope! A great big one!"

At that point I was laughing so hard I barely managed to choke out, "I'm happy for you," before I gave up trying to say anything at all.

After that, it wasn't so hard to head on home and stop worrying about Joe and Lisa. For the time being, I was going to trust him.

Innocent until proven guilty, as a lawyer would say.

CHAPTER 21

After a quick in and out of the shower, a change of clothes, and a glass of wine to soothe my nerves, I was still tempted to drive to the Embassy Suites via Piedmont Avenue, but I resisted. It was out of the way, and I refused to give Sammy the satisfaction of knowing he'd gotten to me. He'd seemed to know everything else, dammit. There had to be a good reason why Joe was with Lisa, and I was sure he'd tell me all about it later.

Absolutely sure.

I could hear laughter coming from behind the door of Room 223 before I ever raised my hand to knock. Those little old ladies were obviously having a good old time in there, but so what? I'm sure it wasn't every day they got to hold a mini "Golden Years" convention to ward off the Evil Eye.

"There you are, dear." Bijou was smiling broadly as she opened the door. She enveloped me in a hug, which I returned. That was followed by several more hugs from various ladies, which I didn't mind; hugging was the equivalent of a handshake among Southern women. The buzz of conversation never stopped, punctuated by comments like, "Oh, this is going to be so exciting!" and "Isn't she just *darling*? Look at that figure!" and "Does she have a boyfriend? My grandson would be perfect for her!" all of which were spoken as though I were deaf.

Luckily, my glass of wine at home had been big enough to leave me mellow but sober, and I ignored the comments with good humor, smiling at everyone as if this truly were a garden party with my grandmother.

"Now you come sit right over here, dear," said Grandma Bijou, "and we'll explain what's about to happen."

I sank down on a chair, which had been placed in the middle of the floor, wondering how so many women managed to fit in one hotel room, suite or no suite. I glanced around, and with a start, realized what I'd failed to recognize earlier at the store—there were thirteen of them. Wasn't thirteen supposed to be an unlucky number?

"First, we'll sweep all negativity from the room, then we'll cast a symbolic circle of protection."

Uh-huh.

"We've actually decided to cast two circles," Bijou went on, quite seriously. "One of air, and one of earth. Estelle, here"—one of the women waved at me from the couch—"will lead us in the Rede—"

Which is where I interrupted her. "You mentioned this before. What the heck is a reed?"

"Not a 'reed,' dear, a 'Rede.'"

Uh-huh.

"R, E, D, E. A code of ethics, if you will." This from one of the women sitting on one of the two beds.

"Words to live by, so to speak," said another.

"Oh."

Bijou went on, unperturbed. "After negativity has been banished, and protection attained, we'll move on to the casting of a warding spell."

"A warding spell." I didn't bother to ask what a warding spell was, just repeated her words like they made some kind of sense.

"To reflect the Evil Eye back upon the one who cast it," piped up an old lady, whose name (I thought) was Betty.

Over in the corner, I heard a familiar grunt, and glanced that way to see Odessa, ensconced in the room's one wing chair. She held a wineglass, half-full. It looked completely out place in her pudgy fingers.

"That would be great," I said loudly, eyeing Odessa as narrowly as she did me. "Maybe I should write it down."

To my surprise, the corner of Odessa's lip curled into what might have been loosely interpreted as the beginnings of a smile, if she'd been capable of smiling. The curl was gone as quickly as it came, though, so I dismissed it as a figment of my imagination.

"You don't need to write it down," Bijou said placidly. "You just need to *believe* it."

And there lies the root of the problem.

"Okay," I said cheerfully. "Let's do this thing."

My grandmother gave me a warning look, and I knew she was onto me. She was a sensitive, after all, and my false cheerfulness wasn't fooling her a bit.

"Try, Nicki," she murmured. "Just try."

I winced, hating to hear my own words come back to me—I'd said the exact same thing to Sammy barely an hour before.

"Pearl will use her besom to sweep negative energy from the room before we begin."

I couldn't help myself. "Her *what*?"

One of the women got up and went to the closet, where she pulled out—of all things—a broom. A very old-fashioned one, too. It looked like a tree branch, with a bundle of twigs tied to the end.

"My besom," Pearl said, smiling at me. She held the broom with its bristles pointing toward the ceiling. "It's a handmade broom that's been consecrated."

I just nodded and tried to look duly impressed, not knowing what to say.

"All right now, girls," said Bijou. "Time to get down to business."

There was a general tinkle of wineglasses as they were gathered up and put down on a table by the door, and a flurry of anticipatory noises as thirteen elderly women got themselves settled on the two double beds. The only one who didn't move was Odessa, who took another sip of her wine and held on to the glass.

Then Pearl flipped her broom over, and began to make sweeping motions over the rug.

"Sweep out evil, sweet out doom,
Round and round and round the room."

I couldn't help but notice that she didn't actually touch the floor with her besom—those twigs must be pretty delicate. She moved along, loosely covering the whole room, between the beds and by the window.

> *"Out with darkness, in with light,*
> *Only good be here this night."*

A grin threatened, but I kept it under control. Everyone was watching Pearl, and they all looked so *serious*.

> *"We banish ill, we banish thee,*
> *And invoke the Law of Three."*

Pearl hardly had the look of a witch—she looked like she'd be more at home baking cookies than anything else.

> *"Thrice around the room I go,*
> *Thrice above, and thrice below."*

On her third trip around the room, she stopped by the door and opened it wide.

> *"Besom, besom, lady's broom,*
> *Sweep out evil, sweep out gloom!"*

And darned if she didn't sweep her imaginary

gloom out into the hallway, just as if she was sweeping dirt out the back door of her house. Then she flipped her broom upside down, so the bristles were pointing up again, and closed the door.

Collective murmurs of satisfaction came from the old ladies on the beds, including an approving grunt from Odessa, but I didn't dare make eye contact with any of them.

"Helen will now cast the circle of air," Bijou announced, very formally.

A tiny little woman with her hair in a bun struggled up off the bed, aided by the women next to her. She picked up something from the bedside table. It looked like another besom, only much smaller—a hand-sized bundle of twigs, tied with twine. Then she picked up the lighter sitting beside it and flicked her Bic like she'd done it a million times. Holding the lighter to the bundle of twigs, she set it on fire. It flared, then subsided, one end glowing red and smoking like a chimney.

> *"Sacred sage, burning free,*
> *Clear our path, help us see."*

Helen's voice was as thin and reedy as her body. She began waving the bundle of sticks over everyone's head.

"Protect us as we gather here,
Banish worry, banish fear."

If I were them, I'd be worried about sparks falling in my hair. Or setting off the smoke detector.

"Cast a circle, round about,
Evil thoughts, get thee out!"

The burning sage made my nose sting and my eyes water. It smelled a little like weed, and I hoped we didn't get busted for it. I could see it now: *Seriously, Officer, we're not smoking pot, we're just burning herbs to drive away evil spirits.*

Thankfully, that part was soon over. Helen went into the bathroom and doused her sage sticks under running water, while one of the other ladies waved a red ostrich plume (probably from somebody's hat) around the room, helping to dissipate the smoke.

"Vera will now cast the circle of earth," Bijou said calmly.

Vera was as round as Helen was thin, and she popped up from the bed with a bowl in her hands.

I assumed it would be dirt—*the maids would've loved that*—but it turned out to be salt, which she sprinkled in a circle directly around my chair, murmuring some chant about purification and protection. Frankly, I'd stopped listening.

Then Bijou stood up and moved to the table beside Odessa. It was a desk, really, where busy businessmen could handle their business while staying at the Embassy Suites. There were candles on it, which I'd noticed before but paid little attention to. Now I quickly counted six white ones, and one black, plus a bowl full of something right in the middle.

Bijou lit the six white candles, while a couple of the other ladies got up and turned off the bedside lamps and the light in the entryway.

And that was when I started to get nervous, the flickering candlelight reminding me of at least two other occasions when I'd ended up scared shitless—once in a hidden voodoo room and the other in the basement of an old house in Savannah. Candlelight and romance were great, but candlelight and rituals seemed to be a bad combination.

I got even more nervous when all the old ladies, including Bijou, formed a circle around my chair, holding hands. No more sweet little smiling faces; no more smiles, period. Odessa was the only one still sitting. For the first time ever, I wished I could join her over there, snug in her corner.

Estelle, the woman who'd waved at me earlier, cleared her throat. As if that had been the cue they'd been waiting for, they all started chanting, in unison:

> *"Bide the Wiccan Laws we must*
> *In perfect love and perfect trust.*
> *Cast the circle thrice about*
> *To keep the evil spirits out,*
> *To bind the spell every time*
> *Let the spell be spake in rhyme."*

Well, that explained at least one question I had as to why everything they said sounded like a nursery rhyme.

Then they recited a bunch of stuff about the moon, and wind, and burning and stuff, none of which made the least bit of sense to me.

> *"Merry meet and merry part,*
> *Bright the cheeks, warm the heart,*
> *Mind the Threefold Law you should*
> *Three times bad and three times good."*

Three seemed to be a big number for Wiccans, for some reason. Maybe I should use it when I played the lottery.

> *"Eight words the Wiccan Rede fulfill;*
> *An ye harm none, do what ye will."*

I figured I was supposed to feel better by now, but I didn't.

Bijou stepped back from the circle, and her place was immediately filled in by the two women on either side of her joining their own hands.

I watched as she went back to the candles and, picking up a white one, used it to light the black one. Then, using the black one, she lit whatever was in the bowl in the center of the candles. A weird scent filled the air, mingling with the lingering scent of burning sage, sweet and spicy at the same time. Then, still holding the black candle, she walked toward me. The women unclasped hands to let her inside the circle, then clasped them again as she stood by my chair.

"After the warding spell is cast," she said to me, "you must say, 'I cast you out', quite firmly. Then blow this black candle out, as hard as you can."

I nodded, to show I understood, but kept my mouth shut. I just wanted this *over*.

> *"Whatever evil threatens here,*
> *We cast you out, we have no fear."*

The women repeated what she said word for word. It was eerie, and I couldn't stop the scene from *Macbeth* from flashing through my mind. All we needed was a cauldron and some cackling.

"Harmful wishes, dark of night,
Be dispelled by the light,
As the moon reflects the sea,
As we will, so mote it be!"

She thrust the black candle in front of my face, startling me.

Taking the hint, I said loudly, "I cast you out!" then blew out the candle.

"Ah." There was a collective sigh of relief from the old ladies.

I looked around, bewildered, as they dropped each other's hands and started chattering like a flock of hens.

"Wasn't that wonderful? I feel marvelous."

The lights came on as the clucking continued. "It was magical, wasn't it? I swear I felt a tingle down my spine during the earth circle."

"That was your arthritis, dear, but I must agree it was wondrous."

My stunned gaze went to Odessa, who regarded me calmly for a moment, then leaned over and blew the white candles out, one by one. The stuff in the bowl wasn't even smoldering.

"Now, I want you to go home and take a ritual bath to cleanse yourself of any lingering negativity," said Grandma Bijou briskly. She thrust a little bag into my hand. "Put this in the water, just like you would bath salts."

"That was it?" I had to admit, I was surprised by how abruptly the whole thing ended. *No lightning? No thunder? No evil spirits popping up to say, 'Boo'?*

Grandma Bijou gave me a little mock frown. "What did you expect, dear? Lightning? Thunder? Evil spirits popping up to say, 'Boo'?"

With a sigh, I gave up. Having a sensitive for a grandmother meant I was never going to be able to truly hide what I was thinking.

Not that I was any good at that to begin with.

"Off you go," she said, making shooing motions with her hands. "Bath time. No dilly-dallying."

CHAPTER 22

I'd already had two showers today, but a long, hot bath didn't seem like such a bad idea. Maybe some Elvis Costello on the CD player and a second glass of wine to go along with it. Might keep me from wondering why Joe still wasn't answering his phone, though it was almost nine o'clock.

Luckily for me, I didn't have to wonder long—his BMW was sitting in my driveway when I pulled up. Breathing a sigh of relief, I put the car in PARK and got out of it in record time.

Joe was sitting on my porch swing, waiting.

"Hey, baby!" I forced myself to sound cheerful and upbeat. Though I was bursting with questions, I only allowed myself one. "Where've you been?"

"I had some things to think about." He didn't get up from the swing, and my heart sank at the quietness of his tone.

I kept a smile, leaning in for a kiss before I unlocked the front door. There was beer on his breath.

Sammy's words came back to me. *They're at the Blue Heron, on Piedmont. A life-or-death emergency requiring copious amounts of alcohol, I'm sure.*

So he'd had a beer. So what? "You missed some great barbecued ribs at Nellie Belle's," I said lightly. "I needed serious sustenance before I went to meet with Bijou and her friends."

A noncommittal grunt answered me as he got up from the swing. "Why don't I have a key to your place?" he asked, abruptly. "You have a key to mine."

Surprised, I stopped, the key in question already halfway into the lock. "I—" Why *hadn't* I given him a key? Shrugging, I just said, "I'll have one made for you tomorrow."

Another grunt. He definitely wasn't acting himself, and it was beginning to make me nervous.

"Is everything okay?" I'd left a lamp on in the foyer and in the living room—coming home to a dark house was a habit I'd left behind once

I'd started seeing spirits—so I could see his face clearly as I put my purse down on the table by the door.

He wasn't smiling. There was definitely something on his mind—the way he ran his fingers through his hair as he walked past me was a dead giveaway.

"I can't stand this," he said quietly.

My heart stuttered.

"I have patients to see, people who were depending on me."

The rhythm steadied, racing now.

"Four years of medical school, a year of internship, two and a half more as a resident." He swung around to face me. "Did you know I'm one of the youngest E.R. department heads in the country?"

I shook my head, not trusting my voice at the moment.

He went on. "I've worked my ass off since high school for a job like this. Scholarships weren't enough to pay my college tuition, so I had to get student loans and part-time jobs. More student loans to get through medical school. Sleepless nights, sleepless days, no personal life." Pacing back and forth in front of the couch, hands on hips. "All of it, taken away in an instant." He snapped his fingers, quick and hard. "Because of a woman."

I seemed to have forgotten how to breathe. Or move. Or speak.

Joe stopped pacing and stood staring down at the carpet. "That Lisa is a piece of work," he muttered.

Breath came back to my lungs with a rush. My knees were wobbly, and so was my voice. "L-Lisa?"

"Oh, yeah." He still wasn't looking at me, not realizing how close I'd come to complete and total heart failure. "She laid it all out on the table tonight. Called me up, wanted me to meet her so we could talk about lifting my suspension. 'I can make it all go away,'" he mimicked, in a mocking falsetto. "She has those old farts on the board eating out of her hand." Shaking his head, he made a disgusted noise. "What a power trip that woman is on. She's actually trying to pressure me into bed with her—how's that for a turnaround on the old sexual-harassment cliché, huh? Can you believe it?" He finally lifted his head and looked at me.

What he saw got his attention—I obviously wasn't as good at hiding my emotions as I thought. "Are you okay?" He came striding toward me, hand outstretched. "You look like you're about to pass out."

I tried to laugh, still shaky. "I might be."

He had me by the elbow now, slipping his other

arm around my waist. I let him lead me to the couch and sank down on it, shaking my head. He went down on one knee in front of me, eyes searching, hands holding mine. Looking him full in the face, seeing the concern all over it, I decided to be honest.

"I thought you were about to dump me."

His eyebrows shot to the ceiling. "What? What are you talking about?"

What a lovesick wimp I was—I knew it, but there was nothing I could do about it. "You were talking about your career, and how it'd been ruined by a woman . . ."

Comprehension dawned. He started to smile.

". . . I'd been trying to reach you, and you weren't answering your phone . . ."

His grin got wider.

". . . and you said you couldn't stand this anymore and I thought . . ."

He burst out laughing.

"What's so funny?" I demanded. "I'm pouring my heart out here!"

"You love me," he said, still laughing.

"Duh," I said scathingly, feeling defensive.

"No, I mean you really love me." He was smiling so big it made me want to smile, too, except I was too busy feeling like an idiot. "You're afraid of losing me."

"And this is funny because . . . ?"

He rose from his kneeling position and sat next to me on the couch, pulling me against him. "Because it isn't going to happen," he said softly. "And because I'm the one who's constantly worried about losing you."

I looked at him beneath my lashes. "You are?"

He made an exasperated noise. "For such a smart girl, you can be pretty stupid."

A gasp of outrage escaped me, but Joe wasn't finished. "I lost you once already, Nicki. I pulled the sheet over your white, sweet face, thinking your eyes were closed forever." The pain in his voice kept me quiet. He paused a second, looking away. "I didn't even know you at the time, but I thought my heart would break at what I must've missed."

He turned his head toward me again, eyes roving my face and hair. "Then you came back. And then I found out I had to share you with invisible people, a gay guy, an elderly transvestite, a twin sister who used to be my wife, and a heart condition." He smiled again, just a little. "And oh, by the way, Satan himself has the hots for you, so I have to deal with that."

"Joe, I—"

"Shh," he murmured, shaking his head. "And you wonder why I worry about *losing* you?" His eyes went all tender, while I turned into a giant pile of mush. "That's what's so funny, Nick. It's kind of nice to see the shoe on the other foot for a change, and have you worried about losing *me*."

The mush overflowed, and I burst into tears.

Much to his credit, Joe didn't try and get me to stop. He just let me cry, let me cling to him—smearing mascara and snot all over his shirt in the process—and let me be a lovesick wimp for a few more minutes.

And when I was all cried out, he got up, went into the kitchen for a paper towel for me to dry my tears and blow my nose in, and handed it to me without a word.

"I am such a wuss," I finally said, throat still clogged with tears.

"Yes, but you're my wuss," he answered, quite seriously.

Rolling my eyes, I attempted to wipe the worst of the eyeliner from my cheeks.

He plopped himself down on the couch next to me, watching as I tried to mop up the after-effects of my waterworks. "You didn't tell me how things went with Bijou tonight." I knew he was just trying to get my mind off my meltdown. He knew all about the plans for the cleansing cere-mony, of course, even if he thought it was a bunch of hoo-ha, just like I did.

"It was fine, I guess." I waved the paper towel vaguely. "A lot of rhyme, not a whole lot of reason. Tons of buildup without a concrete conclusion. Kinda like foreplay, without the orgasm."

He stood up and started unbuttoning his soggy, smeared shirt. "Finally," he said, with a smile and an exaggerated sigh. "Something I can fix."

I couldn't help but laugh, teary-eyed or not. But then I remembered something. "Um, I have to take a bath first."

He quirked an eyebrow at me, tugging his shirt from his jeans. "Why? Have you done something dirty?"

I threw the paper towel at him, giggling at his suggestive teasing. "Not today."

"Ah. Well, we're about to remedy that situation." Now shirtless, Joe tossed the shirt onto the couch and started unbuckling his belt.

"Bijou told me to take a ritual bath as soon as I got home," I said, feeling less and less inclined to do so. "To cleanse myself of negativity."

The sound of a zipper completely stole my concentration. Either that, or it was just the sight of a gorgeous, tousle-headed Joe wearing nothing but a partially unzipped pair of jeans and a smile.

He leaned in, placing one hand on the arm of

the couch, until his lips were inches from mine. "Did she say you had to take it by yourself?"

"No," I whispered, cupping his face with my palms, then letting them slide over the smooth expanse of wide, bare shoulders.

"Problem solved," he murmured.

CHAPTER 23

I woke with a start, knowing something was wrong, but not knowing what it was. The bed beside me was empty.

Then I heard it again—the sound of retching in the bathroom. Throwing back the covers, I headed that way automatically; I didn't think Joe had had *that* many beers.

But it wasn't Joe. I flipped on the bathroom light to see bony shoulders, blond hair, a figure so stick-thin I could count the knobs of her spinal column through her T-shirt. Crystal Cowart was hunched over my toilet, puking her nonexistent guts out.

I stood in the doorway, not knowing what to

do or what to say. Part of me just wanted to go back to bed and pull the covers over my head, but there was another part of me that hated to leave her there, alone and obviously miserable. I'd done my share of puking back in my wild days, and it was no fun. When you were dead, like Crystal, even a cold washcloth to the face wouldn't help.

Finally, she raised her head and sank back on her skinny haunches. "What are you looking at?" she asked me, sullenly. "Never seen anyone throw up before?"

She looked awful. Dark circles beneath her eyes, lanky hair, all angles and elbows. I was hugely relieved to see nothing in or on the toilet—whatever she'd been throwing up was as insubstantial as she was.

"What are you doing here, Crystal?" I kept my voice level with an effort. My own stomach was doing flips, but I didn't want her to know it.

She sneered at me, showing those ugly yellow teeth again. "I'm being punished."

"Punished?"

"He made me eat."

I didn't need to ask who "he" was. What a diabolical thing to do—force an anorexic to eat. That was like making a germaphobe lick an ashtray or something.

"Your stupid boyfriend isn't cooperating with the 'breakup plan,'"—she used bone-thin fingers to make hash marks in the air—"no matter how hard I make things for him." Shaking her head in disgust, she wiped her mouth with the back of her wrist and leaned against the wall. "You must be a hell of a lay."

My chin went up. "Thank you. I am, actually."

She gave a short laugh, looking very tired. "Some guys like fat girls. No accounting for taste."

I didn't bother to argue with her over whether I was fat or not. It wasn't worth it, not with someone who had body-image issues so severe. Besides, now that I knew the truth behind Crystal's spitefulness, she'd lost a lot of the ability to push my buttons.

I repeated my question. "What are you doing here?"

She looked away instead of meeting my gaze. "You're the only one who can see me. The only one who knows I'm still here."

The only one she can talk to.

Standing there, barefoot, wearing nothing but a pair of panties and camisole top, I felt her vulnerability as though it were my own. I should hate her—she'd been making my life a living hell all week. Climbing into my brain, taking over my body, trying to ruin my love life.

But the bottom line was, I still *had* a life, and she didn't.

"What did Sammy promise you to get you to make a deal with him?" I asked the question very quietly.

She shrugged. "A chance to get even." She met my eyes, defiant now. "A chance to be *heard*."

"Get even with who?"

"Your boyfriend," she spat. "The guy who let me die."

I just looked at her.

"With the world, okay?" She was shouting now. "With the whole fucking world!"

I had a button of my own to push, but it was for her own good. "What about Jimmy Boyd?"

The glare she gave me would've shriveled fruit. She was still sitting on the floor next to the toilet, but she moved so that her back was in the corner, drawing up her knees in an unconscious posture of protection.

"You had a chance to help me get even with him, but you wouldn't," she said bitterly.

I made an exasperated noise. "Me going to jail for bashing some guy over the head is *not* what I had in mind. I offered to get your mother to believe you were telling the truth about him, and to keep him away from Amber Marie, remember?"

She looked away, obviously seething. "Yeah, well she didn't believe you any more than she did me, now did she?" The hurt was there, in her voice, behind the fury.

I vaguely remembered reading that anger and cloudy thinking were one of the classic symptoms of anorexia—lack of nourishment affected the brain as well as the body. "You're letting your anger control you, Crystal. It's eating you up inside." It was the wee hours of the morning, I was half-naked, and I was reasoning with a dead girl. The odds were stacked against me, but I kept going. "*Think.* There must be some way to expose Boyd for the creep that he is without murder being part of the plan."

"You don't understand," she muttered. "It doesn't matter anymore anyway."

"Why not?" I refused to give up just yet. She was still here, still talking, so there must be something she wanted, something I could do to help her move on.

"Because I made a deal," she said, glancing in my direction without meeting my eyes. "I made a deal." Her voice lowered. "It's not like I can back out of it now."

I sighed, almost wishing Sammy were here so I could wring his horny neck. This was his fault— all of it.

Squatting in the doorway so we'd be at eye level, I searched for the right words, hoping they'd come. "You know what I think?"

She didn't answer.

"I think the Devil only has as much power over you as you give him."

She started picking at a spot on her jeans, near the knee.

"I think your soul belongs to you, no matter what kind of deal you made." Taking a deep breath, I plunged in deeper. "I think that once your anger is resolved, your spirit will be free, and you'll be able to make a final choice as to where you want to ultimately go."

She finally looked at me, just a little, from the corner of her eye.

I pointed upward. "It's a whole lot nicer up there, I promise."

"Gee, you sound a lot like Jimmy," she said sarcastically. "Streets of gold? Pearly gates and a heavenly choir of angels?" A rude snort followed. "Please."

Undaunted, I shook my head. "No. It's not like that. I didn't see any streets of gold or pearly gates." Now angels—that was something else, but I wasn't willing to call the shifting shapes and colors I'd seen *angels*, exactly. They were something entirely beyond understanding. "It was beautiful, though. Bright, shining. Peaceful. And I wouldn't call it a heavenly choir, but there *was* music, of a sort."

I was at a loss to describe those pure tones, pulsing and changing, color and music and emotion combined. How they filled the air, and how they made me feel part of them—part of *everything*.

"You're full of shit," she said flatly.

"I'm telling the truth."

Suspicious, she eyed me from her spot in the corner.

"Why should I trust you? The last time I trusted anybody religious, it got me raped." She shook her head, disgusted, remembering. "What a stupid, fucking kid I was."

My gorge rose at the mental image that presented. A little towheaded girl, and a man at least twice her age—a man she trusted.

"He did it in the back of a crappy little revival tent in the middle of nowhere." Another ugly sneer. "Hallelujah, sister. Praise the Lord."

I forced myself to swallow hard, and not look away from those hard eyes, just barely gleaming with tears.

"I'm not religious," I said carefully. "I don't even go to church. I just know what I'm talking about when it comes to what happens when you die."

"So do I," she flared, practically snarling the words.

I shook my head no. "You've only seen one side of it. I've seen the other. Darkness and light go hand in hand, Crystal, and you're stuck in the Dark."

She didn't answer at first. A single tear escaped and slid quietly down her cheek. Her face looked like a death mask.

I waited.

"He'll never let me go," she finally whispered.

Taking a deep breath, I said something I knew I shouldn't. "You let me worry about him."

"Nicki?" Joe's voice startled me, coming down the hall from the darkened living room. "What are you doing?"

I rose from my squat and glanced in his direction. He walked into the pool of light spilling from the bathroom, wearing nothing but boxer briefs, holding the remains of a half-eaten apple.

Giving him a halfhearted smile, I said, "Stepped on something. Just looking to see what it was."

He answered me with a sleepy grunt and took another bite of his apple. "Okay," he mumbled, around the bite, heading toward the bedroom. "I'm going back to bed."

"I'll be there in a minute."

When I looked back, it was no surprise to find the corner between the tub and toilet empty. I went in and shut the door behind me.

"Crystal?"

I didn't really expect a reply.

CHAPTER 24

"You need to get yourself to church, girl."

I'd never expected to take advice from someone like Tina Cowart, but the words she'd said when I'd tried to confront her about Jimmy Boyd stuck with me. Going back to Tina's trailer seemed like a bad idea unless I wanted to be arrested for trespassing, so first thing Saturday morning, I decided to revisit the hallowed halls of every self-respecting Gen-Xer's favorite church, the Internet. I Googled everything I could find on a certain child-molesting evangelist/creep, and hit pay dirt.

Hearts on Fire Tabernacle, just north of Atlanta, on the outskirts of Marietta. Services on Wednesday night, Saturday afternoon, and Sunday morning.

Joe had already left for the gym, and Saturday was our busiest day of the week at the store, so I printed out the address, stuffed it in my purse, and tried to figure out what to do next as I drove into Little Five.

Bright lights, flashing blue and red in my rearview mirror, got my attention. "Shit," I groaned. "Shit, shit, shit."

So much for deflecting the Evil Eye with brooms and rhymes and candles. My luck had obviously yet to change.

I pulled over and put the car in PARK, knowing I was about to get cited, yet again, for an expired tag. With everything that had gone on this week, I'd completely forgotten to get my inspection— hadn't paid my tickets yet, either.

Keeping my hands on the steering wheel, I let my forehead fall forward and rest there, too, knowing from past experience that this could take a while.

"License and registration, please."

I lifted my head, expecting to see another big dumb Deputy Do Right with aviator sunglasses and a bad-ass attitude.

"Nicki? Nicki Styx?"

My mouth fell open. "Billy?" My very first boy-friend from the eighth grade, Billy Babcock, stood grinning at me, one hand on the car and one hand hooked in the belt of his uniform.

"Damn, girl, you are looking good!" he said, pulling off his sunglasses. "How've you been?"

The last time I'd seen Billy had been our senior year of high school, almost ten years before, but he still had that boyishly cute quality that appealed to the thirteen-year-old me. Except now he had a crew cut, and a badge.

"I can't believe it." I laughed. "You're a cop!"

Billy had the grace to flush a little under his tan, grinning bigger than ever. "Yeah," he said. "Who'da thunk it?"

I knew he was remembering the time we almost got caught shoplifting at the convenience store near the school. I'd wanted some lemon sours, and he'd wanted a candy bar, and neither of us had any money. We'd snatched our goodies and run like hell, while the Asian woman behind the counter screamed at us in Vietnamese.

"Billy Babcock." I shook my head, still surprised to see him looking so grown-up. "My very first kiss."

Now he *really* blushed, reminding me again of why I'd found him so cute. He'd always been such a sweetheart.

"I'm married now," he blurted. "Two kids. Wanna see?"

Before I say "boo," he'd whipped out his wallet and was showing off his pride and joys. "This is

Adam, and this here's Jessica," he said, tapping a school photo of a little boy who looked about seven, and another of a little girl of three or four. The girl was perched in the lap of a heavyset, smiling woman with long brown hair. "That's my wife, Annie," he added, obviously happy about it. "We've been married nine years now."

"They're beautiful," I said, sincerely. "All three of them." Okay, Annie wasn't beautiful, but she looked *nice*, and that was more important.

"What about you?" Billy tucked his wallet back into his pocket, for all the world as if we'd met in the mall instead of him pulling me over.

"Still single," I said, smiling brightly at him. "No kids. I own a vintage clothing store down in Little Five Points."

"Still marching to the beat of a different drummer, aren't you? Pink hair." He shook his head, grinning. "You need to get yourself a good man, a couple of kids—that'll settle you right down."

"It's all your fault, Billy," I said lightly, flirting just a little. "You ruined me for any other guy after that first kiss—how many thirteen-year-olds get a romantic moment like that?"

It *had* been romantic, actually. I'd been spending the night with one of my friends, who was Billy's neighbor. They lived on a lake. It was a full moon, and while my friend Joy waited on the shore, talking to Billy's brother, he'd taken me out in the canoe. Somewhere in the middle of the lake he'd stopped paddling and just looked at me. Before I knew it, we'd leaned in and kissed. A chaste kiss, but a sweet one. Looking back, we'd probably been lucky the canoe hadn't capsized.

He laughed, slipping his sunglasses back on, probably hoping to hide the fact that he was blushing more than ever. "Okay, okay—no need to butter me up. I'm not going to give you a ticket."

I breathed a sigh of relief. "You're not? Then why'd you pull me over?"

"Your tag's expired, and you're burning oil like crazy," he said. Reaching into the front pocket on his shirt, he pulled out a business card. "You remember my brother, Danny?"

Danny was older, and not nearly as cute. "Sure."

"He owns a gas and lube place over on Euclid and Belmont. Tell him I sent you, and remind him he owes me a favor. He'll get you fixed up."

"Billy, I—"

"No need to thank me," he said, slapping his hand on the door frame in farewell. "Just get that leak fixed and renew that tag, ASAP."

I gave him a mock salute. "Yes, sir!"

He laughed again, backing away as he headed toward his cruiser. "Bye bye, angel eyes. You take care now."

Angel eyes. I'd forgotten how he used to call me that. "Bye, Billy," I called, craning my neck out the window to watch him go. "Thank you!"

A final wave before he got in his cruiser and pulled back out on the highway.

I sat there a minute, filled with good memories and feeling more than just a little lucky. Maybe Bijou and her geriatric buddies had been right, after all. Maybe the Evil Eye curse—or whatever it was—had been lifted.

My smile faded, though, when I remembered what I'd been thinking about when Billy pulled me over.

Crystal Cowart's memories of when she was thirteen were very different from mine.

Tina Cowart, misguided religious fanatic that she was, was right. I needed to get myself to church.

"You're nuts," Evan said to me. "You're likely to burst into flame the minute you walk into that place. Hardly lived your life as a saint, now have you?" He shook his head. "Hearts on Fire Tabernacle—and you've got a bad heart. It's a sign. A bad sign."

I gave him a sour look. "Thanks for the vote of confidence, smart-ass."

We were rearranging the racks as we did almost every morning, making sure the sizing was lined up properly. People tended to put things back wherever they happened to be standing at the moment, and nobody wanted to see size 4s in the size 12 areas.

"I'm just sayin'," he went on, with an innocent air that fooled no one, least of all me. "Bad girls don't belong in church."

"I'm not a bad girl anymore, remember?"

He waved a hand, brushing away my words.

The shop bell tinkled, and we both automatically turned to see who'd come in. Evan's choked gasp barely covered my own.

"What have you done to me?" demanded one of the women who stood there. At least I thought it was a woman—for a minute I thought it was a gray-haired troll. Her face was covered in lumps and ugly red blotches. Combined with her lack of height, extreme roundness, and scraggly long hair, she didn't look quite human. The other woman looked normal, except for the worried look on her face.

"You won't get away with this," the troll said, shaking a finger at me as she advanced. "The Sisters of Circe are a powerful coven. Whatever spell you've cast won't last for long!"

And then it hit me; this was Shadow Starhawk or whatever she called herself, and she was not happy. I should've been freaked—she was certainly scary to look at—but instead I burst out laughing.

"Oh my God," I said between giggles. "It worked. It actually *worked*."

Her face turned redder than ever. "You don't know who you're dealing with, girl."

"Oh yes, I do. Climb back on your besom and fly away, you wicked old witch."

Evan looked horrified, and one look at his face sent me into fresh peals of laughter. I couldn't help it—I felt so *relieved*.

"Mind the threefold law you should," I quoted, dragging the words up from my memory of last night, "three times bad and three times good." Shaking my head in amazement, I added, "You must've cast one nasty spell on me, girlfriend, because now you've got it three times as bad!"

I thought the woman's head was going to explode. "You . . . you—"

"Now, now." I shook my head as well as my finger, and recited, "I'm rubber, you're glue—bounce off me and stick on you." Childish, but appropriate. I knew what I was doing was like poking a stick at a scorpion, but I couldn't help it. She'd started it, after all.

"You broke the Rede," I went on sagely, as if I really knew what I was talking about. "You had to know there would be consequences."

The woman with her grabbed her by the arm, tugging her backward. "Sally," she murmured, eyeing me warily. "Leave it alone. Let's go."

"Listen to your friend," I said boldly, deciding to brazen it out, "before I call in my celestial sisters again, the Silver Belles. They're pretty ticked off about somebody practicing black magic on their turf." Total bullshit, of course, but Sally Starhawk didn't know that.

That seemed to shut the troll up. She was still fuming, but she couldn't quite meet my eyes anymore. The normal-looking one sent me a look of apology, and I was suddenly certain who'd left the white basket of remedies on my doorstep.

"Sorry for the trouble, Miss Styx," the nicer one said. "We'll go now."

"Only mundanes call me Miss Styx." I was having *way* too much fun with this. "You can call me by my craft name—Helen Damnation."

"Let's go, Sally," she said, tugging at her blotchy friend. "I'll make you a poultice."

One final dirty look from the gray-haired troll, and they left.

"Blessed be," I called gaily, before the door shut behind them.

"What the hell was all *that* about?" Evan looked stunned, and more than a little confused. "The Silver Belles? Helen Damnation? Where did all *that* come from?"

"It just popped into my head," I answered, grinning. "I was inspired." I was so glad to see the last of Sally's great big backside that I wasn't going to question where the words came from. "Let's send some flowers to Bijou's hotel, okay? I think my luck has turned."

CHAPTER 25

"Can I get an 'amen'?" Jimmy Boyd shouted, and at least seventy-five people answered, in a full-throated roar.

"Amen!"

"Can I get a 'hallelujah'?" He was striding back and forth on a raised stage area, microphone in hand. The other hand held a Bible, raised high.

"Hallelujah!"

Hearts on Fire Tabernacle was a ramshackle old building that looked like it had once been a barn or a big storage shed. It had been painted white, but outside the paint was peeling, and inside it smelled musty, like mildew or dirty laundry. Or maybe it was just the people who smelled—

several of them had worked themselves into such a frenzy that they were sweating like pigs. One chubby guy near the front looked like somebody had dumped a bucket of water over his head.

"Today we're going to talk about the anointing of the Holy Spirit," Jimmy shouted, "and what it will mean to your lives."

Shouts and moans came from the crowd around me. It was weird to see people behaving like this; hands upraised, bodies rocking back and forth as though they couldn't stand still—Jimmy Boyd had apparently been preaching up a storm before I got there. I'd slipped in the door and taken a seat in the back without anyone noticing me. The pews were just hard wooden benches—no frills.

"The angel of healing is among us today—can you feel him?" Jimmy shook his Bible in the air as everyone shouted an affirmative.

"Oh, I do hope Raphael is here," murmured a silky voice in my ear. "I haven't seen him in several millennia. It would be such fun to catch up."

I was beyond being startled by another surprise visit from Sammy. "You are *unbelievable.*" I turned my head to stare. "Have you no shame? Get out of here."

He looked mildly offended. "It's a free country. We all have the right to worship as we choose."

"Black mass canceled?" I asked snippily.

A gleam of laughter lit his eyes.

He looked fabulously cool today, as usual. White button-down shirt that would've looked boring on anyone else, worn untucked over jeans. His blond hair looked like he'd just rolled out of bed and run his fingers through it, leaving it mussed in all the right places.

"I amuse you, is that it?" Nobody was paying the least attention to us, thankfully. Too much shouting and "holy rolling" going on. "Screwing with my life must be one big laugh riot."

He widened his eyes, faking innocence. "You won't let me screw with anything else."

He got a dirty look for that, which he ignored.

Cocking his head, he remarked, "You've lost all fear of me for some reason. It's quite intriguing. You know what I'm capable of—or have you forgotten our little rendezvous in the basement with Saundra?"

That got my attention, as he'd known it would. I swallowed hard, trying not to remember that night in Savannah—the sight of once-pretty Saundra turning into a three-week-old corpse before my eyes. Purplish green flesh falling from the bone, and the smell . . .

"I understand you've been talking to Crystal behind my back, trying to get her to go back on our deal. How very naughty of you."

"I hate you," I said quietly. Not that anyone could hear me over Jimmy Boyd's shouting—he was whipping the crowd into a frenzy, the chorus of hallelujahs and amens louder than ever.

"No, you don't," he returned. "You want to, but you don't."

To my shock, he reached over and took my hand. Ignoring my attempt to snatch it back, he brought it to his knee and pressed it there, forcing me to feel the muscle and sinew beneath the fabric of his jeans.

I stared down at where our bodies touched, noting the strength in his fingers, the silver thumb ring, the faint blond hairs on the back of his hand.

"I've never put this much effort into seducing a woman before," he said, "nor shown this much patience with anyone who defied me. Doesn't that mean anything to you?"

Raising my head, I looked into his eyes. Pale blue, like the sky. Deceptively beautiful, just like the rest of him.

"Let me go," I whispered, but I wasn't talking about my hand, and he knew it.

"So stubborn," he said. "So sexy. I want to lick every one of your secret places, taste your juices on my tongue."

Somehow, the fact he was saying these things to

me *in church* should've shocked me to my core, but my core seemed to have a mind of its own. Right now, it was heating up, becoming molten.

"Psalms 6, verse 1," Jimmy shouted. "Have mercy on me, Lord, for I am weak."

Wasn't that the truth. If Sammy didn't back off soon, I was very much afraid that I'd eventually succumb. He managed to ignite a flare of lust in my belly every time I saw him. Despite knowing who he was, despite knowing what he was capable of, despite my love for Joe. Like Evan had said, I'd hardly lived my life as a saint, and faced with temptation like this, it was incredibly difficult to start now.

But I was trying, dammit. I was *trying.*

"I came here to deal with Jimmy Boyd," I said, forcing myself to focus my thoughts where they belonged, instead of the feel of Sammy's leg beneath my palm. "Not with you."

"I'm much better-looking." He gave me a naughty wink. "And much better in bed."

Thankfully, that comment worked against him, because it made me think about what Jimmy had done to Crystal, and would very likely do to Amber Marie unless I did something to stop it.

"Don't you care about *anything?*" I glanced at the people around us, keeping my voice lowered. "That guy up there is using religion as a shield, taking advantage of innocent little children. He ruined Crystal's life, and maybe others. There's a little girl in the front row who could be next. You could help me stop it." I'd seen Amber Marie when I came in—her blond head was hard to miss, and she was the only kid here.

"Why would I want to do that?" Sammy sounded genuinely curious. "He's doing all the work for me—misleading the sheep, lying to them, ultimately turning them from good people into bitter, disillusioned souls. Fewer souls for Jesus, more souls for me."

"Please," I whispered, hating to beg, but running out of options.

Sammy sighed heavily, eyes roving my face and hair. "Strangely enough, I'm actually tempted to give you what you want." He grinned, a quick flash of white teeth. "Not a normal thing for me, I assure you. But still . . . I'm not used to denying myself, my love."

My love. I closed my eyes, seeking strength from within. What was it about him that drew me so strongly? Was my dark side really that dark?

"Tell me you don't feel something between us, Nicki." His fingers tightened on my hand. "Tell me."

"The Devil will try and tempt you!" Jimmy Boyd shouted in the background. "He will fill your head with lies and blind your eyes to the truth! Do not be deceived, my friends—do not be deceived!"

I wasn't deceived. I knew the truth, and that's what allowed me to slowly turn my hand in his, and lace our fingers together. Opening my eyes, I looked at him, noting the gleam of triumph in his eyes.

"I'm sorry you're lonely."

His face went utterly blank.

"I'm sorry about what happened in the garden." The fingers that gripped mine so tightly a moment ago were slack. "I'm sorry you've been denied the Light."

"Sympathy for the Devil, little Nicki?" He blinked, and looked away. "How very rock and roll of you. Mick Jagger would be so proud."

Despite the flip answer, I knew I'd drawn blood. Some scabs never healed, no matter how many millennia were involved.

I squeezed his hand, willing him to look at me. "Just because you're damned doesn't mean you have to be a bastard."

He pulled his hand from mine abruptly. "I disagree."

And that's when all hell broke loose.

"I feel the presence of evil in this room," bellowed Jimmy Boyd. A chorus of shouted "No!"s and groans of fear followed this pronouncement.

"It is here, my friends—it walks among us, and we must call it *out*! Be not afraid, for the Lord is with us! Yea, though we walk through the valley of the shadow of death, we shall fear no evil." He shook the Bible in the air, as though it were a weapon. "Thy rod and thy staff, they comfort me!" And then, with unerring accuracy, he pointed the big leather book directly at *me*. "There is one among us in need of spiritual healing, my brothers and sisters. The Lord has brought her to us, and we must not shirk our duty! We must not turn our faces from the face of evil, but deal with it head-on!"

Every person in the room turned to look at me. I shot Sammy a startled glance, only to see him rise, and shout, "It's true! This poor girl is possessed of demons!" Shocked gasps filled the air around me. "Save her, Reverend Boyd! Lift this curse from her, so she may walk in righteousness once again!"

"Oh, you—" The foul names I was about to call him were lost in a sea of shouts. I jumped to my feet, ready to bolt for the door, but he grabbed me by the arm.

"Fear not to lay hands upon her," shouted Jimmy Boyd, from his place on the stage. "God will protect you!"

And before I knew it, a woman had grabbed my

other arm, and I was being propelled toward the front of the church.

"These signs shall follow those who believe; in My name thou shalt cast out devils!"

"I know a devil you can cast out!" I shouted back. "He's right here, holding on to my arm!" But nobody was listening to me, and when I twisted toward Sammy, writhing in his hold, it was another man who gripped me—a red-faced, potbellied man I didn't know. "You sorry-ass bastard," I shrieked at Sammy, craning my neck to see where he'd gone. "I'll get you for this!"

"Ignore the foul words that come from her mouth," shouted Jimmy Boyd. "For she is consumed by forces beyond her control! Oh yes, I have personal knowledge of this woman, brothers and sisters! She has been on television claiming the ability to channel spirits!" His voice got louder and louder, which it had to in order to be heard over the shocked gasps and murmurings all around me. "I sought her out, seeking to help her, but she rejected my aid— the demons within even drove her to raise her hand against me! She has opened herself up to the forces of darkness, but God has brought her here for cleansing! We must drive the devils from body and free her soul from the iron chains wrought by Satan himself!"

Shocked faces, excited murmurings, shouting and crying; everything became a blur of sound and motion as many hands lifted me bodily onto the stage. I hadn't been this disoriented since my last rave party, years ago, when I'd bodysurfed under the influence.

"Let go of me!" The whole scene was like something from a nightmare—I twisted and struggled, but whoever these people were, they were in the grip of a religious frenzy or something.

Jimmy Boyd was right in front of me now, waving his Bible in my face. "Look upon the Word, evil demon," he shouted. "For here is the Way and the Truth, and the Truth shall set you free!"

A chorus of brayed hallelujahs made me cringe. The woman holding my left arm had obviously eaten onions for lunch, and the guy on the right reeked of cigarettes.

"See how she recoils from the Holy Scripture?" shouted Boyd, directing his voice toward the crowd. "Devils cannot stand the manifestation of the Holy Spirit. We must call the angel of healing to our aid, and have faith that God will save her!"

What the hell was I supposed to do? I was seriously worried about getting hurt; there'd be bruises on my upper arms tomorrow as it was. Panicking wasn't working, so I did my best to calm down.

"I'm not possessed of evil spirits," I said to the woman holding my arm. *At least not right now,* I added silently. Ironically enough, Crystal Cowart was nowhere around. "I swear I'm not. This is all a big mistake."

"Peace, child," she said to me, barely even glancing in my direction. "Be still. Trust in the Lord. Reverend Boyd will save you."

"Do not converse with her," bellowed Boyd, having heard this exchange. "For you speak to the demon within, not the girl. To speak to them is to give them power."

The woman's grip tightened on my arm, and she refused to look at me again.

"I'm *not* possessed." I tried again with the guy on the other side of me. "I swear to God I'm not."

"Blasphemy!" roared Boyd. "Speak not the name of the Lord, demon! You will be driven out, and she who you inhabit shall be baptized in the raging fire of the Holy Spirit." He tried to put his hand on my head, which made me start struggling again—I did *not* want his creepy hands touching me. Held as I was, though, there was little I could do. I tried to kick him, but he jumped back, out of reach.

It was then I looked to the left and saw Amber Marie staring at me from the front row. Tina stood next to her, hands clasped in front of her, watching intently. Amber's mouth was slightly open, eyes big.

I forced myself to stop fighting. Maybe the whole horrible experience would get over quicker that way, and I really wasn't into traumatizing children, thank you very much.

"That's right, my brothers and sisters! You see how the power of the Holy Spirit is overcoming the evil within? We must sow the seeds of revival wherever we go, my children, so that many can be saved! As the deacons pass the baskets and collect the offering, reach deep into your hearts and in your pockets, and give so the tree of salvation may spread its fruit over the land!"

I couldn't believe it—Boyd was actually *collecting money* in the middle of this nightmare freak show!

"The more you give, the more shall be returned to you," he shouted, striding back and forth as the crowd swayed and moaned. "The stronger your faith, the more chance this poor girl has to be redeemed!"

My jaw dropped. He was using *me* to drag money from these people's pockets!

"Look upon her, my friends! See how she gasps for the precious Spirit itself, for even now it begins to fill her! The healing has begun!"

"Thank you, Jesus," screamed a woman from the pews. "Oh, thank you!"

I couldn't help myself. "Don't believe him," I yelled, beginning to struggle again. "He's a liar— he's a child molester! Don't listen to him."

Boyd's head swung my way like it had been jerked by a chain. I'm sure nobody but me saw the quick flash of worry on his face, because he covered it well. "Like a beast backed into a corner, the creature within this poor girl knows its power has begun to weaken, so it will fight harder than ever to be heard! Close your ears to its foulness, my friends! Do not heed the spewings of Satan!"

Furious, I had to give the creep credit—he was good. No matter what I said, no matter what I did, I'd only make myself look and sound crazier than he was. Coming to Hearts on Fire Tabernacle had been a *very* bad idea.

Through a sea of waving arms and shouting faces, I could see the one person in the room who seemed unaffected by the mania going on around him. Sammy stood in the back row, eyes intent on my face. I would've expected to see a smirk of enjoyment, but his expression was blank.

"*How could you do this to me?*" I asked him silently, and to my surprise, he answered, inside my head.

You're doing it to yourself, Nicki. Stop fighting me. Give in to the dark side of your nature. You know it's there. You hear it calling.

I looked away from him, letting my gaze take in the openmouthed faces in front of me, hearing the shouts and screams of total strangers who were even now digging into their pockets and tossing money into the baskets being passed through the crowd.

"Sheep," said Sammy, inside my mind, echoing my thoughts exactly. "*Witless fools, willing to believe anything they're told. Why should people like Boyd have all the power and you have none? Take control of your gift, Nicki. Give in to me, and embrace the darkness. Embrace ME.*"

I couldn't do it. Yes, they were witless fools for following a charlatan like Jimmy Boyd, but power was never something I'd sought, and I wasn't going to start now. Particularly when the price was my eternal soul. Choosing Sammy would make me as witless as they were, no matter how much I was tempted.

Shaking my head, I closed my eyes and forced myself to go completely limp against the people who held me. Let them do with me whatever they wanted; they'd have to let me go eventually. I'd find another way to get Amber Marie out of Boyd's sphere of influence—I'd find another way to put

Crystal Cowart's soul to rest. And if I couldn't, I'd live with a bony, angry ghost the rest of my life, and just be grateful that I still *had* a life.

I heard a roar inside my head like that of an angry lion. It made me gasp, wincing.

"Praise God," shouted Boyd, somewhere to my right. "She has submitted! Resist the Devil, and he shall flee from you! Resist . . . resist . . ."

A choking sound made me open my eyes. Jimmy Boyd was two feet away, still clutching his Bible. The expression on his face was one of total shock.

And then I saw why—Crystal Cowart was standing on the stage, staring at him with such hate on her face that my blood ran cold. He could obviously see her, and he was scared shitless.

"The Spirit has come upon Reverend Boyd," shouted the man holding my right arm. "Speak to us, brother, speak to us with the tongue of angels!"

The noises issuing from Boyd's mouth hardly sounded like something created by angels, in my opinion. I glanced around at the crowd, who were swaying and shouting, focused on their leader, oblivious to the very personal drama playing itself out on the stage.

Crystal moved toward him, very slowly, and with every step she took, he took a step backward. Fumbling with his Bible, he held it in front of him, like a shield, never letting go of the microphone. She was between us now, her jutting shoulder blades right in front of me, and I knew what she was about to do.

Poor bastard.

"Bah, bah, back—" he stuttered, sounding more like a sheep than those he led, "back, foul demon!"

Automatically, I looked at Sammy. His face was stern, expression forbidding. Like everyone else, his attention was focused on Boyd.

Crystal's image shimmered, wavering like a heat mirage. And then, as I'd seen her do before, she contracted into a thin wisp of vapor and shot, like a snake, directly at the preacher.

His Bible did him no good. His body began to shake, his eyes to bulge, as the ghost of the girl he'd molested possessed him completely.

"Hallelujah, brother!" yelled a man in my ear. He clearly had no idea what was going on. "The ecstasy is upon him! Praise God and all his saints!"

"Hallelujah," shrieked a woman from the audience. She started gabbling something that sounded like nonsense, eyes closed in some kind of religious ecstasy, hands raised toward heaven.

Jimmy Boyd staggered, swaying on his feet. His face was turning bright red, eyeballs bulging in his head.

Panicky now, I glanced at Tina and Amber, to see Amber looking scared and Tina beginning to frown, as though she'd finally gotten an inkling that something was wrong.

"God forgive me, for I have sinned," Boyd's mouth was moving, but the voice issuing from his throat wasn't quite his own. "I'm a defiler of children, a liar, a perversion upon the face of the earth! Suffer *not* to have your children come unto me, for I shall take advantage of them sexually, as I did Crystal Cowart!"

I watched as faces in the crowd went from flushed and smiling to frowning and uncertain. The room became very quiet, as the magnitude of what he'd said sunk in.

He waved the Bible in the air with a jerky motion. " 'But whoso shall offend one of these little ones which believe in me, it were better for him that a millstone were hanged about his neck, and that he were drowned in the depths of the sea!' " he squealed, obviously unable to stop himself.

Time slowed to a crawl. Now only strangled sounds came from the creep's throat. As I watched, the microphone fell from his hand and hit the stage floor with a loud *clunk*.

Boyd grabbed his chest with his free hand, making wide arcs in the air with the Bible. He took a step backward, then toppled, falling to the stage.

And suddenly, I was free, as the people holding me rushed toward Boyd's prone figure. I stood there, alone and shaken, as several more people crowded onto the stage, all headed toward their leader.

One of the men loosened Boyd's tie and another grabbed his limp wrist, apparently feeling for a pulse. The open Bible lay facedown on the stage, where it had fallen when he collapsed.

Holy crap on a cracker. Don't let it be, please don't let it be . . .

"Call an ambulance!" One of the men bending over the preacher raised his head, grasping at the shoulder of the man next to him. "Reverend Boyd needs an ambulance!"

"Jimmy!" Tina's shriek cut through the chaos as she made it up onto the stage. She shoved her way into the knot of people crouched over Boyd. "Oh no, Jimmy . . . Jimmy!" Collapsing on top of his motionless body, she sobbed as though her heart would break.

And that's when I knew. Sammy had helped me after all, but not in the way I'd hoped.

Looking again toward the back of the room, I saw him staring at me. I heard his voice in my head, clear as a bell.

"It seems your boyfriend was right, for once," he said. *"Your efforts to do good in the world actually could make things worse."* And then he turned and walked out the door.

Jimmy Boyd would never molest anyone again.

But now I had to live with his death on my conscience.

CHAPTER 26

"It's not your fault, it's not your fault, it's not your fault."

No matter how many times I repeated those words to myself, they weren't sinking in. I sat in my car in the parking lot of Hearts on Fire Tabernacle until the paramedics left, hoping against hope to see them working on Jimmy Boyd when they'd come out with the gurney. But the figure on the stretcher had been motionless, completely covered with a sheet, and there'd been no urgency in the way they loaded him into the back of the ambulance.

Knots of people stood around the parking lot, shell-shocked and sobbing. I could see Tina and

Amber sitting on the ground under a tree with a group of women, two of whom kept their arms around Tina's shaking shoulders. Amber Marie was crying, too, shooting worried looks at her mother as she was patted and hugged.

"She's safe now," I said, though there was no one there to hear me. "Amber's safe." As much as I wanted to take comfort from that, the afternoon's events had left me shell-shocked, too.

On autopilot, I started the car and pulled away, not wanting anything more to do with this place or the people in it. Going back to work was out of the question, and I didn't want to go home, so I drove straight to Joe's apartment. I needed to feel somebody's arms around me almost as much as Tina and Amber did.

His Beemer was in its usual spot, but he didn't answer my knock, so I let myself in, making a mental note to do as I'd promised and get him a key made to my house.

"Joe?" His gym bag was on the floor next to the dining-room table, but the living room and kitchen area were empty.

I put my purse down and stuck my head in the hall that led to his bedroom.

The bathroom door was closed, and I could hear the shower running. With a shrug, I went toward the kitchen instead, hoping there was wine. I'd pour us both a glass and be waiting for him when he came out.

A few minutes later, I was sitting on the couch with a glass, staring out the sliding glass doors that led to the balcony. A breeze was moving in the trees, white clouds scudding against a blue sky—a perfectly normal day in a perfectly normal world.

Except it wasn't a normal day. I'd just seen someone die, right before my eyes.

The bathroom door opened. Not wanting to startle him, I turned my head toward the hallway, and called, "Hey, baby, it's me. I opened a bottle of wine."

When he didn't answer, I started to get up.

"Joe went for a run, but I'm sure he'll be back soon."

Lisa Butler walked around the corner into the living room, wearing nothing but a couple of towels—one on her head, and one wrapped around her body. The look on her face could only be described as *smug*.

"What the hell are you doing here?" I stood up so fast I spilled my wine, but I could care less. Slapping the glass down on the coffee table, I faced her, so furious I could barely see straight.

She shrugged. "I'm taking a shower. Isn't it obvious?"

Oh, it was obvious, all right.

"I'm so sorry you had to find out this way," she smirked. "I told him he should be honest with you—a clean break is always best, don't you agree?"

It was on the tip of my tongue to call her every foul name I could think of, and then some, but I didn't. I forced myself to stop, to think, to consider—rushing off half-cocked had already gotten me into serious trouble once today.

"Where are your clothes?" I asked, as calmly as I possibly could.

She blinked, just once, which told me my reaction was not what she expected. A quick flick of her eyes toward the hallway had me heading in that direction.

She moved, too, but I cut her off, getting there before she did. Without another word, I stalked down the hall toward Joe's bedroom.

His bed was neatly made. The door to the bathroom was open, and I could see a pile of clothes on the rug. Lisa's clothes. A pair of panties lay on top, as if they were the last thing she'd taken off. The mirror was steamed up, the shower curtain drawn back. Her purse was sitting on the closed toilet.

Joe wasn't here, and if they'd just made hot monkey love in his bed, I doubted he'd have taken the time to make it before going out to jog. None of which explained what she was doing there to begin with, but I had enough to go on for now.

I bent, snatching up the clothes along with the pair of tennis shoes that lay beside them.

"Hey," she said, "leave my stuff alone."

The look I gave her had her backing up, moving out of my way as I walked out of the bathroom toward the front door, carrying her clothes, purse, and shoes with me.

"Hey," she said, more forcefully, trying to snatch them. "Give those back."

I shrugged her off, reaching the front door in three seconds flat. She was at a disadvantage, having only one hand free, the other still clutching the towel.

Opening the door, I tossed her things out on the landing. "You want them?" I gave her a thin smile, very tight-lipped. "Go get them."

Her gasp of rage warmed my heart. She eyed me, eyed the clothes, then ducked past me to pick them up. I waited a couple of seconds, long enough for her to bend over and get her shoes.

"One more thing," I said. "That's Joe's towel." I grabbed it, just below the point where she was clutching her clothes to her chest, and yanked it off—there was nothing she could do to stop me.

I slammed the door in her face and locked it,

memorizing the look on her face. *Sweet dreams are made of this, baby.*

Still furious, but hugely proud of myself, I walked back over and sat down on the couch to wait for Joe.

"And that's it? You believe me?"

It had been forty-five long minutes before Joe had unlocked the door and walked back into his apartment, and I'd had plenty of time to think. He was sweaty and tired, obviously having been out running, just as Lisa had said.

"Yep. I believe you."

He eyed me like my nose was about to grow like Pinocchio's or something, but that was okay.

I took another sip of my wine and smiled at him over the glass.

"I couldn't believe it when she showed up here," he said, still anxious. "I didn't even know she knew where I lived. Must've gotten it from the hospital records."

Nodding, I answered, "Probably."

He kept going, giving me a worried look. "I wouldn't even have let her in, but she kept going on about needing to apologize, and before I knew it, she was in the living room."

"Huh."

"I tried to get her to leave, but short of shoving

her out the door, I didn't know what to do. I was afraid to actually touch her—she had kind of a crazy look in her eye."

I was listening attentively, even though I'd heard it all once before, right after he came in.

"Kinda like the look you've got right now," he said cautiously.

I giggled, feeling a little crazy, at that.

"Finally, I told her that I was going for a run, and to let herself out. I took an extralong run, figuring she'd get tired of waiting. If she'd still been here when I got back, I was going to call the police. Are you okay?"

With a sigh, I put down my glass and picked up his hand. "I'm okay. Really." It felt so good in mine. "Really, really okay."

"You're scaring me."

I laughed, squeezing his fingers. "That's usually my line."

Totally baffled now, he leaned back against the leather of the couch. "What's going on? If I'd walked in and found a naked man in your house, I'd have punched first and asked questions later! How can you be so calm about this?"

I looked at him, considering. His dark hair was damp with sweat, and so was the rest of him. He smelled like a locker room, and his Boston Red Sox T-shirt had a hole in it, right near the collar.

"I love you," I said, simply. "You told me you loved me, and I believe you. You told me you wouldn't dump me, and I believe you. As much as I wanted to punch Lisa in her fat, naked mouth, I decided that—for once—I'd 'look before I leapt,' and so I looked." I tilted my head, enjoying the stunned expression on his face. "I didn't see anything to leap over, except the chance to toss her and her skanky ass out the front door." Squeezing his hand again, I lay back against the couch. "Which is what I did."

Shaking his head, he started to laugh. "You are something else."

"Aren't I, though?" I loved the way his eyes crinkled when he laughed.

"What brought on this attack of common sense, anyway? No offense, but . . ."

I sighed, giving him a rueful grin. "I know, I know—not my usual style, is it?"

"I love your usual style," he said, "but this one's kind of nice, too."

"As much as I hate to admit it"—I closed my eyes for a second and forced myself to say the words—"I think I may be growing up. Kinda. Sorta. A little."

He rose, still smiling, and headed toward the kitchen. "Something happened today, didn't it?"

"What are you, a mind reader?"

"I know you well enough to know when something's up, Nick." Opening the refrigerator, he reached in and pulled out a bottle of water. "Tell me."

Giving another sigh, deeper this time, I settled into the couch, tucking my legs beneath me. Where to begin? Morning seemed like a long time ago.

"Crystal showed up again last night. I think she needs my help more than she wants to admit, and I—"

"You wanted to help her," Joe said, finishing the sentence for me. His tone was calm and matter-of-fact. He unscrewed the top on his water bottle and walked back into the living room, retaking his seat.

"Yes." No use dancing around it. "I looked up Jimmy Boyd's church on the Internet, and I went there this afternoon to talk to him. I was going to tell him that I knew what he'd done to Crystal and how I knew it."

"You were going to admit you see spirits?" Joe raised his eyebrows as he gulped some water, knowing that telling people that kind of thing was one of my biggest no-no's.

I nodded. "I was going to tell him that I'd go public with what he did if he didn't stay away from Amber Marie. You know—the direct approach, with a little blackmail worked in."

"And?"

I'd expected Joe to get mad at that point; I'd gone off without him—again—to do something potentially stupid. "There was a church service going on." *If you could call that overblown spectacle a church service.* "A revival or something." I frowned, remembering. "It didn't end well."

"Get to the point, Nicki." He took another long slug of bottled water, no doubt knowing he was about to need it.

"He died, right in front of me. Dropped dead, in the middle of the service. It was my fault."

Joe's throat worked as he tried to swallow without choking.

"Well, maybe it was Sammy's fault. But it wouldn't have happened if I hadn't gone there to begin with."

Closing his eyes briefly, he took a deep breath and let it out. "Sammy?" His voice was deceptively quiet.

"He was there. I asked him to do the right thing—to help me keep Boyd away from Amber." I was nervous now, like I was confessing secrets that maybe I shouldn't confess. "Crystal showed up, and instead of possessing me, she possessed Boyd. I guess his heart couldn't take it." I paused, admitting the final truth. "That was how Sammy helped me."

"By striking somebody dead." Joe's voice was flat. He wasn't looking at me, but at his bottle of water.

I hesitated. "Yes."

He stood up, pacing around the coffee table as though he couldn't sit still any longer. "What next?" he muttered, more to himself than me. "What the hell next?" He ran a hand through his hair, a sure sign he was upset.

"Well . . ." I stood up, too, putting a hand on his arm to stop him from pacing. "I'd say a restraining order against Lisa Butler would be a good idea. What she did today might work in your favor with the board of directors at the hospital, too. They need to know they've got a crazy stalker with the hots for one of their doctors on their hands. Do you have an appointment with an attorney yet?"

"Monday," he said, but his mind was obviously not on Lisa. "But how the hell do we get rid of Sammy?"

I shook my head, remembering what Grandma Bijou had told me, months ago. "The Devil can't be gotten rid of, Joe. He can only be overcome by what's in your heart." I reached up, cupping his face in my hands. "And my heart—defective as it is—is full of you."

He stared at me, green eyes piercing, as though he could see straight into my soul. Then he snatched me to him, holding me tight against his chest, burying his face in my hair.

I held him just as tightly as he did me, not caring that he was sweaty and damp. If there had been a way to make the moment last forever, I would have, but instead I just tried to memorize the way he felt in my arms, the way he smelled, the salty tang of his sweat, and the lean feel of the muscles in his back.

Nothing lasted forever, as I well knew; the best we could do was to enjoy the moment. Every moment.

Finally, I pulled back and kissed him: once, twice, three times, lingering on the last one. "I have one more thing I need to do," I said, "but you're not going to like it."

He sighed, arms around my waist now, forehead against mine. "If I had a dollar for every time you'd said that to me . . . What is it?"

"I have to go ask Sammy for one more favor."

Proving once and for all that I had the best boyfriend in the entire world, he answered, "I'll go with you."

CHAPTER 27

That night was the first time I'd set foot in Divinyls; the second time I'd been inside the building since my old friend Caprice, who ran the Jamaican grocery that used to be here, died on the steps outside.

I hated to admit it, but whoever had done the decorating had done a good job—the old hardwood floors gleamed with polish, the walls had been painted a deep Oriental red, and white crown molding had been installed near the ceiling. Cool vintage rock posters from bands like The Velvet Underground, the Ramones and the Sex Pistols were set at overlapping angles all over

the walls, filling the place with just the right at-
mosphere. Wooden crates filled with old vinyls,
modern racks full of CDs, and an area full of
sound equipment in one corner. There was even
a sound booth in the back, full of speakers, turn-
tables, and headphones.

Sammy was flipping through some old vinyls,
his back to the door.

"I'll be right over here in the CDs if you need
me," Joe muttered, eyeing him narrowly.

I gave him a grateful look, knowing how much
it cost him to let me do this by myself. We'd
talked about it in the car on the way over, and I
seriously doubted I'd get much cooperation from
Sammy with Joe listening to every word that was
said.

Steeling myself, I walked toward the vinyl section. Even with the moral support, it was a lot
harder to take the devil by the horns than I'd
thought.

Godsmack's "I Stand Alone" was playing on the
store's stereo system, which I found supremely
ironic under the circumstances.

"How do you feel about the Talking Heads?"
Sammy asked idly, over his shoulder, as I ap-
proached. "David Byrne was ahead of his time, I
think. Still doing great work, by the way."

Should've known there was no surprising him.

"I prefer David Bowie," I answered, refusing to let him rattle me. "Or for older stuff, The Pixies."

"Bah," he answered, letting the album slip back down into the bin. "Mindless noise."

"I would've taken you for a Generation X man, myself. Billy Idol seems to be a particular favorite of yours."

Sammy turned, giving me a grin. It didn't have nearly the wattage of Billy's famous whiplash smile, though. "How very brave of you to face the demon in his den," he said, flicking a glance toward Joe before ignoring him completely. "What do you want?"

I wasn't going to waste my time on explanations. "You know what I want."

"Oh, but I do so enjoy hearing you beg. Aren't you going to plead for Crystal's pitiful little soul?" He leaned a hip against the wooden crate that held the old records, crossing his arms over his chest. "Or didn't today teach you to be careful what you wish for?"

"You didn't have to kill him," I murmured, glad there was no one in this part of the store to overhear us. I had a feeling I was going to carry guilt over Boyd's death around for a long time.

He waved a hand as though brushing away a gnat. "He belonged to me anyway. I just claimed him a little early." His gaze sharpened. "Aren't you glad he won't be raping any more children?"

His bluntness, delivered in such a calm tone, was designed to shock me, but I was beyond that. "Yes," I answered, looking him in the eye, "I am."

"Bravo, little Nicki," he said softly. "I knew the kitten had claws."

I couldn't help the sour look he got for that one.

He chuckled. "Adorable. How I shall miss you." Dropping his arms to his side, he turned away, heading toward the register.

"What? Where are you going?" *And why did I care?*

"Haven't you heard? I'm very fickle. Resist the Devil and he shall flee from you, and all that." Another negligent wave of the hand. "I've grown tired of this particular game."

It was all I could do to keep from grabbing him by the sleeve. "What about Crystal?"

He stopped, turning to face me once again. "What about her?" A blond eyebrow arched.

He was going to make me beg after all, damn him. "Please release her from the bargain she made with you," I said, as humbly as I could (which wasn't very). "Please let her go into the Light."

Silence for a moment, as he stared at me, con-sidering. "I've asked you before, Nicki—what will you give me in return?"

Without thinking, my eyes went to Joe. He was watching every move we made, though he was too far away to hear what we were saying.

"A kiss," I said. "One kiss. Freely given."

I looked back to see both blond eyebrows raised.

"That's it? I'm supposed to give up a soul I've gone to great trouble to harvest for something as paltry as a kiss?"

Setting my jaw, I persisted. "That's it. That's all I'll give you." In case he didn't know it by now, I could be one very stubborn kitten.

Sammy gave another amused chuckle, shaking his head. "All right."

For a moment I doubted my ears.

"On two conditions."

Should've known.

"Three, actually."

"What are they?" I blurted, before he could add a fourth.

Crossing his arms over his chest, he took a very no-nonsense stance.

"One: if you look at your boyfriend one more time while I'm talking to you, the deal is off. I find beta males very annoying. Yours, in particular. I want your full attention."

I wasn't going to argue whether Joe was alpha, beta, or gamma, for that matter—because to me he was perfect, whatever Greek letter of the alphabet he was assigned. Of course, I now wanted to look over at him more than ever, but I studiously avoided it. "Okay."

"Two: if he comes over here and interrupts our kiss, the deal is off."

This condition made me nervous. How many guys would stand idly by while their girlfriends kissed someone? Particularly when that someone was Satan himself? If I had a chance to warn him first, it would probably be okay, but without it . . .

"Either he trusts you, or he doesn't." The smile that played about Sammy's lips told me he was enjoying my nervousness. "Are you willing to take that chance?"

My stomach was now officially in knots. "Yes." What choice did I have? *Don't look, don't look . . .*

"Three"—he took a step closer, lowering his voice—"this kiss is under *my* control. I control the length, the depth, and the duration." The way he drew out those three words sounded distinctly sexual. "There'll be no quick pecks involved."

"And then you'll let Crystal go free?" I wanted it clarified. "One kiss, and your bargain with Crystal is over? Finished? *Finito*? You'll let her go into the Light?"

Tilting his head to the side, he gave me a quizzical look. "Would you like a written contract? In blood, perhaps?"

I had the feeling he wasn't kidding.

"No." I shook my head hastily. "No need for that."

He shrugged, dropping his hands. "Ah, well. Some people like that sort of thing."

"To each his own." I was babbling now, and knew it.

"Of course, we could call the whole thing off," Sammy said, hopefully. "You give in, leave that nasty Light for the glorious Dark, we join forces, mingle juices . . ."

"Not gonna happen. Kiss me and get it over with." *Before I ran screaming from the shop, with my tail tucked between my legs.* Because, damn it all, a teeny, tiny part of me was still tempted, in spite of everything.

He shook his head. "Uh, uh, uh." There was a devilish gleam in his eye. "That wasn't the deal. *You* kiss *me*, remember?"

Oh, this was not going to be easy. Joe was standing right there—*don't look!*—and Sammy was giving me his best smoldering, I'd-like-to-eat-you-for-breakfast, lunch, and dinner stare. If this was going to be over anytime soon, I'd have to dig deep, find some courage, and make my move.

Unconsciously, I wet my lips—I knew I'd done it because his eyes snapped to my mouth, and lingered there. With a deep breath, I took a step closer to him. And then another, praying that Joe would stay back, stay quiet and most of all, stay mine.

Another step, and my nose filled with the scent of forbidden fruit: warm, spicy, and infinitely male. Steeling myself, I lifted a hand and placed it on his shoulder, right where it met the strong column of his neck. I could see the pulse beating there, for all the world as if he were a flesh-and-blood man, not a devil.

The Devil. If I'd ever had any doubt of it, it was gone now; no one could devise a more diabolical torture than this.

He wasn't going to help me, either. His hands stayed by his sides, and though he was gazing down at me, I was going to have to rise on tiptoe to reach his lips, because he wasn't bending. "You smell good," he whispered.

"Shut up," I whispered back, and then I kissed him.

I wasn't sure what I expected: heat, passion, stars, fireworks, lightheadedness; all of that paled in the reality of the moment.

Sammy's lips were firm, yet curiously soft, clinging to mine with the lightest of pressures. His hands came up to touch my waist, but there was no urgency in his grip. My body leaned into his of its own accord, while he kissed me as if we were all alone in the universe, just he and I.

It was overwhelming, but not in the way I'd imagined. Gentle, so gentle. Breathless, expectant, like that moment on a roller coaster when you've reached the crest, just before it plunges toward the earth. The faintest brush of his tongue against the tip of mine, and then—shockingly—it was over. He drew back, and I opened my eyes to see his blue eyes soft. For an instant—just an instant—he looked as he had when I'd seen him in my dream, in the garden. A younger, gentler, kinder version of himself.

And then he ruined it by speaking.

"She's already gone, you know."

For a moment, I had no idea what he was talking about.

"Crystal. She's already gone."

I pulled away, frowning, doing my best to focus.

"It seems you were right, after all, little Nicki." He grinned at the look on my face. "I have only enough power over human souls—whether living or dead—as they give me. Once Crystal's issues with Jimmy Boyd were resolved, and her little sister safe, she had nothing left to keep her here." He was chuckling now, enjoying my confusion. "And no reason left to listen to me, particularly since you'd already shown her"—he lifted a finger toward the ceiling, mockingly—"the proverbial Light."

"Oh, my God," I said slowly.

His lip curled with distaste. "That's right—your God. Not mine." He turned away, leaving me standing there like an idiot. "At least not anymore."

"Wait." I couldn't help it. I had to know. "Will I—will I see you again?"

The tiniest of smiles lifted one corner of his lip, a mere shadow of the devilish grin I'd come to know. "Do you want to?"

I didn't know what to think at this point, much less what to say, so I said nothing. I just watched as he turned and walked away, disappearing down the hallway that led to the back of the store.

"Nicki." Joe's voice at my elbow got my attention. "Are we done here?" His face was set, white lines of tension around his mouth.

"We're done," I answered, hoping very much that it was the truth. I searched his face, not quite knowing what to say to him, either. "Joe, I—"

"'Looking before you leap' is a lot harder than I thought it would be," he said, interrupting me. "Because I'd like nothing more than to leap down that guy's throat." He glanced toward the hallway where Sammy had disappeared, eyes hard. "But I figured if you could do it, so could I." Then he looked back at me. "Still, you better have a damn good explanation for that."

"Only the truth, which is that you're the one I want." I put my hand on his chest, feeling the tenseness that vibrated through every muscle in his body. "I'll tell you everything in the car. Let's go."

It was true what they said about funerals; they're for the living, not the dead. And as much as I hated them, Crystal's funeral was one I would have liked to go to, just to make sure she wasn't still hanging around. But I was out of luck, because Crystal wasn't *having* a funeral.

Cremation, Joe had said, and he should know, because he'd been the one to sign the papers that had ultimately released Crystal's body to the crematory. No service, according to the family's wishes.

It had been six days since I'd kissed Sammy; four days since Joe had met with his lawyer, who'd wasted no time in getting Joe off suspension and back to work. Divinyls was locked up and silent, with CLOSED signs on the front doors. And I was left wondering whether Sammy had told me the truth about Crystal going into the Light, or whether he'd tricked me again with yet another lie.

Lies were his stock in trade, after all.

I was sitting on the couch in my living room. In front of me was the white basket I'd found on my doorstep. The yellow flowers were wilted and faded, the bottles full of powders still there. I picked up one of the little scrolls and unrolled it, already knowing what it said.

SPELL TO SUMMON A SPIRIT

Based on recent experience, I knew there was a chance the spell might really work, but did I want to take that chance? If Crystal was at peace, why should I disturb her? And if she wasn't, would summoning up her spirit start up even more trouble?

Shaking my head, I tossed the scroll into the

basket, picked up the whole thing, and walked out the back door, dumping basket, flowers, powders, spells, and all into the garbage can.

The lessons I'd learned from the Savannah Garden Club were interesting, but despite what I'd said to Sally Starhawk and her friend, I wasn't really all that into Helen Damnation.

Unforgettable, enthralling love stories,
sparkling with passion and adventure
from Romance's bestselling authors

DISCOVER ROMANCE *at its*
SIZZLING HOT BEST FROM AVON BOOKS

Avon Romances
the best in
exceptional authors and unforgettable novels!